# SLEEPER

## KAYLEY LORING

This is a work of fiction. Names, characters, businesses, places, events, and incidents are either products of the author's imagination or are used fictitiously. Any resemblance to actual events, locales, or actual persons, living or dead, is entirely coincidental.

COVER DESIGN: Alyssa Garcia, Uplifting Author Services
COPY EDITOR: Jenny Rarden
BETA READERS: LaLinc Proofreading, Neda Amini, April Pryor

**MERRIAM-WEBSTER DICTIONARY
DEFINITION OF SLEEPER:**

1. *One that sleeps*

4. *Someone or something unpromising or unnoticed that suddenly attains prominence or value*

*//the low-budget film became the summer's sleeper*

## SHANE MILLER SLEEP DIARY – Monday, 6:15 am

**Went to bed at:** *Around midnight. Spent an hour and a half prepping food and packing up lunches for the kids, for the entire school week because I'm awesome.*

**How long it took you to fall asleep:** *Forever. I have insomnia. Duh.*

**How many times you woke up in the middle of the night:** *Infinity.*

**How refreshing your overall sleep was:** *It wasn't. Fuck my life.*

**Number of caffeinated beverages you consumed throughout the day:** *Zero. Thanks for advising me to quit! Fuck quitting coffee.*

**Number of alcoholic beverages you consumed throughout the day:** *As if. I wish.*

**How much time you spent exercising:** *3 hours. How else do you think movie stars stay in shape? My quads are on fire. Fuck my personal trainer and fuck whoever thinks adequate exercise leads to better sleep.*

**Your stress level before bedtime, on a scale from 1 to 5:** *5000.*

**Your major cause of stress:** *On Friday, the fucking nanny quit to get married. I mean, I'm happy for her. Yay for being young and in love and I wish them all the best, but could she maybe have given us some notice BEFORE my ex-wife and her husband left for three months to shoot in the mountains of Poland? Or perhaps waited until AFTER they return? Because Margo will throw a fit if I hire anyone that she doesn't approve of and hasn't met in person. Meanwhile I'm still getting back on a regular schedule after wrapping my last movie and doing night shoots on the East Coast, and as we know, I do not respond well to sleeping pills. So, I AM FUCKED.*

*Also, I don't have a fucking clue how I'm ever going to meet a woman that I can really love if I didn't even like dating in Hollywood when I was a horny teenager. On-location flings are fine and all, but so far I haven't met one woman I'd want to introduce my kids to. I may as well just buy a minivan and a blow-up doll and call it a day. Fuck dating.*

*And you know what—I'm still mad about the last three episodes of* Game of Thrones, *but I guess that's not the "major" cause of my stress at the moment. Fuck you, HBO.*

*But hey, I have this fucking amazing sleep diary, so there's that. I'm guessing this is TMI for your sleep hygiene analysis purposes, since there wasn't enough room for long answers and I've continued onto the back page. But it helps to vent.*

*P.S. I mean no disrespect, Dr. Shaw. Please forgive the f-bombs. I'm just a little cranky because I got maybe two hours of sleep and I have to get the kids ready for school. Maybe I can just close my eyes for another fifteen minutes...*

## 1

## SHANE

"Daddy. Daddy. Daddy. Daddy. Daddy."

"Mmmph?"

"Summer said to woke you up."

"Hunh?"

"I already brushed my teeth, but I'm hungry. Why can't we have toothpaste for eating?"

There's a forty-pound human straddling my back, and I can't move my head to see the clock. "Wha? What time is it?"

"Summer said it's okay."

"Where is she?"

"In the kitchen. Cleaning up."

"Cleaning up what? You gotta climb off me, buddy. I have to get up."

Lucky slides off me and onto the rug with a little thud. "She said don't tell you."

Yeah, that sounds like Summer. It's funny how they take turns being the good twin and the naughty one.

This year, Lucky's the good one. He's already dressed in his private school polo shirt and khaki pants.

"Hey, you're all dressed."

"Yeah."

"Good for you, little man." I reach out to muss up his light-brown hair—perfectly tousled just like his dad's—and with the other hand I reach for my phone. "Fuck." Seven thirty. "Shit. Get your shoes on, buddy." I spring to life. I got this. I pull on the jeans that I'd conveniently left on the floor right by my bed and grab the first T-shirt I can get my hands on.

"I can't find them."

"The ones you wore yesterday?" He has like five pairs of shoes in this house.

"I don't know where they are."

"Then wear another pair."

"I can't find any of my shoes."

*Goddamit.* I bet I know what happened. Margo let Summer watch that Marie Kondo tidying up show, and ever since then, my daughter has been throwing out things that she doesn't think we need and reorganizing everything she could reach in the kids' rooms. Last weekend I came home to find my housekeeper Consuelo crying because she couldn't find anything, and she was afraid I'd think she stole from us.

It's going to be one of those mornings.

Well, the good news is I slept for an hour. Bad news is I have less than half an hour to get these guys ready and on the school property. It's fine. There's time. Twelve minutes to get to school as long as the PCH isn't backed up. Five to ten minutes to make sure my kids are fed and relatively presentable, and who's to say that today won't be the first day in the history of five-year-olds that they'll actually get out of the house when I need them to? Thank God I got their lunches ready last night.

"You checked everywhere in your room?" I hold out my hand to see if Lucky will take it as we walk out of my room and downstairs. He doesn't need to, but I still like to get in a little handholding whenever I can before they turn six and really start asserting their independence. I feel his hand in mine, and my heart melts just a little.

"Is she in trouble?"

"Nah. We'll just ask her where she put your stuff."

"Why is she so weird now?"

"That's a really good question, and I don't have the answer. Sometimes girls get weird, and we just have to wait for them to be not weird again. Right?"

"Yeah."

He's walking so slowly while thinking about this, and I've got one less minute to get to Santa Monica, so I pick him up and carry him downstairs. "Summer!" I call out once we're in the foyer.

"Don't come in!" comes a high-pitched, frazzled, but bossy little voice from the kitchen.

"Summer, did you throw out Lucky's shoes?"

"No! I moved them!"

"I need to know where you moved them to."

"I—I don't remember—don't come in yet!"

I put Lucky down when we get to the entrance to the kitchen, and I'm too caught up in my *fuck this no caffeine shit* thoughts to wonder why she doesn't want me to come in.

And now I know exactly why.

My five-year-old daughter is on her hands and knees, frantically gathering all of the fruits and vegetables that I had thoroughly cleaned and carefully sliced and cubed last night, into one large pile. The crackers and snacks are in another floor pile. The meats and cheeses are piled up on top of the soba noodles. Marie Kondo would probably approve of this, and I would love it she would come to my house right fucking now to tidy this up and make my kids lunches and get them to school on time.

Meanwhile, the hummus and guacamole are smeared all over the floor around her and on the skirt of her uniform dress, as she appears to have used her dress to wipe it up.

"Summer. Stop what you're doing right now."

"I was letting you sleep!"

"Okay. What can you tell me about what happened in here?"

"We're s'posed to bring something red for art class. To paint. Something small," she says with a loud sigh as she stands up and stares at me defiantly. Her jaw is set, like that explains why all ten of the carefully labelled bento box lunch containers I packed up for them are now opened and scattered around on the floor along with the mess of five days' worth of food.

"Uh-huh. And?"

She exhales loudly, exasperated about having to explain this to me. "Soooo, I was looking for apples, but you got green ones! And then I kept looking for tomatoes or red peppers. But you got the yellow ones! You didn't put any strawberries in there at all! Not even red gummy bears! And then I was looking for the round cheese. With the red stuff on them."

"But the containers are see-through. You didn't have to open them to see what was inside."

"But you sometimes hide the snacks!" Her eyes are watery and her lower lip is quivering, but she is not backing down because she is just as stubborn as her mother, only she's a million times cuter. And guess what—she's also right. I do sometimes hide the snacks. As always, this is somehow my fault, and I don't have time to remind her that art class is after lunch, so she probably would have just eaten any red food before getting the chance to paint it because that's what she does. She eats everything.

*Fuck you, art teacher.*

*One less minute to get to school.*

"Am I in trouble?" she asks with a pout.

"I mean, I really wish this hadn't happened, but no. You're not in trouble." *I am. I'm in trouble.* I take a deep breath. "I'm not mad at you, sweetie. Thank you for letting me sleep. But none of us are supposed to sleep in on a school day. And thank you for trying to clean this mess up, but we have to leave in two minutes. You gotta change into another uniform. Let's get this one off you. Shit, have you guys eaten yet?"

"Noooo!" they both yell out.

I'm a shit dad. "Banana!" I declare.

"Banana banana banana!" Lucky chants. "Why do bananas get spots?"

"I have no idea, but we can look it up later." This has become my go-to answer, and it fills me with shame. I grab two bananas from the fruit bowl on the counter, one for each of my spawn. I pull out two containers of yogurt from the fridge and put them, along with two spoons, on the kitchen table. There will be no time for the brushing of Summer's teeth this morning. They can eat in the car. They will be having almond butter sandwiches for lunch, with tortilla chips and a handful of whatever fruits and vegetables I can grab and rinse and—"Hey guys, let's not tell your mom about any of what happened this morning, right?"

I carefully remove the dress from Summer's torso without getting any hummus or guac on her hair or face. I'm starting to think I might not suck at life by the time I've convinced Lucky to wear his sister's sneakers (because they aren't pink), and we are almost to the door to the garage, with our lunchboxes and backpacks and our clean uniforms, our bananas and yogurts and spoons, and my wallet and keys and twelve minutes to get them from the Pacific Palisades to Santa Monica.

"My pen is big…bigger the…than…you…yours."

Summer is blocking the door to the garage, staring up at my chest.

"What?" I look down and realize I'm wearing the gag gift that the crew gave me at the wrap party a couple of weeks ago. *MY PEN IS BIGGER THAN YOURS* "Shit." What a stupid fucking T-shirt. I don't have time to change. If anyone takes a picture of me in this outside the school, I'm screwed. It'll be one of the first images to come up anytime someone Googles my name or the school's. "To the car. Get."

I take the shirt off and put it back on inside-out. I'm a genius, and this is totally appropriate because everything feels inside out and upside-down when I haven't had enough sleep.

"My shoes!" Lucky points at the floor of the back seat of the Land Rover while I'm trying to get him buckled into his car seat. "I don't want to wear Summer's anymore."

"You can take your shoes with you to class and change when you're there. We gotta go."

Summer manages to buckle herself up, but I still go around to make sure she's all snug in there. I kiss her on the side of her head before shutting the car door. She totally smells like banana and hummus, but at least she looks clean.

By some miracle, the PCH is not backed up this morning, and we're halfway to their overpriced private school, at a stoplight, when Summer reminds me that they need something red for art class.

"Does it have to be food?"

"No. It has to be something from home. That we can paint."

"That sounds more like a preschool art project to me."

"We have to really look at it and think about how it makes us feel. And then paint it when we're feeling the feeling."

Well, that almost makes the thirty thousand-dollar tuition worth it. "Red, huh? Can you paint that car?"

They both strain their necks to see the red Prius I'm pointing at.

"Noooo!" Summer says.

"Yes! But we can't carry it to class."

"Hmmm. Can you paint that lady's hair?" I nod toward the lady who's crossing the street in front of us.

"Yes," Summer says, "but I don't like her pants."

"Well, I guess you can't take her to class, then. What else can you find that's red? Should I get out and grab that stop sign?"

Summer crosses her arms in front of her chest, having none of this. "It has to be all red."

"Are you sure? Because strawberries aren't all red. Neither are tomatoes or apples."

I can see her rolling her eyes through the rearview mirror. I swear, she's been rolling her eyes at me since she was a newborn. "Okay, mostly red."

I start digging through the glove compartment. Car title, auto insurance, rolled-up script, green juice box, white and orange smashed-up packet of goldfish crackers, red condom packet—what's that doing in there? I shove that to the back of the pile before my kids can see it.

Red pen!

By the time I pull up to the curb in front of the school on San Vicente, we've got a minute to spare and my twins will be painting their feelings about a red pen and a pair of sandy, mostly-red boardshorts that have probably been in the armrest console since last summer.

Their friend Abby and her nanny Maria are hustling down the sidewalk—thank fuck we aren't the only ones running late today.

"Abby Abby Abby!" Summer yells out.

"No yelling at school," I remind her. "Hey, Maria," I say while helping Lucky get his backpack on and his shoes into his backpack. "Would you mind walking them to the door too?"

"Of course, Mr. Miller. Hello." She smiles at me warmly, notices that my T-shirt's on inside out, and nods politely, looking away. "Come on, kids. We're late, we're late!"

"See you at pickup!" I say, waving.

So that's done.

I got them to school alive and on time.

Now that the adrenaline rush has subsided, I am so fucking tired, I'm considering parking on a side street to take a nap.

I don't think I'm gonna make it through to Tuesday, much less another three months of this.

I start the engine and pull out onto the street,

slowing down as I check out the pair of women who jog by. One of them catches sight of me through the windshield, her eyes widen, and she stops in her tracks to elbow her friend and wave at me. They look like they're in their early twenties. They were probably fans of my Disney Channel sitcom *That's So Wizard* when they were preteens, or maybe the ABC Family one, or the CW show. They don't look like feature comedy fans. They just look hot. My fans are hot. They both start blowing kisses my way. I give them the nod and the grin they're looking for, salute them, and drive off.

Fuck, I need to get laid.

Maybe I should go for a run on the beach.

Fuck that—as soon as I get home, I'm going to call every parent I know to ask for a nanny reference, and if Margo doesn't like it, she can kiss my exhausted ass.

I can't take care of our kids if my basic needs aren't being met.

Shit, did I eat?

I need to eat.

I need to sleep.

I need to buy more groceries.

I need to clean up the mess in the kitchen because Consuelo doesn't come until tomorrow.

I need to call my agent back and tell him to stop sending me scripts unless the projects start at least four months from now.

I need to find out why bananas get brown spots.

I need to hear my name screamed out loud when I'm balls deep in a beautiful woman, but my Dad Dick has been deprioritized, so that goes to the bottom of an ever-growing list.

I feel like the oldest twenty-eight-year-old guy in LA and I just graduated from playing college students.

*Fuck you, insomnia.*

## WILLA TODD SCENT DIARY – MONDAY MORNING

*It's almost spring, and Los Angeles smells like jasmine, skunk, dry shampoo, and the unspoken need for attention and approval.*

*Downtown has the vague scent of urine every now and then in certain parts, but it's nothing compared to Paris. However, it also does not hold quite the same illustrious history. I mean, F. Scott Fitzgerald and Ernest Hemingway probably peed on the sidewalks of Paris. Although, I think Fitzgerald lived in LA for a while. He may have relieved himself all over Hollywood too.*

*But enough about pee.*

*My brother's apartment smells of Nag Champa incense, burnt toast, the lemon oil of his guitar polish, testosterone, a leather jacket that has been clung to and removed by more* girls than I'd care to imagine, and a weeks' worth of sibling tension that has now been heightened by his inability to bring skanks home whenever he wants to.

This morning, I am missing nothing in particular about France and everything in general.

That's wrong.

I miss the scent of every boulangerie I ever walked into or past. Every part of me aches for a freshly baked baguette and a pain au chocolat. Los Angeles is the most gluten-free city I've ever been in, and I hate it.

To transport myself, I've spritzed Frederic Malle En Passant onto this page. If I close my eyes, I'm walking past a lilac bush alongside of a wet sidewalk, moments after the rain has stopped but the storm clouds are still overhead. The wheat note hints at a nearby boulangerie, and the cucumber note keeps it clean and airy. If I could create one fragrance that is as delicate, evocative, and mysterious as this, I would just shit myself. Or something a little more professional and ladylike, hopefully.

To ground myself here to this new reality and cheer myself up, I'm going to burn a simple essential oil blend of lavender, lemon, and Virginia cedarwood and wait for my lazy ass brother to drag himself out of bed so I can make breakfast.

*\* Note: should have used Texas cedarwood. That blend smelled horrible and made me want to puke.*

## 2

## WILLA

*I*t's almost ten.

After a week, I'm pretty much over my jet lag, and I appreciate that Nico was so considerate when I was sleeping at odd hours while he was at home, but now that I'm on LA time, I cannot believe this guy's schedule.

I mean, he got home at two, so I guess it's not crazy for him to sleep until ten, but he's twenty-eight years old. I haven't stayed out past midnight since I was twenty-one. My grandmother has always told people how similar we are. He's an actor-turned singer-song-writer, and I'm a fledgling perfumer. He interpreted characters and became other people as an actor. Now he creates moods and moves people with his voice and lyrics and musical notes. As a perfumer, I help people feel like the person they want to be, creating moods and moving people with layers of fragrance notes. It's a pretty theory, Grammie, but my brother and I couldn't be more different, and just because he has online fan clubs and I don't—my approach to everything is better than his.

That's not sibling rivalry; it's a fact.

Okay, it's a little bit sibling rivalry.

But I'm winning.

Just because he's been making money off his talents since he was a teenager and has this awesome loft in downtown Los Angeles and a bunch of famous friends, while I'm currently unemployed and homeless and have one friend in this part of the country, that doesn't mean my seven years of post-secondary education and life experience in Europe are useless. They just feel useless right now. My carefully measured blending of science and art will prevail. Until then, I'll remind my brother of my infinite sophistication by brewing a way better pot of coffee than his ridiculous pod thing could ever piss out.

I add cinnamon, a touch of cardamom, nutmeg, and a couple of cloves to the freshly ground medium roast coffee, pour hot, not-quite boiled water into my French press pot, and gently stir it with a spoon. The aroma is heavenly. I've already had two cups of Earl Grey tea, but this is the bomb.

Do people still say "the bomb" here? Whatever. That's the other thing about staying with my brother—after four years at college and three years in France, I just feel like a dorky little pipsqueak all over again.

The slumbering beast has finally awoken. Still in his wifebeater and pajama bottoms, rubbing his eyes, he shuffles straight from his bed, which is surrounded by heavy canvas privacy curtains, to the bathroom, to the turntable in the living room area where I have taken over the futon. He puts on some acoustic song that I don't recognize but I'd bet a hundred Euros that the singer has a beard. Nico Todd is exactly as bearish first thing in the morning now as he was when he was a teenager.

"Morning, Sunshine!"

His endless yawn becomes a growl, even as he puts me in a somewhat gentle brotherly headlock and gives me a noogie. "You makin' breakfast?"

"No, I'm cooking eggs and turkey bacon for a new eau de toilette. It's called *Duh, Obvi*."

"Sarcasm only makes you dorkier. Pour the coffee."

"It's not ready yet."

He grabs a mug from the open shelf and slams it down on the counter. "Pour it now or suffer the consequences."

"You're an uncultured ass."

"You're an overcultured dork. That smells amazing."

"It'll taste better in two minutes."

"Fine." He plops down on the bench at the enormous table and yawns again. "I was thinking about it, and I don't want you working at a perfume store or a perfume counter."

"That is unfortunate, because that's the only kind of business I've been sending my resume to."

"Yeah. I don't think it's a good idea."

"I just got a master's degree in Scent Design and Creation. What job do you think would be more appropriate for me while I'm setting up my Etsy store?"

"Anything that doesn't require you to speak to or be exposed to men in any way."

I roll my eyes. Here we go again. "The customers at perfumeries and perfume counters are ninety-five percent female."

"Exactly. Find a job that's a hundred percent female consumer-oriented and do that."

"So I should be a former TV star turned singer-songwriter and sometime bartender?"

"Hey, I have guy fans too. I mean, my friends are fans. But how about this—you can wait tables at The Hotel Café when I'm tending bar or doing a show there." Nico was a bartender for about a year when he was transitioning from acting to his music career, but he still does it sometimes for fun.

"But you only tend bar when you feel like it. That's a ridiculous idea—I'd have to work way more hours than that."

"Well, I'll tell my friends there to watch out for you when I'm not around."

"Brother, dear. I am twenty-four years old. I hate to tell you this, but—"

He covers his ears. "La-la-la-la-nooooooo! Don't say it. You're the baby. Guys in LA are super horny."

"More horny than European men? I doubt it."

"Okay I really don't want to hear about horny European men."

I press the plunger of my French press down slowly then pour my brother a cup.

He still thinks I'm so inexperienced. The little sister in me wants him to keep thinking that because it's cute how protective he is. The twenty-four-year-old woman in me is like, *Dude. I've had sex with two men who were older than you.* Not at the same time. Separately. One was English and one was Italian. Neither were anything to write home about. But still. I've engaged in *soixante-neuf.* In France. With a Frenchman. It was awkward as fuck and I'd rate it about a *cinque* out of *dix* for execution, but I did it. I can handle myself just fine. I've just yet to meet a man who can handle *me.*

I wrinkle my nose at him. "Maybe I should just stay with Harley until I can afford my own place."

"Absolutely not, young lady. That girl is trouble."

"She isn't trouble."

She totally is trouble. Harley is my friend from Cornell. We lived in the same residence hall, and while I was getting my chemistry degree, she was studying Computing in the Arts. Now she does computer graphic stuff for films and stalks male models at gyms, I think. She invited me to stay at her place, but she has a one bedroom and a roommate and there would be no room for me to set up all of my fragrance supplies. Plus, her roommate sprays Febreze everywhere, and it would completely mess up my nose.

And besides, the main reason I chose to move to LA for now is to be with family. I passed up a job as a lab assistant at a major perfume house in Paris so I could be back in the US and start doing my own thing. I can't start my career in our hometown suburb of Detroit, so my brother's futon will have to do. He's just being crabby because he thinks he can't bring a girl home while I'm here. I mean, I don't want him to bring a girl home while I'm here either, but does he not have carnal relations with women who have their own homes?

"This is good," he says, staring down at his mug of coffee and nodding. "This is good. You make good coffee."

"Thank you." I serve him a plate of eggs and turkey bacon. Let's change the subject. "What are you going to do today?"

"I'm supposed to meet up with Shane later. You want to come?"

And there it is. The unmentioned name that has hovered around the edges of every sentence we've spoken ever since I arrived here. Now it fills the loft and steals the oxygen, and I am sucked into the black hole of it. Shane Miller. Do I want to come?

"Who? I mean, where? What are you doing? Going to do? With him? Today, you said?"

*Yeah, I played that totally cool—I'm sure he won't wonder what's wrong with me.*

I concentrate on shoveling scrambled eggs into my mouth and do not meet my brother's inquisitive gaze.

"What is wrong with you?"

"Nothing. I just haven't heard you mention him in ages. I wasn't sure if you were still friends."

"Course we're still friends. Why wouldn't we be?" He sounds defensive. He probably thinks I meant that they wouldn't be friends anymore because Shane went on to be a much bigger star than him. But I didn't.

What I meant was—*I've been dying for you to bring up Shane Miller because I used to be obsessed with him, but I never wanted you to know that, so I've never asked you about him. Ever.*

Shane Miller.

My brother's best friend.

My brother's former costar.

My first non–Disney prince crush.

The only guy I've ever tried to forget and the one I couldn't help but judge every other guy against.

Our first and only encounter may have gone something or exactly like this...

I was a gawky, gangly twelve-year-old girl from a small town in Michigan, and he was the sixteen-year-old star of a new hit Disney Channel comedy about a wizard from a wizarding family who's just trying to be a normal guy in high school. His character's name was Greyson Manning, and he was dreamy. My brother played his best friend on the show and quickly become his bestie in real life too. Our grandmother was Nico's guardian while he was living in Burbank, and I came out to visit them during spring break. We went to Disneyland because my brother had a VIP pass, and that was fun and all, but I was most excited about going to see Nico on set at a studio lot in Hollywood. I wore an all fuchsia-pink outfit, spritzed myself with sweet pea-scented Bath and Bodyworks spray, brought my copy of Tiger Beat magazine that featured an article on the cast for the stars to sign with a silver Sharpie pen, and carried with me an incredible secret: when I did the Tiger Beat quiz "Which Disney Channel character should be your boyfriend?" the answer was Greyson Manning.

Nico made Grammie and me wait in his trailer for an hour while he was in hair and makeup and running lines with the acting coach. Then finally he came back and told me to hurry up and come with him to meet the cast before they all had to do a big scene together. Most of the stars of *That's So Wizard* were hanging out around a big snack table, but Shane Miller was nowhere to be found. I got everyone to sign the cover and back of my magazine, saving the article pages for Shane. I made Nico take a picture of me standing behind the empty director's chair that had Shane Miller's name embroidered on the fabric. When I asked him where Shane was, he just shrugged and said he was "probably flirting with some girl somewhere or taking a dump; who knows." And that was that. I had to go with Grammie to her foot doctor appointment soon, so it didn't look like I'd even get to meet the boy who Tiger Beat had confirmed should be my boyfriend.

Fighting back tears, I let my jerk of a brother lead

me back to his trailer, when I heard someone say, "Hey, is this your sister?"

From the dark recesses of the sound stage, Shane Miller emerged in his character's trademark blazer, white button-down shirt, loose tie, black jeans, and high tops. He was even cuter in real life than on TV, and he was smiling and walking straight toward me. I could no longer move. My hands began shaking. My right eye started twitching.

"Yeah, this is her," Nico said. "This is Willa. Willa-Shane. Shane-Willa." I felt my brother's hands on my shoulders as he tried to move me forward, but I wouldn't budge.

Shane slid the script that he was holding under his left arm and held out his right hand for me to shake. "Hey, Willa. It's good to finally meet you," he said. "I've heard a lot about you."

I didn't say anything, I just thrust the magazine and pen into his chest.

"What is wrong with you?" Nico muttered.

"Tiger Beat!" Shane exclaimed. "Hey, you got everyone to sign it, That's so cool."

I grabbed the magazine back from him and opened it to the page with his picture on it.

"You want me to sign this?" he said, laughing. "They totally misquoted me in this article, by the way. I did not say that blue is my favorite color. I said I like the color of faded blue jeans. Guess they ran out of space."

I tried to giggle at that, but it got caught in my very dry throat.

"It's tough being a misunderstood star," Nico said as he nudged my arm. "You gotta get going, Will."

That's when a guy with a headset came over and told my brother that the director needed to talk to him, so he got dragged off and left me alone with the cutest, most famous boy I had ever met.

"When do you need me on set?" Shane called out to the guy.

"Five minutes!" the guy with the headset yelled back.

There were probably at least seventy other people in that soundstage, but it really felt like just the two of us all of a sudden in this empty space between the snack table and the black curtains that hid the exits to where the trailers were parked on the lot outside. Shane smiled down at me. I swear, he was so friendly, even his hair was smiling at me.

"You having fun in LA?"

"Yeah." I had found my voice, now that my brother was gone. My hands were no longer shaking either, and my eye had stopped twitching. It was like I was meant to be alone with this guy. "It's sunny. It smells like skunks, but people seem happy here."

He looked amused. "Yeah. They do seem happy, don't they? Are you happy in Michigan?"

"I guess so. But I won't be there forever."

"No? You coming out here to be an actor too?"

"Hah! No way. I'm going to live in Paris and make perfume."

"Perfume in Paris, huh? You do smell nice."

"Thank you. It's sweet pea. The flower. P-e-a. Not pee like urine." *Phew. Good thing I cleared that up.*

He grinned. "Got it. I've never met anyone who wanted to make perfume before. How do you do that, exactly?"

"Oh, well, I haven't learned all the different ways yet. I have to study chemistry in college and stuff, but you can use essential oils too. It's just mixing things together until you get the smell you want."

"That makes sense. Where do you learn that stuff? Potions class at Hogwarts?"

"I wish. My parents won't let me spend money on all the stuff I need yet. But I want to have my own company."

"Good for you. I bet you will..." His brow was furrowed, like he was really thinking about this. "How did you—why did you decide to be a perfume maker?"

No one had ever asked me that before. "My grandpa smoked a pipe. The tobacco smoke smelled like cherry vanilla. Every night, after dinner. It's the most delicious and comforting smell, and you'd smell it as soon as you walk into my grandparents' living room. And anyway. He died. He had a heart attack two years ago. It sucked."

"Oh yeah. Nico told me about that. Sorry. Your gram's really cool. But she seems sad sometimes."

"I know. It still smells like my grandpa's pipe in her

living room. It makes her happy-sad. She doesn't always want to feel happy-sad, which is partly why she offered to come out here with Nico. But that smell reminds her—and me—of Grandpa more than anything. It's instant. It's like he's there. That's how I know how important smells are. And I want to make them. I want to make important smells that make people feel things."

"That's really interesting, Willa."

"Thanks."

"Well, they're gonna call me to set soon."

"Okay."

"Hang on. I'm gonna sit down to write on this. It's W-i-l-l-a, right?"

"Yes." I loved how important it was for him to spell my name right.

He sat down cross-legged on the floor, placed the magazine on top of his script on his thigh, uncapped the marker, and began writing and doodling on the magazine.

I sat down right next to him, close enough that my knee touched his. The scent of a metallic Sharpie marker would always remind me of him. He smelled like soap and spearmint, some hair product that I didn't recognize, and Tide detergent. Cute Guy smell.

The rest of the cast had only signed their names, but he was writing other words too, on both pages of the article.

"Yo! Superstar! They need you on set." My brother jogged over.

"Be right there." Shane put the cap back on the pen, closed the magazine, and handed them to me. I was surprised by how serious his expression was. He stood up and then held his hand out to help me up. I took his hand, and he lifted me up, his index finger touching the inside of my wrist. Right on the pulse point. In the time it took me to stand, I didn't *see* our future life together, but I felt it. It felt comforting and exciting and romantic and light and important, and there was a home and kids and...I swear I felt it all in that moment.

I didn't know if he felt it too, and I didn't care. That tiny touch of his finger fired up my pulse, and if I had been anywhere near the same height as him, I would have kissed him on the mouth. But I was a foot shorter than him, so I did the next best thing.

Or the worst. Depending on how you look at it.

Before he let go of my hand, I lifted his hand to my mouth and kissed the back of it. I didn't make a kissy sound or anything, I just kissed his hand like I was some actor in a Jane Austen movie. I had never done anything like that before, but it just felt like the thing to do. I wasn't even embarrassed about it. I let go of his hand, looked up into his stunned face, shrugged my shoulders, and said, "Okay well, bye." Because I knew I'd see him again. We'd have our life together, eventually.

"Yeah," he said, cocking his head to one side and staring at me quizzically. "Okay. Bye."

He turned and jogged away, past my brother,

swatted him on the arm with his script, and disappeared from my view as he was surrounded by makeup and costume people and other crew members.

My brother was now the one who couldn't move. Because he was doubled over laughing so hard. He covered his face and shook his head. "That was the funniest fucking thing I've ever seen." He sighed and wiped a tear from the corner of his eye. "I am never introducing you to my friends again." He finally walked over and patted me on the back. "But that was awesome. Let's get Grams, and then I gotta do a big scene, and we will never speak of this again."

I didn't care what he thought, or if we never spoke of it again.

I clutched the magazine to my heart and waited until I was alone in the foot doctor's waiting room to read what Shane had written.

He had drawn a cartoony speech bubble above his photo, and the words inside it said, *Hey Willa, you're cool and you smell nice!* with his autograph below, near one of his legs. He drew an arrow that pointed to the other leg and wrote, *Faded blue jeans. Fave color.* On the other page, he wrote *Nice to finally meet you! Hope you always get the smell you want when you mix things together. Is that weird? You know what I mean ;-)*

It *was* weird. And I *did* know what he meant. He meant that he knew he was meant to be my boyfriend too.

I may have re-lived that encounter one to five thousand times for a year—or five—afterwards. I wore nothing but faded jeans for the next few years. I only told a couple of my friends about meeting him, once I'd gotten home. It felt like every time I talked about it, it became less real.

So I'd kept it to myself, knowing that we were a match—the performer and the perfumer.

I knew that I would see Shane again.

But I didn't.

Six years later, when I found out that Nico was going to be the best man at Shane's wedding to his costar from that CW show, I burned the Tiger Beat magazine and gave away my V-card to the idiot who'd taken me to prom. Then I was off to college, and I never spoke the name Shane Miller out loud again.

Still, part of me believed that his marriage to Margo Quincey couldn't possibly last.

When I heard that he had become a father, I tried so hard to make all thoughts of him disappear. I had met him one time. It was just an adolescent girl's celebrity crush. He was just being nice to me, the way he was nice to everyone. But it's like trying to remove the dried-down middle and base note scents of an oriental perfume from your skin once it has been absorbed at a pulse point. Even when you can't smell it anymore, others can. I wore my heartache like an invisible veil.

When I heard that he had gotten divorced, well...I was in France. I was just starting to mix things and make them smell the way that I wanted them to. But the heat of my body still emits activated molecules of Shane Miller where he touched me, twelve years later.

It wasn't love, but it was my imagination about what love could be that came alive when he took my hand. It bloomed and reacted with the warmth of my body, and suddenly I felt like the girl that I wanted to be. It's chemistry. I'd tried to smash against the molecules of others, but they'd all been volatile top notes that faded and evaporated almost in an instant.

"Yo. Earth to space nerd." My brother snaps his fingers in front of my face, bringing me back to the conversation.

I suddenly realize that I've been absentmindedly sniffing my wrist and the palm of my hand like a weirdo. "I just meant that I'd almost forgotten you guys were friends," I say to Nico. "I haven't thought about him in so long. But I'll hang out with you guys, sure. Whatever."

## 3

## SHANE

*T*he kitchen is now clean-ish, and I didn't fall asleep facedown in hummus once, so that's a win.

I still have to Skype my ex-wife and deal with the nanny situation, get in touch with my agent, get groceries, and maybe—maybe—I'll have time for a grown-up shower and a nap before picking up the kids.

It's around seven at night in Warsaw, so I might be able to catch Margo. There was a time in my life, long ago, when I couldn't wait to Skype with her if we were in different cities. Right now I'm dreading it. We get along well, but she's so predictable. I always know exactly how our conversations are going to play out before I start talking to her. It's like that with most of the women I've dated, to be honest.

One thing I did not predict from Margo when we were dating—that she'd get pregnant. We had just found out that our CW show *Twice Bitten* would not be renewed for a third season, and it was clear—in an unspoken way—that our relationship would end once the show did. Then one day I was summoned to her trailer, found her sobbing, listened to her explain to me that she had made up her mind and I could be as involved or not involved as I wanted to be, but she would be having this baby. Then I calmly explained to her that I would be as involved a father as legally possible. That meant marrying her.

Was I just trying to do the right thing? Yeah. Were we in love with each other? No. Were we both hoping that at some point maybe we'd both magically fall in love with each other after saying our vows and enduring the trials and tribulations of parenthood? Probably. But we both hated the dating scene in LA, loved the idea of playing house, and to be honest...we did not mind that being young married parents would help casting directors to see us as more than just teenage vampires.

Once the babies came, we grew the fuck up almost overnight and not much else mattered. We both fell head over heels in love with these little people we had created, but...it wasn't enough to keep our marriage together.

We tried.

No breakup is easy when there are kids involved. There's always guilt. But we really did always want what was best for everyone.

I think people have this idea of child actors growing up wild and spoiled rotten, completely out of touch with reality, in and out of rehab. Obviously there are a few of those out there, but every single one I've known is extremely disciplined and maybe even a little hungrier for a stable life than most people—and protective of what we have once we've found some semblance of it. Which is why my ex and I are on the same page when it comes to raising our kids with as much consistency as possible.

We didn't get to have a normal childhood, so it's more important than anything to both of us to give our kids as stable an upbringing as we can. Not that there's anything stable about the life of an actor. Not that there's anything even remotely sane about the lives of two actors who are co-parenting five-year-old twins.

But we try.

Even when Margo fell in love with a very wealthy producer, we tried "nesting" for a few weeks after deciding to end our marriage. Margo tossed the words "conscious uncoupling" around like glittering Holly-wood confetti. I lived in the guest room of our former home in the Hollywood Hills, but every time Landon Gold came over when I was there, it was awkward as fuck. A guy wants to be the king of his castle, and I needed my own castle, no matter how hard it was not seeing the twins every day when I was in town.

But it got easier, eventually. Summer and Lucky were two years old, so I don't think they even remember what it was like before they split their time between us. It was never a question that we'd have shared custody. And the truth is, Landon is a good guy.

He's a much better match for Margo, he's good enough with the kids, and he isn't trying to replace me. So all I've had to do was focus on getting my shit together and figure out how to deal with my ex-wife as a parent.

My shit is pretty together, aside from the fact that I'll probably never sleep or have a significant relationship with a woman again for the rest of my life. Here's what I've figured out about how to deal with my ex-wife as a parent: I just have to pretend that I don't think she's an overly ambitious, mildly self-centered, phony boho-hippie flake, and remind myself that she's a nice person, a good mother, and even a pretty good friend —in her own way. But there always comes a point where I need to put my foot down, and this is one of those points. The foot's coming down.

I find my laptop and try my luck at initiating a video call with Margo. She accepts the call after three rings. The camera of her phone is pointing up at a very high ceiling. I can hear giggling, rustling, and movement.

"I'm here! Hang on!...Owww! You stuck me with the pin that time." The phone moves, and when Margo's hand pulls away, I see that she's in the middle of a costume fitting. "Hi. What's up? We're almost done here." She's wearing a Victorian-era dress and holding her arms up while getting poked with safety pins apparently.

Am I jealous that she's doing a period film that started getting Oscar buzz before they even began shooting it? A little. I'll never get cast in a period film because I have what's referred to as "a modern face and manner." Whatever. The Academy of Motion Picture Arts and Sciences can suck my thoroughly modern balls.

"Do you have a minute? I need to talk to you about something."

"What's wrong?"

"They're fine. I just need to talk to you."

A middle-aged woman with measuring tape hanging around her neck comes into view for a second. "I'll pop out for a bit," she says. "Not to worry."

Margo's voice gets deeper as soon as she's alone. The phone's propped up against something, and she can barely move with a corset on, but she tries to lean in closer to the camera. "What's going on? How are they? You look tired."

"The kids are great."

"Yeah? They're doing okay without Paloma?"

"They're doing just fine without Paloma. They sleep, they get up when they're supposed to, one of them brushes his teeth all by himself while the other makes a fucking mess in the kitchen, and they magically get to class exactly on time."

"You still aren't sleeping?"

"Only from the hours of six thirty to seven thirty in the morning on school days, it turns out."

"Did you try the valerian root tea?"

"It smells like sweaty socks."

"You really need to try meditating again, and I

mean, if you would just practice yoga even for ten minutes a day, it would change everything."

"Really? Will it bring Paloma back? Will it change the location of your shoot from Poland to Vancouver, British Columbia? They have mountains there too, and it's only a three-hour plane ride away."

"No, but it would change your perspective and your response to these things, because that's really the only issue here."

"Is it, though? Is that the *only* issue?"

"We've been over this—it's not like I love being on the other side of the world from my kids. There weren't any neo-baroque castles in Vancouver, last time I checked. God, you're grumpy. I'm going to look up which flower essences would be good for you."

"Fantastic. While you're doing that, I'm going to hire a temporary nanny to help me out until you get back."

"Shane, no."

"Margo, yes."

"Did you talk to your housekeeper?"

"Consuelo has two grandkids to look after when she isn't cleaning houses."

"Can your mom come stay with you for a bit?"

I knew she'd ask that. My mother is a saint. She lives in Sedona, Arizona with her boyfriend, but they're currently driving across the East Coast in their Airstream. When I was a kid, we lived in Flagstaff. On the weekends, she'd drive me two and a half hours away to Scottsdale to meet with agents, audition for commercials, shoot commercials. When I booked the Disney Channel show, she moved with me to Burbank while we shot the episodes, stayed with me during the hiatus when I starred in such stellar straight-to-dvd classics as *Spaced Camp* and *The Santa Blahs*. She continued on with me in LA until I turned nineteen, after my ABC Family show was cancelled, and never blamed me for my dad's affair with his secretary and the inevitable divorce that ensued. So as much as I'd love to just call my mom up and whine that I could really use her help over here—I think she's earned her road trip with a guy named Hank who's seven years younger than her.

"She's traveling for at least a month" is all that I say. "What about your parents?"

"They're both in rehearsals for the Tom Stoppard play. On Broadway. You know that."

"Which is why I'm going to have to hire someone."

She tries to angrily cross her arms in front of her chest, but she can barely move them and just ends up in some stubborn Victorian lady Incredible Hulk pose. Do I laugh at her? Yes. Yes, I do.

"It has to be someone we both agree on. You promised."

"It's not like I'm going to drag someone in off the street. I'm gonna start making calls. I'll keep you in the loop. Skype ya later when the kids are home." I end the call before she can complain.

I'm about to kill two birds with one stone by calling my agent and asking if his wife can recommend someone, when Nico Todd's annoyingly handsome smirky face shows up on my phone and I realize he's calling me. "Yo."

"You on your way?"

"On my way where?"

"To meet me for coffee."

"Oh yeah." *Shit.* I haven't seen Nico in ages. Between us living on opposite ends of LA, me having kids, my shooting on location in Maine and him being on tour, we've only seen each other twice in the past few months. Which is crazy because he's my best friend.

There goes my grown-up shower and nap.

"Yeah. Leaving now. Where am I meeting you?"

"You totally forgot, didn't you?"

"Yeah, I'm having sleep issues and I've had a shit week. Listen, I need to buy groceries and I have to pick the kids up at three, so can we multi-task?"

"Doesn't your nanny do that?"

"She did before she quit."

"Can't you just order online?"

"Yes, but I'd have to be at home to put the cold stuff away when it's delivered—just meet me at Erewhon."

"Which one?"

"On Beverly." Nico and I always meet up midway between his place and mine because it takes a fucking year to get between the Palisades and downtown. I know exactly what he's thinking right now—there are always hot women at Erewhon. Organic cold-pressed green juices plus overpriced superfoods and gluten-free donuts equals starlets in tight little tank tops and yoga pants. It's basic LA math.

"Okay, but I've got my sister with me."

"What?"

"My sister. She's crashing with me."

"Not willingly!" I hear her mutter in the background.

I get a surprising shiver up and down my spine. I remember Nico's sister. Quirky. Adorable. So far, she's still the only person who has ever kissed me on the back of my hand. She was so young, but how could I forget her? "Hey, Willow!"

"It's Willa. We'll be there in like twenty minutes."

"Yeah, I'll be there in half an hour."

"Right. See you in forty-five minutes."

"I'll be there in half an hour."


Forty-five minutes later, I'm walking into Erewhon and scanning the café area for Nico, but I catch sight of a world-class ass in a pair of tight faded jeans and I can't seem to look away. This girl is in the floral section, sniffing a bouquet of flowers and smiling like she's being reunited with a long-lost love. She is stunning. She is surprisingly gorgeous in the way that a sunset is gorgeous. You just have to stop what you're doing to marvel at the natural beauty and remember that it's not your problems and To-Do lists that define you. It's the things that take your breath away and give your life back to you by nudging you off track.

Suddenly, I am not so tired.

Suddenly, I feel wide awake, all over.

She turns her head, as if she senses that she's being stared at.

We lock eyes, and at first, her face lights up. She recognizes me. I'm a man again. There are enough hours in the day. I'm not going to die alone. Everything is going to be okay. I can have it all.

Then, her smile fades, her expression hardens.

And I recognize her.

Same dark hair, same olive skin tone, same golden-brown eyes, same full smirky mouth—as my best friend.

It's Willa Todd.

The unfuckable sister.

A sunset that I can only catch glimpses of in passing, if I'm lucky.

Fuck.

Fuck this day.

## 4

---

## WILLA

*Y*ou know that scene in *The Great Gatsby* where the girl is admiring the ridiculous number of orchids in her cousin's living room when he invited her for tea, and then she hears someone enter, slowly turns around, and sees Leonardo DiCaprio standing there, all rain-soaked in a white suit, with his intense blue eyes? They stare at each other, after years apart, for an eternal breathless moment. The music swells. Finally, she says, "I'm certainly glad to see you again." His jaw clenches and he says, "I'm certainly glad to see you as well." And you just want to watch it over and over again, twenty times, because it's so damn perfect and romantic?

Well, that little cinematic moment sucks donkey balls compared to what just passed between Shane Miller and me in the middle of a fancy overpriced organic market.

For a few magical, floral-scented seconds, I

completely forgot that I was mad at him for forgetting my fucking name when I had spent my entire adolescence believing that we were soul mates.

He is so handsome now and shockingly sexy when he's not being a relentlessly charming goofball in testosterone-fueled blockbuster comedies. He's got bedhead and bedroom eyes that are somehow even more piercing blue because of his day-old stubble. His moistened lips are parted and look like they are on the verge of whispering something dreamy and subtly devastating and then kissing you until you forget your own name. The expression on his face, the way he was staring at me, it made me feel more beautiful and desirable than I've ever felt in my life.

And then I remembered that I am just the goofy little sister that he thinks of as "Willow" and that he's a movie star with two kids who probably only dates actresses and supermodels. And his expression changes. Like I've suddenly come into focus and he's realizing he doesn't like what he sees so much after all. Worse, even. Like I've reminded him of everything that's wrong with the world.

He takes a deep breath, runs his fingers through his hair, and takes a step toward me but stops when he hears my brother say, "Yo! Superstar!"

Nico comes bounding over from wherever he was, abandoning whatever hot chick he was chatting up. Do people still call them hot chicks here? Whatever. I place the bouquet of freesia back into the flower bucket and fiddle with the little gold heart pendant of my favorite necklace, watching as Nico and Shane hug each other. Not just a bro-hug, but a real, full-on, been-too-long-missed-you-old-friend embrace. It's sweet.

When they finally pull away from each other, I start to make my way over to them, but some woman, about my age, goes over to ask if she can take a selfie with them. She inserts herself between them, and they all lean in together so she can take a picture with her phone. It seems like the kind of thing that happens all the time. I know that girls used to love the idea of them being friends in real life. My brother instantly lowers his chin and makes his smirky musician face at the camera, but Shane is looking beyond her phone, smiling at me. Like he's remembering something amusing.

Probably thinking about how I kissed his hand.

Whatever. I'm sure tons of girls have done spazzy things like that to him.

It's a good thing I'm not a naïve, impressionable twelve-year-old anymore, because it would be really easy to misinterpret that look as something meaningful.

But I won't. I've learned my lesson. I've moved on.

The girl says something gushy to them and then immediately steps away, probably to post the pic on Instagram. Nico grabs Shane's shoulders and squeezes them, musses up his hair. and starts catching up with him. They seem completely unaware of anyone else's presence here, so I go back to perusing the floral offerings.

A minute later, my brother calls out my name.

I slowly remove my face from the eucalyptus branches that I've been inhaling and place them back in their bucket.

Nico brings Shane over to me. "You remember my little sis? Willa."

His face is so serious now. "I do. Sweet pea. P-e-a, the flower, not urine."

Great. *That* he remembers, but not my name.

"What?" My brother laughs. "What does that mean?"

"Nothing," Shane says, grinning at me now. That trademark flirtatious but safe and friendly grin that sells tickets and dreams and wastes years of a girl's life. "Hi." He holds his hand out, and I glance down at it before taking it because I'm afraid that despite being twelve years older and ten times wiser than I was the last time I touched that hand, I will do something idiotic like kiss it.

I need to say something amazing but understated and memorable.

"Hi. Your shirt's on inside out."

He lets go of my hand as soon as he's given it a good firm shake. "Yes. Yes, it is."

Well, that was underwhelming, but at least there's no way either of them can tell how I used to feel about him.

We both look back at my brother and wait for him to steer the rest of this conversation in the right direction. He shakes his head at me, silently wondering what is wrong with me, but he suggests we order coffee and take it to the covered outdoor seating area. Shane orders decaf and informs us that he has insomnia. I have about a thousand things to say about that, but it's probably not my place.

He still smells clean, but in more of a house-cleaning product way, with a hint of something earthy or nutty. Hummus?

I take a seat at a small table, Shane takes the seat across from me, and Nico pulls up another chair.

Now that my brother is around, Shane has barely made eye contact with me. It's fascinating. And it sort of makes me want to capture his attention again.

"Let's see the kid pics," Nico says to him, like he wants to get it out of the way. Asshat.

Shane laughs. "You don't have to indulge me. They're just as cute as they were the last time you saw them."

"I want to see them," I say, tossing my long hair over my shoulders and leaning forward. His tired eyes barely slip to glance at my exposed cleavage in this silk camisole before staring down at the table in front of him as he reaches for his phone. I'm wearing a blouse over the cami, so my brother can't see any boobage from where he's sitting. *That was just for you, tired daddy.*

He flicks through a few images and then turns his phone to face me. "This is Summer Rain and Lucky Scout."

I gasp. It's not even a fake reaction. Those are two

of the cutest, most beautiful children I have ever seen. They have their father's blue, blue eyes and his wavy brown hair. I suppose I can see their mother in their pretty faces too, but mostly Shane. "Oh, Shane. They're wonderful. What are they—five?"

"Yeah, they're in kindergarten." He tilts his phone for Nico to see.

"Yup. Still cute," my brother says.

Shane swipes to another photo to show me.

"You took these pictures, right?" I ask.

"Mmhmm."

"I love how they look at you. Summer's a little bit sassy and Lucky kind of reveres you."

"Yep. That about sums it up." Shane shifts around in his chair and places his phone facedown on the table, still avoiding eye contact with me.

My brother looks back and forth between us. "You know...Willa was a nanny in France. You should hire her to help you with the kids."

I practically sprain my neck when I snap my head around to widen my eyes at him.

"What? You need a job. He needs a nanny. You need a live-in, right?" he says to Shane. "This could work out well for all of us."

"You don't—uhhh—I've been applying for jobs at perfume shops," I explain to Shane.

"Yeah, that sounds more..."

"But you'd rather make your own perfume and set up your Etsy store, right?"

"Well, an Etsy store is just the first step."

"Whatever—you could do that if you stay at Shane's. Right? The kids are still in school. She'd have time to do her own thing sometimes."

"Sure, yeah. Are you—would that interest you?" he asks me.

I think we both want to kill my brother right now. "I mean. I wasn't..." *Would it interest me?* "Yes. It would," I hear myself saying. "If you... I don't want you to feel..."

"No, I just—it's a really good idea, actually, if you..."

"Yeah, I would...I mean, we should talk about this."

"Sure, let's talk about this." He smiles and shakes his head at Nico.

Meanwhile, my brother's attention has turned to a model-y looking blonde who is entering the store.

"Holy shit," he mutters, craning his neck to watch her through the window. "I've seen that girl around. I'm gonna go get a green juice or...something." He stands up, pats Shane on the shoulder. "You guys figure this nanny thing out. I'll be back." And the fucker's gone.

Shane and I just stare at each other for a few seconds and then laugh.

"You wanna go 'get a green juice or something' too? I can sit here and drink coffee by myself. It's fine."

"I don't think green juice is what I need right now."

"Oh yeah? What do you need?"

"A three-day nap."

"Have you always had insomnia?"

He shrugs. "Off and on since...since right before I

got married, actually." He says it as if he's just realizing this now.

*Interesting.*

"And you need a nanny now because…"

"Because the regular nanny quit on Friday, so I have the kids while Margo and her husband are shooting a movie in Poland for a few months. I'm taking time off from work so I can be with the kids, but it's been so long since I've had a good night's sleep, I can barely function. The weekend was okay, but I almost didn't get them to school on time today."

Poor guy. This is a man who's led a charmed life. He's not used to feeling overwhelmed and out of sorts. I look down at his hands, both of them holding on to his cup of decaf coffee.

He needs so much more than caffeine to wake him up right now.

"Have you ever had your palm read before?"

He quirks a brow at me. "No. Have you?"

"Yes. By a woman in Versailles." *She told me that I met the love of my life before I was in high school.* "I'm pretty sure everything she said was a crock of shit, but she was very charming and convincing."

I can't tell from his expression if he's a cynic or not.

"Let me see your right hand." I hold out both of my hands, palms up.

"Wait a minute," he says, smirking and cocking his head to one side. "Are *you* the charming and convincing crock-of-shit palm reader from Versailles?"

"The grandmother of the family I boarded with

taught me a few tricks." I beckon him with the fingers of my outstretched hands.

He pushes his coffee aside and stretches his hand across the table without hesitation. *Surprising.* I take his hand in mine and examine the shape of it. I am fully aware that this would play out very differently if we were at a bar instead of a supermarket and if my brother were half a world away instead of at some counter inside the store, chatting up a hot chick. I am also aware that the last thing I should be doing is pulling out the party trick I've employed to flirt with guys who are either too pretty or too shy to make the first move. But I guess this is what's happening.

*His hand.*

*Oh Lord, his hand.*

The texture of his skin is not quite rough and not exactly smooth. *It feels good.* "You're down-to-earth, but you're also sensitive."

"Am I?"

I turn his hand over to press my thumbs into his palm. It's firm and resilient. "You're very practical and hard-working."

"And you're still kinda weird, huh?"

"Am I?"

His skin has a pinkish hue. *I bet his penis is really pretty.* "Well, the lack of sleep isn't affecting your overall health. That's good." He's loving and support-ive. Margo Quincey is a fucking idiot for letting this guy go. "Oh, you have a square palm."

"What does that mean? I'm good at opening square jars?"

"It confirms that you have good energy and you're a hard-worker. You don't mind a challenge." *His long fingers are capable and sexy, and I want them on my body. Shit.* "You're responsible and you finish what you start." *I want these fingers inside me. Fuck.* "This is your heart line," I say, tracing the major line across the top of his palm with my fingertip. It's long and strong. *I want to see him wrap this hand around his cock, and I want him to ram that cock into me. He could really give it to me good. Goddammit, what is wrong with me?* "This tells me something about your emotional life."

"Oh yeah? What's it telling you?"

His heart line is curved. Shit, it's really curved. Sex is very important to this man. "I, uhhh...That's about the extent of my palm-reading abilities. Sorry."

He pulls his beautiful hand away to rake it through his amazing hair. "Well, I learned a lot about myself, thanks."

I place my hands at the edge of the table in front of me and push myself against the back of my chair. This is a passionate man who will stop at nothing to make a woman come, and I can't be that woman and I need to shift gears. "So, are you doing an ad for hair products later today or what?"

"No, I'm not."

"Then why do you look like that?"

"Like this?" He points to his perfectly tousled hair.

"I literally wake up with awesome hair every day. I couldn't make it look bad if I tried."

"That's kind of annoying."

"I know, but to be fair, it's my only annoying quality."

"Unless one considers the inability to select a decent movie to star in a quality." *Shit. Too far. I'm going too far in the other direction.*

And yet, he seems totally unoffended.

"Once again, to be fair, that's just my inability to fire my agents for encouraging me to do those mainstream movies that pay me millions of dollars so I can feed my children."

"And you couldn't possibly feed your children with money earned from films that don't star former wrestlers? I'm curious—do you even read the scripts before you agree to make these movies?" *Oh my God, Willa, he's a nice dad who is exhausted and he really needs your help. Don't be a dick.*

Where's my idiot brother?

I need to shift gears again.

And Shane Miller needs to stop staring at my mouth or I'm going to fling myself across this table and never stop kissing him.

## 5

## SHANE

*T*his girl is giving me whiplash.

I never know what she's going to say next, and I love it.

She needs to stop staring at my mouth or I'm going to lean across the table and kiss her.

But also, why is it so adorable that she's being such a little turd to me?

"First of all, yes I do read every script that my agents read first and then pass along to me. Secondly, John Cena is a hilarious and talented actor who was a costar—not the star—of that movie. And third, it just so happens I recently wrapped a fantastic little independent film that I was only paid scale plus ten for."

"I don't know what that means."

"It means I didn't do it for the money and if it doesn't get into Sundance I'm screwed."

"Uh-huh. So you also didn't do it because you loved the script."

"I did love the script. It's a great script... You know, it's funny—I'm remembering now that Nico once mentioned that you've been sort of a dick ever since you moved to Europe, but I didn't believe him."

"And now?"

"And now I think that was an understatement."

She blinks once and then looks down at her coffee cup. "Yeah. Sorry. It seems the only way my super impressive science degrees actually benefit me in Los Angeles is that they make me feel superior enough to ridicule attractive, successful actors who make more money in one month than I'll probably make in five years. If I'm lucky."

"Wow, there is a lot to unpack in that sentence, but all I really heard is that you find me attractive, so I'm gonna let you continue to make fun of me."

"Thanks. I would have continued even without your permission, but your mild narcissism makes it even more rewarding."

"You aren't a dick to the kids you look after, are you?"

"Not really."

"That's comforting."

"I generally prefer kids to adults, so..."

"Yeah? Hang on—my brain's a little slow today, but I just realized something. It sounds to me like you're very familiar with my entire body of work."

She scoffs and looks away. "No."

"And yet, you speak as though you are familiar with the scripts of the films I've starred in."

"Movies. You've starred in movies. And I did not watch them willingly."

"Go on."

"No. Are we just going to sit here and talk about you and your hair for half an hour, or would you like to tell me about your children?"

"You're the one who started talking about my hair."

"I don't think so... Okay you know what—this is weird, so I'm just gonna tell you something and get it out of the way so things don't get weirder, and then you can decide if you want to hire me as a nanny or not."

"Okay..." This should be interesting. If she tells me that she's been arrested, I think I can still make this work, as long as it was for a nonviolent crime.

She takes in a huge breath, grabs on to the pendant of her necklace, and tilts her head up, squeezing her eyes shut. I take this opportunity to briefly admire her slender neck and elegant collarbones, the impossibly smooth skin of her chest, and the strap of that pale-pink bra that's peeking out from under her blouse and tank top, and *fuck me she's pretty. Not just pretty—she's lovely and odd and sexy in a way that I've never encountered before. I want to take her to dinner and go for a walk on the beach and talk to her for hours and hours while Netflix and chillin', and I want that gentle, knowing hand and that pouty sassy mouth on my cock. Oh fucking hell, I want to suck on those beautiful tits until she comes, and I want to spank that round ass and fuck her with my tongue and make her scream my name, and then I will bend her over and give it to her until she—whoa.*

She takes another deep breath, and I look around for Nico. He could take one look at me from inside the store and know that I've been thinking about coming all over his little sister's tits, and there would be one hell of a cleanup needed in Aisle Me. He is nowhere to be found, but I need to clamp down on this train of thought regardless.

"I used to have a crush on you."

*Fuck. That's not helping.*

"A big one. Years ago. When you worked with my brother. And maybe for a few years after that. I mean I was basically a zygote and we only met once, and you barely even knew I existed. I realize I was just one of thousands of little girls who had a thing for you, but anyway. You were the first famous guy I'd ever met—I mean the first cute young one. I had met the local weatherman in Detroit, but he was old and creepy. Anyway. You were so nice to me, and it meant a lot to me, so...I had fond memories of meeting you."

*Goddammit. It's so cute that she's telling me this.*

"But I'm over it. So over it. That was then. This is now. Between now and then, I've dated tons of other guys. Mostly European ones. And not all of them were chemistry nerds either. So. It's not a thing anymore. Let's just focus on your kids and your sleeping problem and the job you need me to do and not get weird about the fact that I might be living with you for a few months. Right?" She wrinkles her nose, finally looks over at me, lets go of her necklace, and bites her lower lip.

*Fuck me. I don't want her to be over it.*

"Yeah. Right. Thanks for making it not weird." Fucking hell, why does she have to be Nico's sister? "First of all, there were hundreds of thousands—possibly a million or more girls and moms who had a thing for me when I was on *That's So Wizard*, just to clarify. Secondly, I'd like you to define *tons*. Tons of guys—is that Girl Speak for three?"

She smirks. She clearly did not mean three. "Sure. So, we're cool, right? Potential friends who might be living and working together-ish? Obviously don't tell my brother I had a crush on you, because he would lose his mind and never let me see you again."

"You think?"

"Oh yeah. He had no idea how I felt about you. I'm gonna stop talking about how I felt about you now."

"Good, yeah, great... You should probably stop talking about that now."

"Okay, I need to do something though." She slaps her hands on her thighs. "It would be better if you cover your eyes."

"Sure." I cover my eyes with both hands and totally sneak a peek through the cracks of my fingers just in case this thing she's about to do involves giving me another glimpse of her cleavage. She stands up, takes one step to the side of her chair, and starts jumping up and down while flinging her hands around. It would probably be a strange and not at all sexy thing if someone else were doing it, but her tits are all bouncy and carefree, and nothing else really matters right now except for that. She's jogging in place and tilting her head from side to side, and now she's jogging away from me and back again, once, twice, three times, and now she's back in her chair.

"Okay, I'm done."

I remove my hands from my face. "What are you done doing, exactly?"

"I just had to release some nervous energy and do something even more embarrassing than disclosing my former crush to you."

"That makes sense."

"Now *you* tell me something embarrassing about yourself."

"I'm not doing that."

"Fine. I guess that penis shirt is embarrassing enough."

I look down at the front of my inside out shirt. "Pen shirt. My pen is... You can read what it says?"

"I'm pretty sure everyone can."

"Whaddya know...shit—what time is it?" I flip over my phone to check the time. "I should start shopping. I've gotta get back home to unload the groceries and then pick up the kids." Jesus, those are the least sexy sentences a guy could ever say right there. "You want to come with? We'll keep talking. About the kids. Not about the huge crush you used to have on me."

"I'm super glad I confided in you. Thanks for not making me feel awkward about it."

"I'm super glad you brought it up, even though I've practically forgotten about it already."

. . .

I text Nico to let him know we're shopping, but I saw the model he's hitting on. He won't be joining us anytime soon. And I'm glad. This is the first time I've been out grocery shopping with anyone other than the kids in years, and it's nice to just push a cart up and down the aisles and not have to worry about things being dropped or knocked over or someone getting lost. Although I could easily get lost in that voice and those eyes and that hair and those hands and that body and the way she smells—Jesus, she's a buffet of sensory delights, and I can't indulge in any of them.

But I can tell she's trying just as much as I am to find a rapport that will work for us.

Kids.

Focus on the kids.

"So how old were the kids you looked after in France? Versailles, right?"

"Yes, right outside of Paris. That's where the post-graduate school is, where I got my Master of Science."

"In perfume."

"In scent design and creation."

"So now you've learned all the different ways to mix things together to get the smells you want?"

She smiles and blushes. "Pretty much. Anyway, I boarded with the Angier family. Noelle and Leo are the kids. Noelle was six when I first got there, Leo was eight. School-age. I'd look after them when their parents were at work or traveling. My class schedule was similar to theirs, so it worked out quite well. They're good kids. It was easy."

"Well, mine are good kids, but they aren't easy."

"No?"

"No, they're a nonstop adorable nightmare. Like an animated Disney movie that follows you around and just won't end."

She giggles. "I don't believe you."

"You'll see. They're really smart, though. Probably a little too smart for my liking." We're in the produce section, and I reach for a bunch of organic bananas. "Hey, you don't happen to know why banana skins get brown spots, do you?"

"Enzymatic browning," she says without whipping out her phone or even stopping to think. Her face lights up as she explains, "Polyphenol oxidase reacts with phenolic compounds and oxygen to create brown pigments. During the ripening process, amino acids transform to ethylene gas, which is a hormone, to break down the complex sugars. They also go brown from bruising if they're dropped, because that makes them produce the gas faster. It's actually best to eat a banana once the brown spots have started to develop. Sugar is easier to digest than starch."

*I am an undereducated moron.*

"Right. Chemistry. I'll just tell Lucky it makes the bananas sweeter." *Moving on.* "Do you speak Spanish?"

"I'm pretty fluent in French, but I learned how to say 'please leave me alone, I'm not interested' in five other European languages. Why do you ask?"

"Because the kids learn Spanish at school. Our other nannies would speak it with them quite a bit. Don't worry about it. It sounds like you were very popular in Europe."

"I could probably pick up Spanish really quickly," she says, ignoring my last comment. "They're both Romance languages."

"Really, don't worry about it."

"No, I should learn Spanish if I'm here. You must speak it pretty well by now."

"*Sí*." That's it. That's the extent of my spoken Spanish. This girl is out of my league.

"Where do you live?"

"Pacific Palisades. Overlooking the ocean. It's between Malibu and Santa Monica."

"I've been dying to get out to the beach."

"My house is on the bluffs, with a view. I gotta warn you, though. I mean, has Nico told you anything about my neighborhood? It's no place for a single twenty-four-year-old. Every restaurant in the village is closed by ten. It's really family-oriented and quiet."

"Has Nico not mentioned that I'm a boring dork?"

"I don't think so."

"I am."

"Really? Because you seem like a fairly exciting dork to me."

"Really? Thank you, but you seem like you have fairly limited experience with dorks."

"It's not for lack of trying. Can you cook? You don't have to."

"I cooked for the kids in France sometimes, sure. But I learned a lot of tricks from their grandmother, and they all involve butter, so..."

"My personal trainer will hate that."

"Sorry."

"No, I hate my trainer. That's a good thing."

When we pass by the Wellness and Beauty department, Willa places her hand on my arm for half a second, and I feel things that I haven't felt in ages. "Have you tried lavender essential oil?"

I shake my head. "For what?"

"Insomnia. You should get an essential oil burner."

I let her guide the front of the cart down the aisle and listen to her explain in a sing-song voice about aromatherapy and how breathing in the scent molecules of lavender essential oil can transmit signals to my limbic system to relieve stress and promote deep, relaxing sleep. She doesn't harass me about it the way Margo does. She just presents me with the information and lets me decide for myself if I want it.

I want it.

I'll take it.

"Do you have a current driver's license?"

She blinks at the abrupt change of subject as she places a burner, tea lights, and essential oil in my cart. "I do."

"How's your driving history?"

"Minimal but fantastic. I went to college in Ithaca, so I didn't have to drive much there, and I sometimes drove the kids around in France, but not much. I've been driving Nico's truck here."

"His old Nissan pickup?"

"Yeah. I like it."

"Well, I'd have to rent you a car if you're going to drive my kids around."

She shrugs. "Okay." She looks up, directly into my eyes, for the first time since we've been walking around the store. "So, you really want to do this?"

*Yes.*

Fucking hell, I need this woman in my life.

I'll take her any way that I can have her. Dick in pants. Heart on lockdown.

My kids need this woman in their lives.

I can make this work.

I can sell this to my ex-wife.

Margo loves this natural beauty, aromatherapy shit. She fancies herself a Gwyneth Paltrow for millennials. She will eat this girl up in a totally different way from how I want to.

"Well listen, I'll have to talk to Margo, and then you'll have to Skype with her, but I really need a nanny, like yesterday. This could definitely work. If *you're* really interested."

"Do you want me to meet the kids first too, though? Make sure they like me?"

"Oh, they won't like you. They've never liked any of their nannies or babysitters."

She guffaws. "Seriously?"

"It shouldn't affect the way you do your job."

I have now replaced all of the food items that my daughter transferred to the kitchen floor this morning and push the cart over to checkout. I don't think about how easy it is to talk to Willa, and I don't think about how good I feel, and I don't dwell on how impossible it will be to restrain myself from kissing her. I just ask her to stay in line with the cart while I go over to the floral section and pick out the flowers that I saw her inhaling when I walked in. Back in the good old days, when I didn't know she was Nico's sister. I grab all of them. Five bunches of these sweet and peppery-smelling blooms.

When I place them on the checkout counter, she smiles and helps me place everything from the cart onto the counter. We don't say anything until the cashier scans the five bouquets and I take them from her to present them to Willa. "For you. Welcome to Los Angeles."

"All of them?"

"It's a big city. You deserve a big welcome."

"Thank you." The way she's blushing and smiling at me now, it's just like when I first met her. When she was a zygote who had a big crush on me. "Well, why don't I take one of them back to my brother's and you can take the other four to your house? I mean, since I might be there too. Eventually." She places four of the bouquets back into the cart.

"That also works."

Is the lack of sleep clouding my judgment?

Is this the best or the worst idea ever?

Do I have any other choice?

No. I don't have any other choice.

Having Nico's hot, weird younger sister help me with the kids and sleeping and showering in my house is the only choice I've got.

*Fuckin' A.*

*I love this day.*

"Sorry we didn't hang more," Nico says, putting his arm around my shoulder as we carry the groceries to my car. Willa is waiting by his Jeep and sniffing those flowers with a dreamy look on her beautiful face. "I've got a show coming up. Maybe you'll come."

"Yeah, no, it's fine. I'm glad you got to spend some quality time with yet another model in yoga pants."

"Somebody's gotta do it." He grins. "Hey man, no pressure about hiring my sister or anything…"

"Not at all, man. She's great. I'm in. I think this is happening. I'll just have to clear it with Margo, you know."

"Yeah, good. It's just that she needs a job, and I don't know if she's ready to handle LA guys if she's at a sales counter or waiting tables or whatever, but I trust *you*." He squeezes my shoulder, and I'm pretty sure he doesn't mean to do it in a menacing way, that's just how my dick's reading it. "You'll look out for her. Like a brother."

"Yup." *I will definitely keep her away from other LA guys.* "You can count on me."

## 6

## SHANE

"So...you really didn't get in any trouble for this?" I tape Summer's latest masterpiece up onto the side of the fridge, above Lucky's painting of my red board shorts.

"No. Why?"

"No reason. And your teacher didn't say she wanted to talk to me?"

"No. Why? I did what I was s'posed to."

"You did, baby. You really did. It's beautiful. Yours too, Lucky. These are really, really good. I'm proud of you." Summer did a really good job painting a big red pen and writing out the words *MY PEN IS BIGER THAN YORS*. "Really, really proud." I toss their empty juice boxes into the recycling bin and put their snack dishes in the sink.

"What are those flowers doing here?" Summer stares at the flowers that I put in a pitcher in the middle of the kitchen table.

"They make the kitchen more homey, don't you think?"

"Yeah. What's homey mean?"

"A place where you feel good and comfortable."

"Why do they smell like that?"

"I'm not sure, buddy. To attract bees, maybe?" *Why the fuck don't I know anything?* "Hey, Lucky, do me a favor and find my iPad. I think it's in the living room. We gotta Skype with your mom before she goes to bed."

"Why does she have to go to bed so early?" Lucky asks.

"It's not early where she is, remember?"

"But why is it different for her?"

I bet Willa can explain time zones to a five-year-old. "That's a really good question, buddy. There's these things called 'time zones,' and we'll have to look them up later. Summer—brush your teeth."

"Why?"

"Because you didn't brush them this morning."

"But I'll have to brush them again before bed!"

"Get to the bathroom now. We can't Skype your mom until you have clean teeth."

She makes a cartoony *harrumph* sound, and I follow her as she stomps to the guest bathroom. "I. Will. Only. Brush. My. Teeth. If. You. Sing. to meeeeee!"

"I'm not doing that."

"Yes! From a musical!"

"Nope."

I squeeze some toothpaste onto a little pink toothbrush and hold it out to her after she stands up on the step stool, but she just crosses her arms in front of her chest and shakes her head.

"Brush your teeth."

"Sing to me!"

"Ask me to do anything else—I don't like to sing."

"Why not?"

"You know why not. I'm not good at it."

"Why not?"

"Because nobody's perfect. I can't be a good comedy actor, have great hair, a six-pack, *and* sing and dance. I'm not Zac Efron."

"Can Uncle Zac come over?"

"No. Brush your teeth, or I will brush them for you."

Her lips disappear inside her stubborn, adorable face. She looks like an angry Muppet.

"Summer. We all have to brush our teeth at least twice a day. Come on."

She shakes her head slowly, maintaining eye contact with me, reminding me who's boss.

I am so fucking proud of her for knowing what she wants and being so strong-willed, but I also want to rip this sink from the wall.

I open up her hand and place the toothbrush in it. "*I…*"

Her face lights up, and she lifts the toothbrush to her mouth, which is still closed.

"*I am the very model of a modern Major General.*"

She smiles, and I maneuver the toothbrush so it's touching her teeth.

I can memorize all of my dialogue after reading a script twice, but I only know the first couple of lines to every song I've ever heard. Singing breaks my brain, but I swear, Margo can tell if someone hasn't brushed their teeth from six thousand miles away and I'll be damned if I'm going to look like a totally incompetent father today. *Fuck you, Pirates of Penzance.*

"*I've information vegetable, animal, and mineral.*"

She starts moving the toothbrush up and down.

"*Keep brushing Summer Miller or you're gonna be in big trouble. If not your teeth will all fall out and it will look just terrible. Go up and down and front and back and don't forget the bottom ones. La-la-la-lah-bah-puh-buh-bah!*"

"Enough!" she orders, shaking her head like a tiny Simon Cowell with a mouth full of foam. "Stop!"

"What? You don't like that song?"

She spits into the sink and wipes her mouth with the back of her hand. "I don't like your voice on that one."

"You've heard me sing before, so why do you keep making me do it?"

"I thought you'd get better!"

I fill a little cup with water and hand it to her. "Such an optimist. Rinse."

"Found the iPad!" Lucky calls out from the hallway, sounding like he's been searching for hours.

"Thanks, buddy. Wipe your mouth with the towel,

not the back of your hand," I say to Summer as I walk out of the bathroom.

"Abby's dad can sing!"

"Yeah, but Abby's dad can't act and he isn't funny. Trust me. I've seen him on *Saturday Night Live*." I take the iPad from Lucky. "Actually, you know what, I have to have a little chat with your mom first. Why don't you guys wait for me in the family room."

"Can we watch—"

"No!"

"Mean!" Summer stomps down the hall to the family room.

"Ohhhh no! You gotta sit in the family room for two minutes without watching TV! Your life is so hard!"

I initiate a Skype call with Margo as I carry the iPad back into the kitchen, sliding the door shut.

The video window opens up after two rings. "Finally. I can barely stay awake."

"Welcome to *my* world."

"Where are they?"

"In the family room. Just listen. I've found a nanny."

She purses her lips, just like Summer did.

"Nico's sister is staying with him. She just came back from France, where she was a nanny to two French kids while she was getting her master's degree in...perfume design or something. She's a perfumer. Her name's Willa."

"I forgot Nico had a sister."

"So did I. But she's here. I just met up with them

this afternoon. She's twenty-four, super nerdy and responsible and down-to-earth. She's into natural stuff and aromatherapy, and she's about to open up an Etsy store and she wants to make perfume for a living. She's trained for it."

I know my ex-wife so well—I can literally read her thoughts as she processes this information.

*Gwyneth.*

*Goop.*

*Margo.*

*Signature scent.*

*Margo.*

*Synergy!*

*Marketing campaign.*

*Next level.*

*Margo Margo Margo.*

"She sounds interesting. Let's set up a time for me to Skype her. Wait—I'll Skype Nico. I don't want her to have my information in case it doesn't work out. Make sure they're together. Can we do it tomorrow?"

"I could literally be dead from lack of sleep tomorrow, but sure."

"I'm quite sure that's not physically possible."

"It definitely feels possible."

"Well, she'll have to sign our nondisclosure agreement. What about her salary?"

"Oh shit. We didn't discuss that."

"Well, what did you discuss?"

*She read my palm. She told me she used to have a crush on me. She alluded to dating a lot of European men.* "Her excellent driving record, her fluency in French, her preference for kids over adults. You'll like her. She's a good vibes person."

I would never say the words "good vibes person" out loud to anyone but Margo, and only when it involves getting Willa Todd to be my kids' nanny.

She studies my face for a few seconds. "Okay. Well, I hope it works out. Did you talk to the kids about it yet?"

"No, I wanted to talk to you about it first."

She smiles at that. "Okay. Take me to them. I need to see them, but I have to go to sleep."

I take the iPad to the kids in the family room, tell Lucky that his mom's going to explain time zones to him, and while they're talking, I go back to the kitchen to text Willa.

When she programmed her information in my phone, she put it under **Willow SweetPeaNotUrine Todd**. I change it to **Willa Todd** before typing out: **Yo.**

Shit. Why'd I send that? Why am I texting like a creepy old dude?

**WILLA: Hey. Why are you texting me like a creepy old dude?**
**ME: I hit send before finishing the sentence... YOU are the lucky winner of a Skype call with Margo Quincey. She's excited to meet you. We'll set up a call for you and her on Nico's phone tomorrow. That okay?**

Good save, Miller. Good save.

WILLA: Word!
ME: Why are you texting like a boring dork who's trying to sound cool? Oh wait, never mind.
WILLA: Booyah.
ME: I really hope some of your '80's hip-hop awesomeness rubs off on my kids.
WILLA: Fo' shizzle.
WILLA: I hope some of me rubs off on you too.

   *What?*

   Shit, is that flirting? Is she flirting? Now I can't stop picturing her rubbing off on me.

   Fuck, this is a bad idea.

WILLA: Um. It just occurred to me that you might have read that the wrong way.
WILLA: To be clear, I have no intention of rubbing off on you. Ever.
WILLA: Or on anyone else, for that matter.
WILLA: Do people even call it that here anymore? In France there's a term for jerking off that literally means 'to wobble oneself.' Like you're walking a tightrope and wobbling from side to side? Which always made me wonder if the French are wanking themselves off properly.
WILLA: I'm going to put my phone away now.
Thanks for the job opportunity, sir. Byyye!

Fuck. She's adorable.

This chemistry between us is a living thing that I can't seem to control or predict. New and energetic and wobbly like a toddler. Or like a single dad who's walking a tightrope and wobbling from side to side.

Yeah. This is a bad idea.

## SHANE MILLER SLEEP DIARY – TUESDAY, 11 AM

**Went to bed at:** *Around nine thirty. No, really.*

**How long it took you to fall asleep:** *Not long. Took a shower after putting the kids to bed and...felt some relief.*

**How many times you woke up in the middle of the night:** *Once. And I never got back to sleep.*

**How refreshing your overall sleep was:** *It wasn't great. But it wasn't terrible. I used this lavender essential oil thing. It may have helped at first. But then I think it made things worse, because the smell just reminded me of...something.*

**Number of caffeinated beverages you consumed throughout the day:** *Zero. Really don't see the point of abstaining, Dr. Shaw.*

**Number of alcoholic beverages you consumed throughout the day:** *I fucking wish.*

**How much time you spent exercising:** *One hour. Trainer just left. Fucking asshole. Sixty straight minutes of upper body work, circuits, and supersets, and I still have mental energy to burn. Physically, I'm tired. But I've got something on my mind, and it's keeping my brain stimulated. Focused on one particular issue. All the time. This isn't like me. It doesn't make sense.*

**Your stress level before bedtime, on a scale from 1 to 5:** *5-50.*

**Major cause of stress:** *Guilt.*

*Still a little anxiety about not working for a few months, but if I left the kids to work while Margo's out of town, then I'd have even more guilt. And also, I'd never do that. So fuck my career.*

*Except no—don't fuck my career. I need my career. I should probably go for a run on the beach. Maybe if I run ten miles, I'll be tired enough to sleep for an hour or so before I have to pick up the kids. Maybe if I run twenty miles, I'll be too tired to think about her.*

## WILLA TODD SCENT DIARY – TUESDAY AFTERNOON

*I don't need to burn any essential oils today because the yellow freesias are so powerfully fragrant. Sweet and spicy. It's strange to me that this flower is supposed to symbolize innocence, because when I smell it now, all I can think about is how pretty someone's penis probably is and how I really shouldn't be thinking about how pretty it probably is, because as of tomorrow he will be my employer. And I can't think about my employer's penis. Especially while I'm responsible for the well-being of his five-year-old children.*

*Actually, I should breathe in some neroli essential oil to calm down. I have been impatiently waiting for my brother to get out of here to meet up with some record producer so I can finally take a shower and...get some relief.*

*I've already started thinking about fragrance notes for Margo. I can't believe I am now on a first-name basis with Margo Quincey. I really can't believe she wants me to design a natural, nontoxic signature scent for her. It would be my first commission in the US, so I guess I'm happy and grateful. I checked out her wellness website, and it did not make me nauseous. I may have even liked it. Obviously this woman wants a fragrance that represents who she wants to be. As opposed to who she is. Because if I were to design a fragrance that evokes who she really is, it would smell like a phony idiot who somehow managed to get the greatest guy on earth to marry her and then fell in love with some other entitled idiot like a bitch. I'd call it Phony Idiot Bitch. Top note: Phony. Middle note: Idiot. Base note: Bitch.*

*Okay, the truth is she was nice. She said she checked out my Instagram and loved it (but said she won't follow me yet "for obvious reasons." No, please explain to me what the reasons are. Because you're a fancy famous actress and you don't want your fans to see you following a commoner on IG? No, I completely get it obviously. Hopefully you'll also understand why I won't be following you either).*

*Nico has only good things to say about her. And she seems like a good, caring mother. Aside from the whole cheating on the cutest dad on earth and leaving her kids for a three-month job in Poland thing. But—if it weren't for that, I wouldn't be going to live with her amazing ex-husband and beautiful children, so... Yay Margo. Guess I'll make her smell good.*

## 7

**WILLA**

"*A*re you still on Sunset?"

I'm on speakerphone with Harley, who is breathing heavily because she's on a treadmill at the gym. I think she's been doing a walking pace this whole time—the heavy breathing is from staring at some male model who's doing deadlifts in her eyeline. We live very different lives.

"Oh my God, yes. This street is endless. I'm actually in the Pacific Palisades now, though. Very different vibe from every other part of LA that I've been to so far."

"It's called boring rich people vibes. Make a legal U-turn ASAP and get back to the east side while you're still cool enough for me to talk to."

"You and I both know that I've never been cool enough for you to talk to."

"True."

"I think I might love it here. Oh, look, there's a hardware store that's not a Home Depot! All the buildings on this street are two floors at the most. It seems really chill, and everything's clean and pretty!" I roll down my window. The air is cleaner here. I can't see the ocean, but I can feel it. People are actually walking around in this village. Willingly. Happily.

"Oh God, I'm losing you."

"Can you hear me now?"

"Yeah, I mean I'm losing you to the Westside, and I've only seen you once since you got here. This is tragic."

"I will still hang out with you. Hang on, I have to turn here. I think I'm almost at his house. I think...I think that's Tom Hanks coming out of a Starbucks."

"Stellar. I bet he doesn't look half as good in compression shorts as the guy doing squats twenty feet in front me. Okay, send me pictures of the house, I need to go flirt with Mr. Leg Day before he hits the showers."

"I'm not going to send you pictures of the house. That would probably be in violation of the nondisclosure agreement I'll be signing."

"Ugh. Girlfriend needs to get over herself."

"No comment. Have fun squatting on Mr. Leg Day."

"See now, *that's* the kind of fun you should be having in LA."

I end the call and lift the inside of my wrist to my nostrils to inhale my homemade vanilla and amber perfume oil. I smell like a sexy, soulful bakery, and it makes me feel calm, feminine, and warm—not at all like the horny girl who pleasured herself in the shower yesterday while thinking about her poor, tired, hot-as-fuck new boss.

Now that I'm off the phone, my navigation app is telling me to turn onto a residential side street. This neighborhood is gorgeous. There are red and fuchsia bougainvillea bushes and small trees everywhere. The sky is a more vivid shade of blue here than it was downtown, and the wispy, windswept white clouds are so inviting. The houses aren't as big and fancy as the ones I could see right off Sunset when I was driving in, but I like that. They're built into the hills and designed to favor the views.

I love it here.

When the app tells me that my destination is on the right, I slow the truck down and my heart starts racing.

*Stop it.*

This is where I'm going to be living for three months?

*Stop. It.*

I can see the ocean from the driveway.

The rest of the property is gated with a privacy fence, but not in an obnoxious way. Through the horizontal slats I can see a young eucalyptus tree and ornamental grasses, Russian sage, and lavender plants. The house is modern, understated, friendly, eye-catching. Just like its owner.

I park the truck, leave my belongings inside of it, and skip to the gate. At this point, I might even be more excited to see the rest of the house than I am to see

Shane Miller's gorgeous, sexy face. It's just after eleven, so the kids are still in school. I press the button on the intercom, running my fingers through my hair and trying to control my facial muscles so I look a little less like a lunatic who fantasized about getting drilled by a former Disney Channel star and more like a responsible caregiver who really appreciates good architecture and landscaping.

I am all ready for a little joke-y home security banter, but the gate buzzes and clicks open. I push the gate and step inside the front yard. It is narrow, with landscaping on either side of a wide path that extends up a sloping hill to the street and down to the front door. The front door opens, and Shane Miller steps into view, breathing heavily and chugging a bottle of Gatorade. His brown hair, though sweaty and disheveled, still somehow looks like it has been styled that way. He's wearing a tight tank top and gray sweat shorts, and his skin is flushed.

"Hey," he says, a little breathless. "My trainer just left. Sorry I'm all sweaty. Welcome. Come on in."

He allows me to step into the foyer past him, simultaneously giving me a glance of this magnificent home and a whiff of the most amazing man sweat I have ever inhaled.

Let me take this opportunity to nerd out and briefly discuss a chemical substance known as pheromones... Pheromones are like hormones that are secreted externally by an animal's body—they subconsciously cause a physiological response and affect the behavior of other animals of the same species. It's an incredibly effective form of chemical communication that is detected within the olfactory system—despite the fact that they may seem odorless. Ever wonder why ants follow an invisible trail to a tiny piece of food? Scent pheromones. Curious as to why your cat keeps rubbing his face against the leg of your coffee table and absolutely everything else in your house? Scent markings—he's marking it with facial pheromones.

There is great debate among scientists as to whether or not humans actually produce pheromones, because it has not been definitively proven, but it is surmised that if humans do emit pheromones, one of the main ways they do it is through their sweat glands. This has led one university researcher to conduct a study of women's brain responses to polyester pads that were placed under men's armpits while the men were watching porn, as well as pads of men's sweat when they were not sexually aroused. Guess what? The MRI scans revealed that the sexy sweat stimulated different parts of the women's brains than the normal sweat did, and the scientist then suggested that women can subconsciously recognize the scent of a man who is attracted to her.

Because, science!

Well, alert *Scientific American*, because I am one hundred percent certain that Shane Miller has just detonated a sex pheromone grenade in my face, and I fucking love what I smell. I'm not saying he's lying about recently working out, but perhaps at some time in the very recent past he has also worked a little something else out, if you know what I'm saying. And I say this as a professional perfumer—if I could bottle up and sell this man's scent, women would try to hump everything you sprayed it on. I would be financially secure for life. *For life.* But I wouldn't. I'd keep it for myself. Because I want it all over me.

Fortunately, I am not an insect and my rational brain is perfectly capable of overriding this primal urge to rip off our clothes and plaster my mouth to my employer's mouth.

I think.

Yeah.

I can definitely transform this primitive sexual desire into sarcasm.

"Wow. What a shithole," I say, looking around. "You should probably call your agents and tell them you need to do a few more crappy blockbuster action comedies."

He blinks. The corner of his mouth twitches. He nods once. He is not amused.

"If you're trying to laugh, it's not coming out right."

"I'm just too fatigued to express my appreciation for your delightful sense of humor."

"So this is what you're like when you're at home?"

"This is what I'm like when I've had a grand total of eight hours sleep in two days."

"Did the lavender essential oil not work for you?"

"It did, but then it didn't." He gestures and leads me farther inside this glorious and spacious house.

"Wow." The back of the house is almost all windows, and the view is all ocean. "To be clear—I think your house is gorgeous."

"Thanks. I'll let my agents know they can stop sending me crappy scripts, then." He leads me to the counter of the island in the center of the kitchen of my dreams, but I go straight to the kitchen sink and the window that overlooks the bougainvillea-covered bluffs and narrow highway and beach and glimmering ocean below.

"Wow" is all I can say. "Seriously. Well done."

"I'm glad you like it. Can I get you something to drink? Eat?" He guzzles the last of the Gatorade and walks over to where I'm standing. I can feel the damp heat emanating from his skin. It's giving me goose bumps. My physical response to this man is strangely intense, even though our interactions are decidedly unsexual. "'Scuse me," he mutters as he reaches down to open the cupboard door under the sink. His fingers don't even touch my denim-covered leg, the empty plastic bottle does, and yet I feel a ridiculous little jolt and step aside.

Pheromones, I tell you.

Clearing my throat, I ask, "Can you walk to the beach from here?"

"Not really. There's no direct path down the bluffs, so you have to go back up to the village and then down along Temescal Canyon. It's a bit of a hike, especially with the kids. But it's doable. Was that a 'no' regarding something to drink?"

"I'm fine, thank you."

When we both finally look away from the view and at each other, I see a flash in his eyes of something just as primal as what I was feeling. Or maybe he's horrified by what my pores look like in this bright natural light. Whatever he was feeling, he blinks and looks away, and any sign of it is gone. He goes over to the island and picks up two printouts from the counter, along with a pen. "I feel weird about doing this, but this is a standard NDA and the employment contract that Margo's lawyer has all of our domestic employees sign. Sorry—I hate calling you that."

"It's fine. That's totally what I am to you now."

He clears his throat. "Right. You don't have to sign it now. You can look it over or have your attorney look at it..."

I scoff at that. "Sure. I'll have my legal team go over it first." I pick up the pen and sign both pages without reading them.

"And my business manager is supposed to e-mail you about setting up payments."

"Yes, his office has reached out to me, thank you."

"Cool. Also, he said it would be better to buy a car and then sell it, rather than rent one for three months, so someone's going to deliver a Volvo with car seats tomorrow morning. Hope that's okay."

"Are you kidding? I love Volvos."

He manages to laugh at that.

"No, really."

"Well, just don't go on any joyrides and crash it."

"I mean. I'll try not to."

"I'll give your e-mail address to the kindergarten teacher, Mrs. Babcock, so you'll get cc'd on their class updates and schedules. Get ready for a stuffed inbox." He winces and then shakes his head as soon as he says that, probably wishing he could erase that phrase from my memory as I simultaneously try to stop picturing this man stuffing my inbox.

"Great. And I've got Margo's e-mail address now, so I'll be sending her pictures of the kids and keeping her in the loop."

"Oh good. She'll like that."

"Yup. All good. If you want to take a shower, don't let me keep you."

"I'll help you bring your stuff in, get you settled first. Unless my workout stank is offensive to your highly trained nose, then I can shower first."

"Nope. I am definitely dealing with it. Let's get me settled."

Shane carries my enormous duffel bag full of clothes and pulls my even more enormous hardside suitcase that contains carefully bubble-wrapped perfume supplies, while I carry my portable perfumer's organ into the nanny room. This room is just down the hall from the kitchen, with an adjoining bathroom. I place the perfume organ on the floor by the desk that's under the window.

"It's called an organ?" he says, wrinkling his untrained nose.

"That's what a perfumer's workbench is traditionally called, yes. This one's basically a fancy folding spice rack for containers of materials that I use for creating scents. My little fragrance lab." I carefully open it up on the floor so he can see all of the little amber, blue, and clear bottles on the shelves.

"Cool. You're going to set that up in here?"

"Yeah, on this desk, but I'll have to move the desk away from the window so the sunlight doesn't degrade the contents."

"I don't think this room gets a lot of direct sunlight, but I'll help you with that." He comes over to lift up one side of the desk.

"Oh, now? Okay." I take hold of the edge of the other side of the desk, and we carry it to the nearby wall.

"We should tell the kids not to come in here. You want me to put a lock on the door? Or can you keep the bottles locked up in this thing when you aren't using them? I don't want the twins to break anything."

"I've found that it's better to just show kids exactly what's in the bottles and let them handle them. It's curiosity and the lure of the forbidden that tends to lead to broken things and messes." *For kids and grown-ups.*

He nods, as if he's agreeing with me, but says, "Maybe with French kids, but literally everything leads to broken things and messes around here."

"Yeah. Your house is a disaster."

"The housekeeper came yesterday. There should be plenty of towels in your bathroom. Consuelo made the bed. There are extra sheets in the closet and tons of hangers, I think. The laundry room is downstairs. I'll show you later."

I can't help smiling. He's very considerate for a male host. When I got to my brother's loft, all he said was, "There's your futon; there's the bathroom. If you get your girly things all over the place, I'll throw them out."

Shane puts his hands on his hips and looks around, his gaze pausing on the bed for a second before returning to meet mine. "Anything else you need? I should probably hit the showers now."

"No, I'll start unpacking. Then maybe you can show me the rest of the house before we pick up the kids." I slide the elastic hair band from my wrist and lift my hair up to put it into a ponytail so I can get to work, but a few strands seem to be caught in the clasp of my necklace. "Ow."

I tug on my hair and struggle to untangle the mess, but all of a sudden I feel Shane's fingers graze mine, his breath on the back of my neck as he pushes my hair to one side.

"I'll get it. Hold your hair up."

It's a gruff command, and I do as he says.

He carefully unhooks the necklace and meticulously frees each strand of hair from the gold chain and clasp. I can imagine how patient he must be with his kids. But I can also imagine how thorough and focused he must be with women.

He may or may not be breathing in the scent that's emanating from my wrists and my neck.

I may or may not be holding my breath and squeezing my inner thighs together.

"You want me to put it back on for you?"

I nod. "Yes, please. Hang on. I'll put my hair up first." I pull my hair up into a high pony while he holds the necklace in place around my neck.

When I lower my hands, sliding them into the front pockets of my jeans, I remain perfectly still and face forward as he fastens the clasp.

The fingertips of one hand drag down just an inch of bare skin at the base of my neck and then over my T-shirt between my shoulder blades, making my breath catch, sending a delirious shiver all through me.

I turn my head the tiniest bit.

If he doesn't move, I will turn my whole body to face him. I have to. How can I not, in this moment?

But he's out the door without a word.

Leaving me here with a tension between my legs that may never be resolved, a pulse that has skyrocketed, and my hand over the little gold heart pendant that I bought years ago to remind myself of how important it is to protect that vital organ from the likes of Shane Miller.

"hat was your favorite part about school today?" I ask the kids.

"Lunch!"

"Yeah? What did you have?"

"Noodles with chicken bits that we ate with our fingers! And cucumber and carrot sticks and goldfish crackers! And Daddy hid the red gummy bears under the crackers!"

"He did? That's funny. What about you, Lucky? What was your favorite thing?"

Lucky is considering his answer very carefully. "Hmmm. I liked it when Mrs. Babcock tooted and pretended she didn't. Everyone laughed, and then she laughed too, and she said she had a soda for lunch." Lucky and his sister both cover their adorable faces as they laugh hysterically.

"I seem to recall Mrs. Babcock had a soda for lunch last week too," Shane mutters from the driver's seat.

"She did! She toots a lot. But not the smelly kind."

"Wow. Mrs. Babcock sounds like my kind of teacher."

"Why do some toots smell bad and some don't?"

"Good question, Lucky! Willa's an expert on smells. Willa?"

I smile, and my eyes meet Shane's in the rearview mirror. When we picked up the twins. I decided to sit in the back seat between them. Partly because it seemed like a good idea to be closer to them and partly because sitting next to their dad on the drive to school was silent, awkward agony. He's barely said a word to me since his shower, and the only time he's made eye contact with me since then is through the rearview mirror.

"Well, I can tell you exactly why that is, actually. You see, when you toot, your body is passing gas and chemicals out from the belly, and the type of gas that comes out of you depends on what you ate. So, if you ate something that has *sulfur* in it, like meat or eggs or broccoli, your farts are going to be silent but deadly! But if you drink bubbly drinks like soda, your belly might get filled with those gas bubbles, but there's no sulfur in them, so when the gas comes out it doesn't smell."

So this is what our life is going to be like together for the next three months. Fart talk. That should make it easier to keep it in my pants.

"Did you know our mom and dad are famous?" Summer grins up at Shane while asking me this.

"Yes, I do know that. Did you know that I first met your dad when he was a famous teenager?"

"You did?" Lucky's voice gets squeaky. "Did you know our mom too?"

"No, I actually met your dad when he was working on a TV show called *That's So Wizard!* with my brother Nico. Do you know Nico?"

"I know Nico!" Summer yells out as she flings her arms in the air. Typical female response to my brother's charms. "Wait. Nico is your brother?"

"Uh-huh."

"Is Nico coming to live with us too?"

"No."

"Why not?"

"Because Nico has his own place. And I'm better at looking after kids than he is."

"Because you're the nanny?"

"Exactly, Lucky. Because I'm the nanny."

"Was our dad the same as he is now when you met him?"

"Well, that depends. How is he now?"

"Tall. Funny. Nice," Lucky says.

"Tall and weird and tired all the time and sometimes nice and sometimes a big grumpy bear."

"Hey," he says without looking back. "I'm not tired *all* the time, and I'm nice even when I'm a big grumpy bear."

Honestly, it's hard for me to believe he's grumpy with the kids. The way their faces lit up when they saw him waiting on the sidewalk. The way they ran to him and giggled when he caught them both and somehow managed to pick them both up at the same time...my right ovary wept while the other one shoveled ice cream into its mouth.

"Sounds like he hasn't changed much," I say. "Only I don't think he was tired all the time when he was a teenager. Maybe we should let him take a nap when we get home. What do you think?"

"Dads don't take naps. Naps are for little kids."

"They don't? Not even tired dads? Do you take naps sometimes?"

"Nooooo!" Summer says.

"Sometimes! When we're tired we do!"

"See. Anyone can take a nap if they're tired. Even dads."

When we get back to the house, I ask the twins to show me what they want for a snack and tell them they'll see their dad again at dinner. Shane looks uneasy about leaving me alone with them so soon, or perhaps he also does not feel that masculine grown men are allowed to take naps. I tell him to go do whatever he wants, just do it up in his bedroom with the lights off. And then I skillfully distract him from the accidental innuendo by telling awesome, hilarious jokes.

"Hey, guys—if your dad refuses to go upstairs and take a nap, we're going to have to charge him with resisting a *rest*. Get it?"

That one went straight over their little heads, but Shane just blinks and grins appreciatively.

"We should give your dad a report card on his napping skills. If he does good, he'll get straight zzzzz's!"

I can tell that Lucky and Summer don't get the joke, but my delivery is so comical, they laugh politely anyway. They're good kids. Shane shakes his head, gives each of his kids a kiss and then says to me as he passes by, heading out of the room, "See you at dinner. If you don't quit before then."

"You won't get rid of me that easily. Hope you get some zzzzz's!"

Summer and Lucky show me to the pantry, where their favorite afternoon snacks are kept. They are all packaged, organic, and Margo-approved. While they eat, I take a picture of them to send to their mother, rinse salad ingredients for dinner, and encourage them to make up more jokes about napping.

"Why did the chicken cross the road?" Lucky barely manages to ask because he's laughing so hard.

"To take a nap!" Summer says, giggling. "What's black and white and red all over?"

Lucky's head falls back before she's even finished the sentence. "A nap!"

I guess this is how twins tell jokes to each other.

After I've wiped their mouths and hands with wet wipes and they've helped me to put the dishes in the dishwasher, Summer asks for pocket snacks.

"What are pocket snacks?"

"Snacks that I keep in my pocket. For later," she explains, as if she shouldn't have to explain this to me.

I look over at Lucky. "Is that a thing?"

He shrugs. "I don't need them. But she gets really grumpy if she doesn't have snacks."

I don't want to wake up Shane to ask if it's okay for her to have double snacks, and gosh darn it, I want her to like me. "Okay, but just something small, like a packet of goldfish crackers."

"But I'll take Lucky's too. I have two pockets—see? And he forgets that he likes snacks sometimes."

"Hmmm. Okay, but only if you both brush your teeth first."

"Why? I brushed them this morning!"

"Because you ate lunch and snacks. I like to brush my teeth whenever I get the chance. Brushing your teeth is fun!"

Neither of these two little people is buying it.

Summer screws up her face and tilts her head at me as she slides snacks into her pockets. "Do you know any songs from musicals?"


"*By the sea, by the sea, by the beautiful sea! You and me, you and me, oh how happy we'll be! When each wave comes a-rollin' in, we will duck or swim, and we'll float and fool around the water. Over and under, and then up for air, Pa is rich, Ma is rich, so now what do we care? I love to be beside your side, beside the sea, beside the seaside, by the beautiful sea!*"

Summer has barely brushed her rear upper quadrant by the time I reach the end of the first kid-friendly song that popped into my head, courtesy of all the ocean views. Without removing the toothbrush from her mouth, she says, "Again."

"No ma'am. One song, that's the deal. Finish brushing all of your teeth so we can do something else."

Lucky is definitely the good twin.

"What are we going to do?" he asks.

"Well, that depends. Do you guys feel like being big right now or being little?"

"What can we do if we feel like being little?"

"I can read you a book, or you can play dress-up or some kind of game."

"What can we do if we feel like being big?"

"Well, I heard that Summer hid your shoes and some other things, so maybe she can show us where she hid all of it and we can put everything back where it was so everyone can find everything and that will make life easier for everyone."

Summer spits into the sink, frowns at me, and crosses her arms in front of her chest. "I did not hide them. I put them in better places."

I fill a little cup and hand it to her to rinse with. "Okay. Well, why don't you show us where these better places are. Or we can make it a game! Lucky and I can look for his shoes, and you can tell us if we're getting close to finding them or not!"

She puts the cup down, wipes her mouth with the back of her hand, and huffs.

"Or...I can show you my room and all of the things I use to make perfume and you can help me mix together something that might help your dad sleep better at night. And then you can help me make dinner."

Summer and Lucky have now sniffed all fifty of my essential oil bottles, and after calmly explaining to Summer that no, I do not have more than I need because this is for my work and if she ever throws my things away I will be very, very mad, she and Lucky have narrowed the scents that they think will help their dad sleep down to spearmint, lemon, and rosemary. They're all stimulants. But they'd smell great together!

"Why don't you try this one again." I open up the neroli oil. "Don't you think this one's nice?"

They both lean in to get a whiff.

"It smells like Grandma's hands."

"She probably has a soap or a lotion with this ingredient. I'm going to leave this one out for you to think about. How about this one?"

I open up the rose essential oil for them to sample again.

"I like it," Lucky says.

"It's too girly-foo-foo for daddy."

"Well, he's not going to put it on his skin. This is for burning in an essential oil burner in his room before bed, remember? We'll put a little bit of water in a little soapstone bowl, add a few drops of these oils, and then we light a tealight candle under the bowl and it makes the room smell like the essential oils."

"Why?"

"Because the heat from the candle warms up the oil and water, and that releases them into the air. That's called evaporation."

"But why does it make the room smell? Because of gas in his belly?"

I can't help but laugh at that. "Sometimes. But this will make the room smell really good and help him to relax and fall asleep."

I feel my phone vibrate in my back pocket.

"Why don't you guys sample some more, and then we'll decide on three of them before we start making dinner."

I pull my phone out, and my heart skips a beat when I see a message from Shane.

SHANE: Have you set your own hair on fire and run away screaming yet?

ME: No, but I accidentally set the twins' hair on fire. Is that okay?

SHANE: Yeah, just keep it down. Trying to sleep over here.

ME: Maybe put your phone away and try harder.

SHANE: I just wanted to say thanks. For explaining farts to us. For being here. You're good with them.
ME: Well, now I just feel bad for burning their hair.
SHANE: Naw. It'll grow back. Okay, I'm gonna go to sleep, but I have one question for you.
SHANE: What do you call a male cow who's taking a nap?
ME: A bull dozer. Nico and I learned every dumb joke on the Internet. It was basically the only way we could communicate with each other when we were kids. So if you want to dazzle me with something I've never heard before, you'll have to try harder.

The moving dots by his name appear immediately, continue to move for about twenty seconds, and I brace myself for some amazing dazzling thing that I've never heard before.

But the dots disappear.

No more messages come through.

Maybe he fell asleep.

Maybe I should stop texting my boss to try harder to dazzle me.

But hopefully he just fell asleep.

## 9

## SHANE

*I*t's seven thirty, Summer is about two blinks away from falling asleep, and we're only halfway through *Green Eggs and Ham*. This is awesome. She usually makes me go through a few books before finally nodding off.

Willa is in Lucky's room, reading to him. I took on bath time duties since I had gotten a couple of hours sleep before dinner and have been feeling great. Now I am simultaneously impatient for and dreading the moment when Willa and I will be the only two people awake in this house. It is bizarre, how quickly she has assimilated into our life.

I try my luck at turning a chunk of about ten Dr. Seuss pages at a time and hope that she doesn't notice when I continue reading, but Summer knows this book by heart. "Daddy."

"What?" I ask innocently.

I expect her to turn the pages back, but instead she says, "Is Willa always going to live here?"

"No. She's just here to help me out with you guys until your mom is back from making the movie she's making now. Then we'll hire a different nanny. Why? Don't you like having her here?"

"Yeah. She's better at singing than you. I think she should live with us all the time."

"Well, I don't think that's something she'd want to do. Being a nanny isn't her normal job. She needs to get her own place eventually. But you can enjoy her while she's here, right? You tired?"

She nods.

"Did you have fun today?"

"Yes."

"Hey there," Willa whispers as she tiptoes into the room. "Sorry to interrupt."

"Lucky asleep?"

"Out like an adorable light." She stops at the foot of the bed and clasps her hands behind her back in a way that pushes her chest out and makes me want to die a little. "I just wanted to say good night to Summer, but —wow." She grins at me. "I never would have guessed you'd look so good as a redhead."

*Fuck.*

I remove the child-size Little Mermaid wig that I had forgotten was on my head and toss it on the floor. "She made me wear it."

"I would have too if I'd known about it. Keep reading."

"Actually, I think we're done, right, sleepyhead?"

Summer can barely keep her eyes open. "What are you going to do when we're asleep?"

"Nothing," I answer quickly.

"Separate stuff," Willa says.

"Nothing together."

"You should watch a movie," Summer says.

"I'm sure Willa has more important things to do."

"Not really. What movie should we watch?"

Summer smirks. "Austin Powers."

Willa gasps. "That's one of my favorite movies to watch—all three of them, actually."

"Oh, really? You like *those* movies, but you think mine are stupid?"

"Well, the Austin Powers movies know they're stupid."

"Uh-huh."

"And I never said your movies are stupid. I would love to watch Austin Powers tonight, Summer, that's a great idea."

"Say it," Summer says, pointing her finger at me without moving her head from the pillow.

"Nope. Good night."

"Say it, or I won't close my eyes." She tries so hard to keep her eyes open.

"*You* say it."

She giggles. "Throw me a frickin' bone here."

"Yeah, bay-bee, yeah!"

Willa snort-laughs. "Oh, behave!"

"Yeah!" I kiss Summer on her forehead before

standing up. "You get your groovy self to sleep now, bay-bee!" I may not be a good singer, but my Austin Powers impression is shagadelic.

"Good night, Summer." Willa walks over, leans down, and kisses my daughter once on each cheek. "That's how French people kiss each other when they say hello and good-bye," she explains.

"Are you saying good-bye?" Summer sounds so worried.

"No! I mean, they do that when they say good night too. I'll see you in the morning."

"Okay. 'Night."

Willa smiles at me and walks out of the room, leaving an unbearably fragrant trail in her wake. I've never been much into desserts, but today I find myself wanting to eat out an entire bakery. I mean, eat up. Eat up an entire bakery.

I turn off the bedside lamp. Summer doesn't respond when I tell her I love her. That was—hands down—the most struggle-free bedtime routine I have experienced with Summer since she turned five and realized she was a Jedi Knight who can make me do whatever she wants. I don't know what kind of aromatherapy or voodoo magic Willa is practicing on us, but I am all for it.


Willa is looking out the family room window when I get there. It's a clear night, the room is bathed in moon-light, and the dark outline of her figure is beckoning me. What do you call a horny guy who can't touch the strange, beautiful woman he's quietly staring at from the doorway like a creeper? Me.

I press the dimmer switch to turn the overhead lights on low, causing her to jump.

"Sorry."

She starts fiddling with the pendant of her gold necklace. "Guess we missed the sunset."

"Yeah. I usually miss it on school nights this time of year. But on the weekend—if you're not busy doing something more exciting—we can go for a walk on the bluffs in the evening. With the kids. That's kind of the thing to do around here."

"Sounds like my kind of thing." She smiles at me as she crosses over to one of the armchairs.

I go over to my Blu-ray collection. "We don't have to watch Austin Powers if you don't want to."

"Oh, I want to. Yeah bay-bee!"

I am now remembering that Nico and I used to crack each other up on set by saying our lines like Austin Powers during read-throughs. "You let Nico know you got here safe?"

"Yes. While you were in the shower this morning. I'm sure he's already gotten to second base with that model by now."

I wonder if she knows that second base for Nico is doggy style.

I try to shake all thoughts of sex out of my head as I start the movie and go over to sit on the sofa, as far from where Willa is sitting as possible.

"You're a good dad."

I have to chuckle at that. "I try. I mean. I like to be good at things, you know? But ever since I had kids, I've felt like I'm failing at everything except keeping them alive and preventing them from murdering anyone."

"You're a really good dad. Trust me. You need to absorb that. The father of the family I lived with in Versailles was absent even when he was there. Same with my dad. You really pay attention to your kids. All the time. That's not a small thing."

I feel uniquely humbled and moved by this. "Thanks. I don't think anyone's ever told me I'm a good dad before."

"Well." She flicks her hand dismissively. "Most people are idiots."

"I've noticed that. Did you want popcorn or anything?"

She shakes her head. "I'm still stuffed from dinner."

"Me too. I'm going to have to do extra cardio tomorrow."

She guffaws and makes some wry comment, but now I'm too busy thinking that I should put my personal training sessions on hold while Willa's here, or at least move them to the gym. My trainer's a fucking stud and he will be all over her.

I mean...I did promise Nico I'd keep her away from guys like that.

Willa's chair is angled to face the TV, so I can easily

shift my gaze from the TV over to her without it being obvious.

She is so pretty and fun and so comfortable with my kids and in my house.

Too bad she can't stay here all the time.

"Shane. Shane. Shane. Shane. Shane." That voice. That sexy fucking voice. I never want to stop hearing her say my name.

"Mmph."

"You should go up to bed."

I open my eyes a crack to find a shapely pair of legs in tight jeans in front of me, and my instinct is to reach out, hook my fingers into the waist of those jeans, and pull down.

"Whoa."

I open my eyes all the way and realize I've just yanked the nanny down onto the sofa beside me. She places her hand on my chest for balance. I realize I'm lying down. I realize I fell asleep. I realize that she covered me with a blanket. I realize that I was having a raunchy sex dream about her while she was ten feet away and I was about to act it out right here, while my kids sleep upstairs.

I remove my fingers from between the waist of Willa's jeans and her smooth bare skin. "Shit. Sorry. I fell asleep."

"Yes. You did." She pats my arm and stands up.

I sit up immediately, unable to think of many more things I could have done that are less cool. "Is the movie over?"

"Yes."

"Sorry. I was half asleep..."

She walks over to the TV to turn it off. "It's fine." She looks over her shoulder at me coyly. "Do I make you horny, bay-bee?"

*Yes. Fucking yes.* But I shake my head, frowning. "Don't even joke about that."

Her face falls. "Alrighty, then."

I have no idea why I just snapped at her, other than to hide the fact that my answer is 'yes, fucking yes.'

"I ran the dishwasher, so I'll put the dishes away and go to my room. Don't forget to use the essential oil diffuser. The kids spent a lot of time deciding which ones to use."

She leaves before I can apologize or get up to grab her, press her up against the wall, and kiss her. I want to do both of those things, but tonight I can only do one of them. I fling the fuzzy blanket off me and rub my scalp vigorously to wake myself up. I barely know her, but already there is so much that I want to do with this woman, and all I can do is apologize to her.

"Sorry," I say, as I enter the kitchen.

She doesn't look up from stacking the clean plates on the counter. "You don't have to apologize." She forces a smile. "My Austin Powers imitation isn't half as good as yours anyway. Good thing I'm not trying to be an actor."

"Yours is better than most," I say as I transfer the plates to the cupboard. "You ever consider acting?"

"Don't even joke about that," she deadpans.

She continues removing dishes from the dishwasher and handing them to me so I can put them away. We're quiet for a good minute. Until I can't stand how comfortable and right this feels anymore.

"I hope you find time to do your perfume thing while you're here. I mean, I'll make sure you do. You won't have to pick up the kids every day. I'll start taking some meetings here and there, and I'll have to do ADR at some point, but..."

"What's ADR?"

"Automated Dialog Replacement. You've heard of looping?" She wrinkles her nose and shakes her head. "Where I have to re-record certain lines of dialogue if the sound got messed up on location or whatever. For the film I just shot. In Maine."

"The one with the script you loved and got paid scale plus ten for."

"Right. Anyway. Set up your Etsy shop. Do whatever you need to do for you."

"Actually, your ex-wife has asked me to design a scent for her. She told you that, right?"

"Oh yeah. That's official?"

"She said she'll have her lawyer draw something up."

"Yeah. She says stuff like that a lot."

"She's, uhhh, she's nice. She's very pretty. Obviously. Do you miss being married?"

"To her? No. Not at all. But I do miss being married. I mean. I think I'd like being married to someone I actually...you know..."

I glance over at her. She's got a confused look on her face. "No. Someone you actually what?"

I clear my throat. "I mean, it's not something I want the kids to know." I lower my voice. "We got married because she was pregnant."

She looks so surprised and maybe relieved to hear this. "Oh. I did not know that. Does Nico know that?"

"Yeah. He was one of the few people who knew she was pregnant before we got married."

"Wow. I guess he can be really discreet when he wants to be."

"I wouldn't have made him my best man if he weren't." I don't like talking about this with her. "So what are your plans? Your perfume plans? What would the sweet smell of success smell like for you?" I really fucking wish I had not just said that. I don't know why, but now that she's the nanny, I just feel like Old Dad Guy around her. Horny Old Dad Guy, if I'm being honest.

"Well," she says, grinning and clearly finding it hilarious that I just said something so lame. "I want to set up my own niche perfumery. Grow a client base and reputation through Etsy, and then set up a separate online store and then a brick and mortar. And then hopefully more of them."

"Instead of working for like...Chanel?" The only kind of perfume I can think of.

"I mean, that's another way to go, obviously. And it would be a steady paycheck. Ultimately, it's more important to me to have my own company and create natural, nontoxic fragrances. But if I were to take a job at one of the major perfume houses, I would get a lot of valuable experience and connections."

"And where would those major perfume houses be? Paris?"

"Paris, London, New York."

"Nothing in LA, huh?"

She shuts the dishwasher and slides her hands into the back pockets of her jeans. "No, but there is a burgeoning niche perfumery scene here. Which is why I came."

I shut the cutlery drawer, lean back against the counter, and shove my hands into the front pockets of my jeans. "Well, I hope you get whatever you want."

"Thanks." She shrugs and smiles at me. "I'm gonna go work on a logo for my store. In my room."

"Yeah, cool."

"Yeah."

She is so fucking pretty, and I've never noticed how quiet it is at night in this house before. All I can hear is the hum of the refrigerator, her uneven breaths, and my pounding heart. When she starts taking slow steps toward me, my heart beats even faster. She tilts her head and reaches one arm out, and holy shit this is happening.

Her hand reaches just past my head. "Sorry. I just need a glass of water to take to my room."

"Oh." I step aside. "Good idea."

She opens the cupboard that was right behind me and grabs a glass.

I stay exactly where I am, watching her beautiful ass as she crosses to the refrigerator to use the water dispenser.

When she turns back to face me, she says, "Okay, good night."

"Good night." My hands grip the edge of the counter, when all they really want to do is grab on to that beautiful ass.

Holding her glass of water, she walks toward me again, smiling. Before I can step out of the way, she stops right in front of me, stands on her tiptoes, and kisses me on one cheek and then the other. She pauses. I loosen my grip on the counter. "Sorry. It's what the French do." She lowers herself back down, avoiding eye contact. "I guess I shouldn't do that again."

I loosen my grip on my sanity just a little and mutter, "Probably not. Are both people supposed to kiss both cheeks?"

Her eyes flick up to meet mine. She nods, just barely, holding on to her glass with both hands. I look down and see ripples in the water. Her hands are trembling.

"I want to get this right, then," I say as I hook one finger under her chin to tilt it up. I lean down to kiss her right cheek, soft and slow. I spread my fingers to gently grip the back of her neck as I kiss her left cheek, hearing the quiet gasp by my ear and feeling it all over. I inhale the subtly hypnotic scent of her and whisper, "Did I do that right?"

"Mmmmhunh."

I let go, pull back. Her eyes are closed, her lips parted. If there was ever a girl who I should kiss on the lips and a moment for me to kiss her, it's this girl right now. But I don't.

"Good night."

"Good night," she says, eyes still closed, standing still. And then she shakes her head and opens her eyes, clears her throat. "Good night."

And then she's gone.

I stay exactly where I am until I hear the door close down the hall.

I stay where I am, and if that door opens again, nothing is going to stop me from going through it.

But it doesn't.

And I don't.

## SHANE MILLER SLEEP DIARY –
## THURSDAY MORNING

**Went to bed at:** *Before ten.*

**How long it took you to fall asleep:** *Not long.*

**How many times you woke up in the middle of the night:** *Not once.*

**How refreshing your overall sleep was:** *Very. Slept eight hours straight. Probably in large part due to the essential oil thing that my kids and the nanny mixed together for me. Woke up five minutes before my alarm to the sound of laughter from the kitchen and the scent of the most amazing coffee I have ever smelled.*

**Number of caffeinated beverages you consumed throughout the day:** *Not gonna lie to you, Dr. Shaw. I had a cup of that amazing coffee this morning. And I have zero regrets. If I can only have one vice at this point in my* *life, it will be caffeine. More specifically, it will be the caffeinated beverage brewed by the new nanny. Never had anything like it. Works on every level. Still feeling it, hours later.*

**Number of alcoholic beverages you consumed throughout the day:** *Still none. Yeah, I really need to stay away from alcohol.*

**How much time you spent exercising:** *One hour. Wanted to punch my trainer in the dick and dropkick him out of my house. For reasons. But other than that I'm starting to feel like my usual relatively happy self again.*

**Your stress level before bedtime, on a scale from 1 to 5:** *3?*

**Your major cause of stress:** *Being a fucking good guy.*

## WILLA TODD SCENT DIARY – FRIDAY AFTERNOON

*Had the twins help me cut some lavender sprigs from the front yard. There are now pretty little relaxing lavender bouquets in every room of the house. Until Summer decides there are too many of them and throws them out.*

*Took the twins to the beach after school while Shane was having a coffee meeting in the village with some director. It's a good beach. Very few people, although I guess it's not that surprising on a Thursday afternoon in March.*

*I asked Summer and Lucky to tell me what they could smell there. They said, "stinky toots." They aren't wrong. The bacteria that eat dying plankton produce a sulfur compound through the digestion process. That sulfur helps with cloud formation and controls the planet's temperature. It's amazing.*

*The faint smell of actual sewage didn't even bother me,*

*maybe because the salty air was coating my nostrils. And because I knew I'd see Shane again in an hour.*

*I feel good.*
*I like it here.*

*One day I'll want to create a scent that evokes my memories of this time in the Palisades, but thinking of a time when I won't be here makes me sad. It has only been a few days, but this already feels like a place I could call home. I swear, it's that feeling I had when Shane held my hand twelve years ago. It's not something I'd ever try to explain to him, but I can admit it to myself. I guess I had assumed it would be something else, but if it was about me being a nanny to his kids, then I don't mind. It's nice.*

*I'm working on the Margo scent. I really fucking hope she doesn't actually want to call it Margo, but if we're taking wagers—my money is on "Margo." She asked for cherry blossom essential oil as an ingredient. Told me she has "lovely memories" of being a girl in Manhattan during cherry blossom season. So fucking lovely. It's not possible to make essential oil from cherry blossoms, but I can formulate something that evokes it. Using Osmanthus, ylang ylang, sweet orange. She definitely wants something fruity and floral. She needs something more earthy, but who am I to tell her that.*

*What I really want to do is create a scent for Shane. He's been on his best behavior since the first night. Unfortu-*

*nately. If I can't rub myself all over him, then I at least want him to wear something that I've created on his skin and for it to make him feel all of the amazing things that I want to make him feel. Like a man. Like a wanted man. Like the kind of man who'd step into the shower with his nanny when the kids are at school—because hey, life's short and this nanny's a lot dirtier than he thinks she is.*

## 10

## WILLA

"What does a banana do when it sees a chimpanzee coming?"

Summer and Lucky just stare ahead, frowning. Shane bites his lower lip and shrugs his shoulders.

"The banana splits!"

Shane shakes his head, smiling. The twins just keep staring ahead at the chimpanzee exhibit. Tough crowd. We're at the LA Zoo for a fun Saturday outing, but something passed between Summer and Lucky at the meerkat exhibit, and now they're having what Shane refers to as a "twin fight." It reminds me a lot of the fights that Nico and I had when I was five and he was nine, but quieter and more intense. Minus the name calling and wet willies. Summer is two minutes older than her brother, and she milks it for all it's worth.

They both napped on the way here, since it took an actual year to get to this Griffith Park location from the

Palisades. So, I thought they'd be in a better mood. But nope. They've been complaining about the animal poo smell—which I personally like and find quite relaxing and earthy—and they don't feel like walking, but they also don't want to be rolled around in rented strollers or carried like babies. Not even the highly un-Margo-approved churros are floating their boats. Shane muttered to me that it will blow over eventually, but I won't give up that easily. This is one of the nicest zoos I've ever been to, and it's a beautiful spring day, and I'm happy to be here with Shane (who is wearing a base-ball cap and sunglasses and looks exactly like a hand-some star who's trying to go incognito), and I want everyone to be happy.

"What did the banana say to the chimpanzee? Nothing! Bananas can't talk! Wokka wokka. No? Not even a little smile?"

All of a sudden, for no reason that I can see, Summer whacks her brother on the head with her churro. Lucky basically growls into her face, and it turns into a shoving match. I grab Summer, Shane grabs Lucky, and we pull them apart.

"Hey!" Shane says. "Knock it off."

"She started it!"

"You started it by being a poopie doopie head!"

They both scrunch up their faces and stick their tongues out at each other.

Shane and I signal to each other that we're going to separate them for a bit.

"Come with me, little lady." I take Summer's hand

and drag her away. "We do not hit people with churros or shove them when we're angry," I say to her firmly but quietly. "Got that?"

"He's so dumb!"

"I don't think he is, but why don't you tell me why you're mad at him."

She stops in her tracks, throws her churro on the ground, balls her little hands up into fists, and growls just like Lucky did.

"Okay, you know what?" I pick up the big stick of deep-fried dough, take her hand again, toss the churro into the nearest trash bin, and pull her over to a nearby bench. "Sometimes when we're really mad at someone, we can't find the words to talk about it right away, and that's fine. But we have to find other ways to get rid of the anger that don't hurt anyone or anything. Do you feel mad?"

"Yes!"

"You feel it all over your body?"

"Yes! And it's his fault!"

"Well, let's figure out a way to get that mad feeling out of your body."

I hop up from the bench. "When I feel angry, I do this." Fortunately, I'm not wearing tight jeans for once, so I jump around on the pavement in front of her and kick and punch the air with absolutely no regard as to whether or not any other zoo patrons are watching me, because fuck 'em. This is an important life lesson. And then I just fling my arms around while jumping up and down. "This feels really good!"

Soon, Summer is jumping up and down and kicking and punching the air next to me.

"Good! Don't you feel better?"

She's smiling now.

"Now fling your arms around like this to get rid of the rest of that energy!"

She does just that.

I stop jumping. "Better?"

She stops jumping and nods her head. "You're weird."

"Yes, I am. But you aren't mad anymore, are you?"

She shrugs her shoulders and then shakes her head.

"Good. I feel great. And you know what I feel like doing?"

"What?"

I look around quickly to make sure I've got room, and then I do a cartwheel. I'm fucking awesome at doing cartwheels, and I've got so much pent-up sexual energy that I will do literally anything to work it off so I don't start dry humping their dad's leg in the reptile house. I execute a perfect cartwheel, except that my blouse drops to my neck while I'm upside-down. Fortunately, I'm wearing a bra. Unfortunately, it's not a family friendly bra. I pull my shirt down as soon as I'm right side up.

"I saw your undies!"

I swing around to see if anyone else saw and find Shane standing about twenty feet away, with an expression on his face that is caught somewhere between *what the fuck is wrong with you?* and *show me that fucking bra again right now*.

I regret nothing.

"You know how to do a cartwheel?" I turn to ask Summer, but Summer's eyes have lit up and she gasps when she sees something that is not me.

"Abby, Abby, Abby!" She runs over to a little girl who's walking next to a woman who is blatantly eye-fucking Shane.

"Yaaaaah!" the little girl who must be Abby exclaims as she runs over to Summer and they jump up and down in front of each other. Lucky runs over to them too, and there doesn't seem to be any trace of animosity left between the twins.

I, however, have very quickly developed some animosity for this blonde woman with blown-out hair and a fake tan, probably fake boobs, and tight white jeans—I mean come on… Tight white jeans at the zoo on a Saturday afternoon?

I take a seat on the bench and monitor the kids in my peripheral vision while keeping a closer eye on this woman who keeps tossing her hair, putting her hand on Shane's arm, and throwing her head back when she laughs. She must be a single mom. Well, isn't that cute. A single mom and a single dad at the zoo. How fucking perfect.

I thought it was so funny how overprotective Shane was being when his personal trainer was flirting with me at the house the other day, but this feels really shitty.

I mean, that's probably what he needs—a rich, fake-boobed single mom who probably used to be married to some other actor.

Shane keeps glancing over my way, but he's wearing sunglasses so I can't see his eyes, and he is such a friendly guy that I cannot for the life of me tell if he wants me to rescue him or not. Because I would very much like to rescue him. Or rescue myself from this terrible situation.

Shane waves me over to come join him. I'm by his side in less than two seconds.

"This is our new nanny, Willa. Willa, this is Abby's mom," he says, and I can tell from the way he says it that he doesn't remember her name.

"Hey, Willa," she says, offering me a limp handshake. "I'm Jillian."

*You used about three too many spritzes of Calvin Klein Obsession today, Jillian, but you have a vintage bottle— good for you.* "Nice to meet you, Jillian. Looks like the twins are pretty fond of Abby."

"Yes, they get along great. Well, you should bring the twins over for dinner," she says, touching Shane's arm again. Somebody came to the zoo on a single dad safari. Can't say I blame her. "I bet you could use a good home-cooked meal." She whips out her phone. "How about next Saturday? We can take the kids to a matinee first. Make a day of it."

"Actually, you can come to our house if you want— the two of you. We've got a nice view of the sunset at dinnertime."

*Our house.*

He puts his arm around my shoulder, just for a second, but he makes a point. "Willa here is kind of an amazing cook. She uses a ton of butter, but we like it anyway. Dinnertime is fun at our place."

*Our place.*

"You're welcome to join us sometime." I give her my best hostess smile.

*Us.*

Jillian's coral-stained lips are sticking to her bleached-white teeth, but I can tell she wants to kill me, and I am fine with it.

"Yeah, we'd love to have the two of you over for dinner. Sometime."

Jillian puts her phone away. "Fantastic. Sounds fun. Let's go, Abby! Time to go! Great to see you, Shane." She nods at me, grabs her daughter, and strides away in her four-inch mules.

"Can we see the giraffes now?" Lucky asks. He and his sister are holding hands, and it's pretty much the cutest thing I've ever seen.

"Let's go find those giraffes," Shane says.

All I really want to do is drag him to the reptile house and dry hump him, but I get a shot of the twins holding hands in front of us to send to their mother later.

"Well, I sure hope Jillian takes you up on your offer," I say as we stroll down the path to the giraffes.

"Sorry. I didn't know how else to get out of that."

"No, I think you chose the perfect way. Happy to be

your friendly domestic cockblocker." I give him a side-glance.

He's grinning, and he's so hot in that baseball cap and those sunglasses, but instead of dragging him to the reptile house, I bump against his arm with my arm. Classic move from the handbook of seduction techniques for eight-year olds.

He does it back to me. And then he rests his arm on my shoulder again. Not in a sexy way—in the way that my brother would. But still. We're in public. We're with the kids. I'll take it.

And then I hear his back pocket vibrate. He uses his other hand to check who's calling. When he removes his arm from my shoulder, I know immediately who it is.

"Yo, superstar!" I hear my brother say. Talk about a cockblocker. He must have sensed that a man was touching me.

"What's up?...No, we're at the zoo, actually. Wanna join us?...Oh yeah, is that next week?"

I catch up to the twins so Shane can feel free to converse without me eavesdropping. "What's your favorite animal here so far?" I ask them.

"Lucky!" Summer says, lifting their connected arms up in the air.

"Summer!" her brother says.

"Awww, you're my favorites too!"

Shane catches up with us, sliding his phone back into his pocket. But instead of putting his arm around me again, he walks on the opposite side of the twins from me.

"Is my brother coming to join us?"

"No. He was just calling about his show next Friday."

"Oh yeah... Are you going to that?"

"I mean...are you going?"

"Well, one of us should probably look after these guys, right? You should go."

"But you haven't had a night off yet."

"I just started working for you."

"You probably haven't seen your brother play in ages, though."

"No. I haven't."

"You should. He's great live. The Hotel Café is a great place to see him. You go."

I keep looking over at him, but he won't look at me. "Okay. I'll go."

"You should. You should go out. Take your friend." He nods, like he's trying to convince himself.

"You really don't have anyone else who could babysit them?"

"Nah. You go." He nods again, still not looking over at me.

"Okay. I'll go."

## 11

## SHANE

*I*t's almost eight, Friday night.

The four of us went for a walk on the bluffs right after dinner. I watched Willa watch the sunset over the ocean. I watched how her skin tone changed as the color of the sky changed and couldn't decide if she looked prettier against the glow of an electric pink, fiery orange, or muted purple backdrop. Because she's always pretty. She's ever-changing and always pretty and as untouchable as the clouds.

The kids are asleep in bed.

Nico's supposed to take the stage at the bar in Hollywood at nine thirty, but Willa and I have been taking our sweet-ass time clearing the table and loading up the dishwasher.

I'm having a beer. Fuck it. It's Friday night. I've been drinking coffee for almost a week now and I can still sleep. Lavender trumps caffeine, apparently. One beer can't hurt. Now that I've drained almost a whole bottle, it hurts a little less to stand this close to her. Now that I've texted Nico to wish him luck, now that I think about how much fangirl ass he'll be getting, I feel a little less guilty about how many times and ways I've imagined drilling his little sister. I mean, his sister is hot. She's going to get with someone eventually. Wouldn't it be better for everyone if that someone was me?

Wouldn't everything be better if I had another beer?

But I don't. Because in the back of my dad mind, I'm always reminding myself that I might have to drive my kid to the hospital at any given moment. So that's it for me tonight.

But she's so fucking pretty.

And this is going to be her first night away from me since she started staying with us.

She washes her hands in the sink, dries them, and comes over to the island counter that I've been leaning against while ogling her like some pervert at a bar.

"You should probably start heading out soon."

"I guess."

"You going by yourself?"

"No, I'm meeting up with my friend."

"Oh, good. Which friend?"

"Harley."

*Who the fuck is Harley?* "Oh good. Cool. Harley. Sounds like a fun guy."

"Harley is a girl. She's the friend I told you about. From college."

"Even better."

"Do you want to go with us? Or meet us there?"

*Fuck yes, obviously, yes. I want to meet you anywhere. I want to go with you everywhere. Just not anywhere your brother can see us together.*

"I can't think of anyone I can call to babysit on such short notice."

"Right. So you're just going to hang out here by yourself?"

"Believe it or not, I've gotten pretty good at keeping myself entertained at night. Kind of a necessity when you're an insomniac."

"But you aren't an insomniac anymore."

"Good point." *Everything is different now that you're here. Don't go.*

"I don't have to go. I can see him play some other time."

*Yes. I'll come to your room. You can sit on my face all night, and I will make you scream into the pillow. I will fuck us both senseless, and then things won't be weird between us anymore. Or it'll be even weirder, but it won't matter because we fucked each other senseless.*

"No, you should definitely go. I know how excited he is for you to see him on stage. Seriously, it would mean a lot to him. Don't worry about me."

"Okay, well, I've got two plus ones, but I'll text Harley to let her know she can invite Remi."

*Who the fuck is Remi?* "Remi. He sounds fun too."

"Remi is also a girl."

"Good. Good for her."

I watch her type out a text. Her thumb hovers over the Send icon as she looks up at me through those long dark eyelashes. "Last chance."

"Maybe next time. When Margo has the kids."

She sends the text and slides her phone into her back pocket. "Next time. I've never been to The Hotel Café before. Obviously. I'm not sure what to wear. Nico said it's casual."

"Yeah, it's definitely casual. You can just go like that. With maybe a bulky sweater or a puffy jacket over your T-shirt or something."

"Sounds about right. Maybe I should change into a pair of old sweatpants and wear a baseball cap."

"You'd still look good," I mutter.

The awkward silence that follows is a giant gaping hole that I wish I could crawl into, but no. It's there. I'm here. She's here, staring down at the counter and gently stroking the smooth concrete with the tip of her index finger while exhaling. No snarky retort. No eye roll. Just this silent, honest torture.

"You need me back here to make breakfast?"

"Are you not coming home tonight?"

"I was just going to crash at Harley's. She lives in Hollywood."

"Ahh."

"There's some other bar she wants to go to after Nico's show."

"Cool."

"And then she wants to go to some club after that, but I doubt I'll be able to stay awake that long."

"Is Nico going with you guys?"

"No."

"Uh-huh."

"But I'll be back in the morning. To drop the kids off at the birthday party."

"Right. The trampoline one?'"

"Yes. Unless you need me..."

*Fuck yes, I need you, I want you, I crave you... Can't you see that?*

"I can definitely manage breakfast. You have a good time. Not too good."

"I will have exactly the right amount of good time."

"So will I."

"I have no doubt... So I'm gonna go change into some overalls and an oversize sweat shirt, maybe some rain boots, and be on my way."

"You're driving?"

"Yes. The truck. Not the Volvo."

"You're not drinking, then?"

"I'm driving to Harley's, and we're going to walk to the thing. She lives like five blocks away."

"You're walking? In Hollywood? On Cahuenga? At night? Absolutely not, young lady. I'll give you money for an Uber."

"Oh my God, it's only five blocks."

"Does your brother know you plan to walk to his show?"

"No, and I'm pretty sure he wouldn't care. Is there rampant gang activity in that part of Hollywood or something?"

"No."

"Then I think I'll be okay. There will be three of us. I am a big girl. You do realize that, right? I can handle all kinds of things." She straightens up. She's looking at me, really looking at me, daring me to look back at her.

This girl. She can explain sunsets to a five-year-old and convey her maturity to a twenty-eight-year-old, and I'm starting to wonder if *I'm* the one who can't handle *her*. She is so many things, and I don't want to risk losing any of them.

"I'm just looking out for you. You're kind of my responsibility right now."

"Even on my night off?" She arches an eyebrow and takes a step closer.

"You're still my kids' nanny. You'll always be Nico's little sister."

"I know who I am. And I'm a lot more than that." She frowns and pushes herself away from the counter. "I keep wondering when you're going to figure that out," she says as she brushes past me.

I hear the door to her room close, and I don't have a fucking clue what just happened.

But if she doesn't like that I'm the responsible guy, then it's not my job to explain everything to her. That's who I am. That's who I've always been. It's one thing to fuck around with someone on location, but this is real life. This is my life. She's better off with some twenty-four-year old asshat who can take her to hipster downtown cocktail bars on a Tuesday night and to a party in Los Feliz on Saturday because his buddy's house-sitting for Jon Hamm and it's totally cool for them to hang out there! And then they can just fuck all night in his shitty studio apartment that's off of Fairfax and grab Sunday brunch, maybe catch a matinee at The Grove.

Fuck, that sounds great.

I wouldn't trade my kids for anything, but just one Saturday night of mindless twenty-four-year-old fucking and then doing whatever on a Sunday? I could have used one of those. I could still use one of those.

But that's my life, not hers.

Her future is still wide open.

"Okay, I'm off," she says from the doorway.

Fucking hell.

She's wearing a tiny leather jacket over an even tinier top that does not cover her belly button, and why does she have to wear those black high heel boots over those tight faded jeans? Why should any other guy be allowed to see how good her ass looks in those boots and those jeans? Why is her hair all fluffed up? She put on eyeliner? Lip gloss? Oh hell no, little girl.

"Not exactly the outfit vibe we discussed."

"If I wear a bulky sweater and sweatpants, Harley will just force me to wear something of hers that's even sluttier." She shrugs. "Good night." She turns to walk toward the garage, and I watch that ass walk away from me, and *fuck you Other Guys—fuck you for thinking about all the things you want to do to that ass. I know what you're thinking.*

"Wait."

She pauses, resting her hand on the doorknob. "Yes?"

"There's no garage door opener in the truck. I'll close the garage door for you."

She lowers her head, laughing. "Great. Thanks."

She flings open the door, and I catch it before it slams against the wall.

*Well well, look who has a fiery temper.*

Fuck, she smells good.

Fuck.

"Drive safe," I say sternly, knowing it'll piss her off. "Don't drink too much."

"I'll drink however much I want to—it's my night off."

I shut the door behind myself, grab her arm, and pull her to me.

"Don't drive angry."

She glares up at me, chest heaving, eyes shining. "Stop trying to push me away when you know I can't go anywhere."

Goddammit, why does she have to know everything?

I put both hands around her gorgeous, exasperating, frowning face. "I'm the one who can't go anywhere."

"Then let me stay with you."

I lower my lips as close to hers as I can without kissing them. "If I do, I won't ever want you to leave."

She stares hungrily at my mouth. "Good."

Her purse hits the floor just as my lips crash against hers.

Those lips, those glistening, juicy lips. I've heard so many surprising things come out of them, but this little humming sound that she's making as her tongue tangles with mine is my favorite.

She's spicy, but she tastes so sweet.

I push her two steps back, against the side of my Land Rover, lift her up by her thighs, and she wraps her legs tight around my waist. Hands gripping the side of my shirt, she gasps, and her head drops back as I tug on her hair so I can kiss her smooth neck.

"Oh my God, Shane," she whispers, arching her back.

"This is how we say good night in America," I grumble into her ear.

After a beat, we both burst out laughing for about three seconds—because that was a bad line, but I had to say it. And then she's threading her fingers through my hair and we're kissing again.

The truth is, I've never kissed someone with this much feeling without having a director yell "cut!" before changing camera angles.

She wriggles around. It's fucking unbearable how much she's wriggling and writhing around. I realize she's removing her leather jacket and tossing it aside. She can move around more freely now, and there's one less layer of clothing between my chest and her beautiful swelling tits. I lower her until her feet are back on the floor so I can slip my fingers up under that blouse that is far too small and place my hand on one soft, perky breast. Her bra is lacey, and her nipple is so hard.

She strokes my throbbing hard dick through my jeans.

"Fucking hell, Willa. You're making me crazy."

This has already gone too far.

She's unbuttoning and unzipping her jeans. She puts her hand on mine, the one that's squeezing her ass, that sexy little heart-shaped ass, and brings it around, slides it down inside her panties. "I want you to feel how wet I am for you."

"Jesus." The slippery warmth of her is so much more than proof of how much she wants me. It's proof that there's life after Dad Dick. "Willa. We need to stop."

"No, don't stop."

She slowly turns around to face the car door, my hand still down the front of her jeans.

She places her palms flat against the car and rocks back and forth against my hand while rubbing her ass against my crotch.

My groan echoes around the garage, and my fingers find her clit and rub slow and steady.

My other hand reaches around to massage her breast, and there are about fifty other things I want to do to this woman, but right now I just need to make her come fast and quiet.

She is already right there on the edge.

I whisper into her ear. "You wanna come for me right now, Willa?"

"Yes."

"This is who you are? This is what you want?"

"Yes. Yes!"

"You better stay quiet."

"Uh-huh."

My fingers slip inside her. She moans as she clenches around them. She is so hot and wet and tight. She reaches behind herself to grab on to my hair and whimpers while I fuck her with my fingers. I bite down on the fleshy part of her shoulder—not hard, but I can tell she likes it.

"Oh shit," she sighs.

She starts to undulate and moan. I have to let go of her glorious tit so I can cover her mouth because I can tell she isn't going to be quiet at all.

I rub hard and fast against her clit to make her buck and swear and scream my name into the palm of my hand, and I don't stop until she's clenched up one final time, I don't pull my hand out of her panties until the aftershocks have subsided and she's collapsed against my chest. My breaths match hers. She turns to face me, runs her fingers through her hair, runs her fingers through my hair, kisses me tenderly.

"I'm...I'm gonna stay." Her voice is trembling. "Should I stay?"

Fuck, she seems so young and innocent all of a sudden.

I rest my forehead against hers, catching my breath, before letting go of her. "No. You should go.

Nico's expecting you. Your friends are waiting. I'm sorry. I shouldn't have done that."

She snorts and rolls her eyes, which shouldn't be sexy at all, but it totally is. "Really? Which part?"

I pick up her jacket and purse for her while she zips and straightens herself up.

"I have to change. I can't go like this."

Five minutes later, she's changed her clothes, and she's backing out of the garage. I refrain from reminding her to drive safe and not drink too much. I wait until she's out of sight before shutting the garage door.

Well. That wasn't too shabby for a Friday night in the Palisades.

After checking on the kids, to make sure they're still fast asleep, and taking care of myself in a very quick shower, I send Willa a text: **I lied. I'm not sorry. But I shouldn't have done that.**

A minute later, I get a reply.

**WILLA: I'm not sorry either. But I'm very glad you did that. I just wish you would have let me get you off too.**

I nearly swallow my tongue.

ME: Great, but it's illegal to text while driving here and also very dangerous.

Willa: Calm down. I pulled over.

ME: Good girl.

WILLA: I'm really not.

ME: Yeah, I'm starting to get the hint.

WILLA: Well, I have to hit the road again. I don't want to miss Nico's set. Thanks for being so responsible for my well-being. I'll be sure to tell my brother you're taking such good care of me. <winking face emoji>

ME: Not funny.

WILLA: Kinda funny.

ME: Let me know when you get there.

WILLA: Yes sir.


I am in so much trouble.

Just as I had suspected, Willa Todd smells fucking delicious inside and out, and I know that I won't sleep again until I've tasted every inch of her too.

## 12

## WILLA

"Okay, don't look now, but I think that guy over there was in that movie last year with whatsername from *Twilight* where she was a singer. Or maybe she was a nurse. Or was it Hermione?" Harley's roommate Remi might be an idiot.

"I didn't see it."

"Neither did I—don't look, but he's really cute and he keeps checking you out."

"I'm not going to look, and I don't know who you're talking about." We're seated at one end of a long table. The Hotel Café is crowded, mostly filled with young women my age who are here to see my brother, and I wish he would take the stage already so this person would stop talking.

"Okay, well, he's super cute and his friend looks really familiar too."

There's a guy on stage who's setting up microphones and a keyboard and drums. Is he my brother's roadie? Is that what you call him even if my brother's not on the road? Does that mean my brother will be starting soon? How is it possible that my panties are this wet, even though I changed them before coming here?

Harley puts her hand on my shoulder. "Willa's living with a much cuter, much more famous actor, Rem. She's not going to go slumming with no-name below the title actors that she doesn't recognize."

My cheeks are on fire.

"Wait—who are you living with?"

"Not like that—I'm his nanny."

How is it that no one has been able to tell just from looking at me that I had a massive orgasm like one hour ago? How is it not obvious to everyone that I'm not really here? I'm in a garage, pressed up against a Land Rover, disappearing into the hypnotic rhythm of the most intense kiss of my life?

"I mean, I just started looking after his kids, but he's my brother's best friend."

"Who is it?"

I don't think I can say his name out loud right now without arching my back and moaning.

"Shane Miller," Harley tells her.

Remi's eyes nearly pop out of her head. "Shut up! From *Twice Bitten*?"

"From *That's So Wizard*," Harley corrects her. "And that movie with John Cena that we liked."

Is the hum of the crowd's chatter and the muted funky bass groove that's blasting from the speakers really so loud that no one can hear me screaming Shane's name in my head? God, I hope I didn't wake up the twins. God, I hope we get to do that again.

"Wait... I thought he was married to Margo Quincey. They were so cute together on that show."

"They got divorced after two years and she married someone else," I snap.

"Wait. You're living with him?"

*Yes, and I'm still feeling the aftereffects of his one-handed virtuoso performance on my clitoris. Is there an Oscar category for Best Male Finger Banger? Because we have a winner.*

"Not like that. I'm the nanny."

"He has kids?"

"Yes. That's why he hired me as a nanny. To look after his kids."

"Awww. I love kids. Should we get mojitos?"

Both Harley and I ignore that question—me because I'm still in a garage with Shane Miller's beautiful possessive hand on my boob and Harley because she's been busy scanning and categorizing the entire male population of this establishment since we got here.

"Okay, there are like fifty guys here, mostly under forty, predominantly singer-songwriters like Nico, Hollywood and music industry assistant-types. Possibly a few junior music executives. A few B-list actors. I see potential in about five of them."

*None of them. I see potential in none of them.*

"I say we blow this hole as soon as Nico's set is over

and you say your hellos and goodbyes, little sister, and then we head down to The Three Clubs to meet up with my friends from work. Then hit up either the Rooftop at The Standard downtown or The Exchange, because I know the DJ who's on at midnight and I should be on the list. Depends on how we're feeling vis-à-vis guys with degrees and jobs or whatever."

Tired. I'm already feeling tired of all of this. I already miss the twins. I miss the house. I miss Shane, and not just because he's such an amazing kisser.

"Is Netflix and wine really not an option?"

Remi laughs because she doesn't know me well enough to realize that I'm one hundred percent serious, and Harley rolls her eyes because she knows me so well, she totally called this a week and a half ago.

"I knew it. I told you I'd lose you to the Westside."

"I'm here, aren't I? I'm out with you." I raise my hands in the air and do a little butt dance in my chair. "Woohoo! Friday night in Hollywood!" *When can I go home?*

"Actually, I think it was Jennifer Lawrence," Remi declares. "The movie that guy was in. He's still looking over here. Don't look, though."

"Don't worry. I won't."

Harley is frowning at me, and I don't blame her. I am the oldest twenty-four-year old in Los Angeles. Thank God the house music fades and my brother steps out on stage. I am so happy to see him that I almost forget that his best friend's fingers were inside me not very long ago. Nope. Now I'm thinking about it again. The way these young women are hooting and hollering for Nico, that's what I want to do when I think about Shane.

Shane.

He needs to see this.

I pull out my phone and take a little video of the enthusiastic female crowd and the way my brother is standing there in front of the microphone, casually tuning his guitar and smirking out over the darkness. He doesn't say anything. He just launches into one of his upbeat fan favorites, and the hooting and hollering kicks up a decibel. Okay, I'm proud of the fucker. This is cool. I yell out, "I love you, Nico!!! Wooooo!" My brother grins in a way that tells me he heard me and recognized my voice.

I send the video as a text, to Shane, with no message. I email it to my Grammie, explaining where I am. I slide the phone into the back pocket of my jeans so I can give my brother the attention he deserves. Until I feel it vibrate. I move my phone to my lap and discreetly check the screen.

SHANE: What a stud. Guess this means you got there safely.
ME: I sent you that picture of our feet walking down Cahuenga!
SHANE: That was not evidence of your safe arrival at The Hotel Café. Those boots are really fucking hot, though.

ME: Well thank you, but they're made for walking and they got me here safe and sound.
SHANE: Good. Have fun.
ME: You too.
SHANE: Not too much fun.
ME: You too.

"Seriously?" Harley is reading over my shoulder. "Why are you even here?"

"Sorry. Putting my phone away."

"Like hell you are," she whisper-yells into my ear. "I mean, what are you doing here when you should be in the bathroom taking a boob pic for sexy daddy boss?"

"I am not sending him a boob pic! I do not send boob pics."

Right?

## 13

## SHANE

It's almost one. I've been tossing and turning in bed for an hour, after a night of catching up on e-mails with Netflix on in the background, getting up to see if Willa came home every time I think I hear something, and trying to read one page of a Steve Martin book for forty-five minutes. I came this close to waking up the kids just so they could keep me company.

The lavender isn't working anymore.

I shouldn't have had the coffee.

I shouldn't have had that beer.

I shouldn't have finger fucked the nanny in my garage right before she left to see my best friend.

Everything was good and on track, and now this shit again.

It's been hours since I heard from Willa. I keep wondering where she is. Who she's with. How many guys are trying to get into her pants. If she's still thinking about what happened earlier. If she still feels good about it. If she can still remember the feel of my fingers between her legs, because I can't forget her silky warm wetness. *"I want you to feel how wet I am for you."* Jesus. Was that really the same girl with the Tiger Beat magazine who kissed the back of my hand? Is it actually possible that the same woman who's great with my kids is also a randy little minx? Am I the luckiest man alive, or is this some big test? Would having sex with Nico's little sister mean that I pass or fail? Fuck. I may never sleep again.

"You awake?"

I open my eyes and turn my head toward the bedroom door.

She's there.

She's there, in my doorway, dimly backlit by the nightlight in the hallway. Wearing pajamas. Hair brushed straight and to one side.

Is she there? Am I dreaming?

She steps inside, carefully shuts the door, and tiptoes over to stand near the foot of my king-size bed.

"I just checked on the kids. Fast asleep."

She's here. I am the luckiest man alive. "Hi."

"Hi. I think Summer snuck a pocket snack to bed. There are little cracker crumbs on her pillow."

"Well...that way she'll be able to find her way back to her pillow if she gets lost."

"Is it okay if I sit here for a minute?"

I lift up the covers for her.

"Oh. No thanks." She sits at the edge of the foot of

the bed. I sit up. Okay, maybe I am being tested. "I don't think I should be anywhere near your amazing hands or your beautiful mouth or your probably very pretty penis right now."

"'Pretty?'"

"Pretty badass penis is what I meant to say."

"That's more like it."

"This is weird. It seemed like a really mature thing to do when I was downstairs, but it's weird that I just came into your bedroom, isn't it?"

"It's weird that it's not weird."

"Okay." She sighs. "I just wanted to make sure you don't feel bad. About what happened tonight. Because I really don't. Whether it was a bad idea or not. Whether it happens again or not. I just want to make sure we both feel good about it."

"Okay. I feel good about it."

"Okay."

She stares at the door. I don't want her to go.

"Did you have fun? With your friends?"

"Not really. I mean, I'm glad I went. It was great to see Nico perform, and he was so happy that I was there. I've never seen him with a band behind him before. I'm proud of him. Did you have fun? By yourself?"

"No."

"Are we really this lame?"

"Pfft. Lame? Speak for yourself. I don't know if you've heard, but I'm a movie star with a pretty badass penis, so I'm cool no matter what I get up to at night."

She yawns. "Yeah. I should get to bed. I partied *so* hard." She rolls her eyes.

Goddammit, I want her to get in bed with me. But not now. She's right. When the kids aren't here. When we can really be in bed together. Is that what she means? She stands up.

"I'll make breakfast tomorrow so you can sleep in," I tell her. "If you want to."

"You sure? Did you get any sleep yet?"

I shake my head. "I will now, though."

She smiles, so sweetly. She's probably blushing. I wonder if she's still wet for me, because I could be completely hard for her in three seconds.

But not now. She's right.

"Good night," she whispers.

*Fuck it.*

Before she reaches the door, I'm blocking it and my hands are up in her hair and I'm kissing her—not on the cheek, not with the intensity of earlier tonight... I'm kissing her to let her know that I'm glad she came back and I can't wait until tomorrow to kiss her again. She's surprised and relieved and responsive. Her hands press against my chest—not pushing me away but leaning into me. Her head falls back so I can kiss her neck and all over her beautiful clean face. "Good night," I whisper, kissing her on the mouth one last time.

Her eyes are still closed and she's swaying a little when I reach for the door handle to open it.

She bites her lower lip, opens her eyes, and punches my bicep on her way out.

"Badass," she whispers.

"Damn straight."

I stand by the door until she's downstairs and I've heard the door to her room close shut, and then I check on the kids before getting back into bed.

My alarm's set for six and I'll sleep soundly until then, knowing that everyone is home where they belong.

"Who's ready for more pancakes? Chocolate chip this time." This is my third batch of pancakes this morning. First batch was plain and a little burned. Second batch was blueberry and fucking awesome. This one is weird-looking but with chocolate chips, so who cares.

"Meee!" Maple syrup is dripping from Summer's mouth. She always claims that she's still hungry after I've cooked a meal, but I'm going to win this breakfast. It might take a few hours to clean this mess, but my breakfast game is strong this morning.

Lucky barely raises his left hand, elbow on the table, like an old drunk guy ordering another bourbon. Meanwhile he can barely lift his fork to get the turkey sausage and scrambled eggs into his mouth because he's so full.

I've been keeping myself busy cooking every breakfast item I can cook, to keep from sneaking into

Willa's room and crawling between her legs. That counts as good parenting, right? It's after eight, and she's still not up yet. Is she in the shower? Should I check?

"Can we watch *Pokémon*?" Summer asks as she reaches for the remote for the kitchen TV.

"Pikachu!"

"You guys are watching *Pokémon* now? When'd that happen?"

"Willa showed us it. It's fun. And weird. Like Willa," my daughter says while turning on the TV before waiting for permission.

"Yeah? What's the show about?"

The twins start explaining something about Ash and Pikachu and adventures, but I don't really hear a word they're saying because Willa has just walked in wearing a casual, loose-fitting dress that hits above the knee, with bare legs and bare feet and her hair is wet. The birthday party doesn't start until eleven, but I'm wondering if we can drop the twins off a couple of hours early. Is that wrong?

She just smiles at me from across the room and kisses the twins on their heads as they keep talking.

*Should I make coffee?* she mouths to me.

I nod. Yes. I want coffee. I also want to lay her out on the table and lick maple syrup off her naked body.

But not while the kids are here.

I haven't completely lost my mind yet.

"Sounds fun," I say once the kids have stopped talking. They could have told me they're watching a snuff film as far as I know. I can't stop staring at Willa's legs.

"You sure you made enough food?" She glances over at me, grinning.

"Are you saying I shouldn't also make waffles?"

"I want waffles!" Summer shouts out without looking away from the TV. Her plate is still piled full of pancakes, eggs, and turkey bacon.

"You guys are going to the trampoline party in a couple of hours, remember? For Riley's birthday. Maybe don't eat too much."

"Oh yeah!" Lucky turns to look over at Willa. "Riley's gonna be six!"

"Do we have birthday presents for Riley?" I ask Willa with an expression on my face that probably reads more like *are you wearing panties right now, young lady?*

"They're in my room. I just wrapped them." She smirks at me, daring me to carry her to her room and unwrap her.

I stroll over to where she's making coffee and reach around her for a paper towel that I don't really need. "Are you okay driving them there, or should I?" Her damp hair smells so fucking good, she must have used sexy mermaid shampoo and then rolled around in a flower bed while sultry nymphs did a striptease by her head. Jesus, what is wrong with me?

"Yeah, I was planning on dropping them off. If you don't mind tidying up the kitchen?"

"I fully intend to take care of this mess." *And I fully*

*intend to take care of you as soon as we're alone in this house.*

"The trampoline place is in Woodland Hills," she says, dusting pancake mix off my chest. "They'll be there for two hours, and then all the kids get shuttled to Riley's house in Brentwood for lunch and cake. So we pick them up there at around two. You need to sign a waiver for the trampoline place online. Did you do that?"

I sign the waiver online, releasing the trampoline company of liability if my kids get injured. Meanwhile I'm doing some frantic sex calculations in my head—on a Saturday morning, it'll take Willa 35 to 50 minutes to drive each way. That'll give us maybe two hours alone together, tops. I can live with that. We can get a lot done in two hours.

*Happy birthday, Riley. I can't wait to start celebrating.*

When Willa brings me a cup of her amazing coffee, she whispers, "Just letting you know in advance that I'm on the pill. So take that into consideration."

Fuck me.

Maybe I should hire an Uber to drive the kids to Woodland Hills. People do that, right?

Oh my God, give a girl a break, traffic gods! Some of us have to get home to get naked with Greyson from *That's So Wizard* over here!

I accidentally lean on the horn and then wave apologetically at the driver of the car in front of me. One of five thousand cars in front of me. The 405 suddenly got completely backed up about a mile from my exit. Not funny, Los Angeles! Not cool.

I did the right thing by *not* dropping the kids off at the curb. I went inside the trampoline gym to make sure they were all comfortable there with their friends, made small talk with Riley's mom and the other parents and nannies for a minute, and then bolted back to the car while visualizing all of the amazing things I want to do to Shane's penis. I'll be lucky if I get back to the house in the next fifteen minutes, which means I'll only have time to do like ten awesome things to him. He deserves more. Or maybe it's fine. Hopefully this will be the first of many penis things I'll be able to do to him. We should probably take it slow.

Not the traffic—dammit. The traffic needs to take it much, much faster.

I accidentally honk the horn again. Shrug and wave apologetically again. I'm probably going to get shot. I need to calm down.

This is going to be the first time I have sex with a guy I actually care about.

The guy I was somewhat mildly obsessed with for my entire adolescence.

My brother's best friend.

My employer.

Shit.

Is this the worst idea ever?

Have I lost my mind?

Telling him that I'm on the pill while his children are eating breakfast in the same room?

He must think I'm a total tramp.

I must be having an allergic reaction to his pheromones.

Maybe we should wait a few months, until I'm not working for him anymore.

I've waited this long. A few months of getting to know each other better as friends could only make it better when we finally...what? Bone each other a couple of times and then he's off to do a movie with the girl from *Twilight*? Or Hermione? Because what actor wouldn't rather be with them?

I let the minivan in the next lane get in ahead of me.

By the time I've turned onto Shane's driveway, I have convinced myself that I should just tell him we need to chill.

By the time I've parked the Volvo in the garage, I am thinking it would be a good idea to tell him that it may have been a mistake, what happened last night, but it was my fault.

By the time I've opened the door to the house, I am sure of it.

But as soon as I step inside, Shane's arm is around my waist and he's pulling me to him.

"Fucking hell, I've been dying for you, Willa."

My eyelids instinctively close and my hands reach for his face.

He breathes in the skin of my neck, massaging my hips, sliding his hands up and down my waist. His hands, oh God, his hands. He touches me like he owns me, and I want to give him everything.

His hair is damp, and he's wearing an unbuttoned shirt and jeans. I'm pressed up against his warm, bare chest. This is heaven.

I'm smelling cologne on him for the first time. Dear God, it's a Giorgio Armani absolu. Top notes—bergamot, marine notes, something fruity. Middle notes—hints of lavender and rosemary. Base notes—oh fuck it, he smells hot. He just smells hot. I want to eat him up.

I pull my head back so I can see his handsome face. His eyes are hooded, blue like the late-afternoon sea, his jaw tense. So serious. *Don't even joke about that.* I tilt my head up to press my lips against his, a half-kiss. Savoring this calm before the storm of our bodies crashing against each other.

He rests his forehead against mine, hands up in my hair, slowly exploring my breasts, my waist, my hips. "Beautiful girl, what have you done to me?" His hands cup my face. He smooths his thumb across my bottom lip, and I suck it into my mouth, moaning and watching him as I do.

Heat flashes in his eyes. He licks his lips. Makes a deep, guttural sound, like a shot fired, and the race to do as much to each other's bodies as we can begins.

I pull his shirt down off his shoulders, running my hands down the smooth, toned muscles of his arms. He tosses the shirt to the floor and pushes me against the wall, kissing me hard on the mouth, practically growling, and then dropping to his knees and disappearing under my dress.

Oh sweet Jesus, he tugs my panties down. I feel his thumb brush up against my clit, and then he grabs hold of my ass, slides one hand down the back of one thigh, hiking my leg up over his shoulder. He licks and then bites the flesh of my inner thigh and proceeds to do all of the amazing things he did last night to my lady parts with his fingers—with his tongue this time.

I cannot do any penis things to him from this position.

My eyes roll back inside my head. "Oh, shit." I melt into the wall, into his hands, into his tongue. His flicking, circling, sweeping tongue. His gentle, punishing, determined tongue. I'm whimpering and floating up and caving in on myself. My hands slap against the wall, trying to find some leverage, bracing myself. And now his fingers get in on the action too.

"Shane. Oh my God. How many of you are down there?"

He answers by moaning, pushing his fingers up to my hips and pulsing his tongue in and out and in and out. My entire being is struck by a hot jolt of electricity, and then my hips follow his rhythm, warmth radiating up and out from my center and back to where his tongue penetrates me. It feels too good. I scream out his name and then cover my mouth because I'm making such loud noises.

"I want to hear you," he says from under my dress. "I want to hear you come."

I uncover my mouth and whimper. I squeeze my thighs together, wriggling away from him. It has to stop. It's too much. I've never ever gotten enough from a guy, but this feels like so much more than my body can handle and it's just the beginning.

"Shane."

He continues licking me, pressing my trembling thighs together even more with his palms and then sucking on my clit.

"Oh God!"

My life flashes before my eyes, and it turns out my life has just been one long pre-orgasm leading up to this.

He goes back to kissing me down there and doesn't stop until my hips have stopped rolling, until my body has stopped jerking and tensing, until every cell of my body has gone from screaming to whispering his name.

His head finally reemerges from under my dress, but I still feel little electric shocks in my core.

*What just happened?*

I'm limp as a ragdoll, but I also feel like I could run a marathon.

Before I can even mutter his name again or say the other thing I'm thinking—*That was so wizard*—he's carrying me in his arms to my bedroom. He kicks the door shut. Just in case the kids come home, I guess. Or to keep me from running out—as if.

He lowers me to the foot of the bed, lifts me up to sit, kneels before me to untie my Keds. *Such a dad move, oh my God.*

When my shoes are off, he stands up, takes my hands and holds them up, pulling my dress over my head. The dress gets tossed aside. I can barely keep my heavy eyelids open, but his eyes are wide and appreciative. I am completely naked before him in this white filtered natural light, and I'm not even afraid of him seeing me.

"Willa…look at you. Goddamn."

I run my fingers through my hair and toss it all behind my shoulders so he can see everything, dragging my fingertips down the side of my neck, between my breasts.

He groans and reaches for me, but I reach for his jeans, looking up at him as I unbutton and unzip, maneuvering them so they can drop to his ankles. He steps out of them, kicking them aside. The bulge in his black boxer briefs is magnificent.

"Wow, your pen really is bigger than mine," I mutter.

I cup it with one hand while tracing my fingertip along the inside of the waistband and then pulling the elastic away from the taut skin of his pelvis. He watches me as I uncover this fully erect beautiful thing.

*Oh my God, it's so pretty. I knew it. I knew it would be. It's so clean and well-groomed and big and friendly, and it matches the rest of him. I can't stop staring.*

I need to refrain from talking about it.

No need to share everything that pops into my brain.

Just keep it to myself.

"I just...I just have to say that if the penises in porn looked like this, I would actually watch pornos. You should show your cock in movies. Seriously. This puts Michael Fassbender's penis to shame."

"Once again, I'll be sure to pass that along to my agents."

I push the boxer briefs down until they drop to the floor. My mouth is watering, staring at his erection. *All this for me?* I cup his balls, wrap my hand around the base, and lick up the underside, all the way to the crown and then suck on it.

We both groan at the same time.

His hands are in my hair again.

*I can do fantastic things with my tongue too, Shane Miller, just you wait.*

"Willa," he says so quietly. "Fuck, that feels so good."

I stroke and lick and suck and squeeze.

He tugs on my hair. His hands grip my shoulders. "Willa, stop."

I don't stop. I want to do all the things to this cock.

"Willa." His voice is so growly. "What do you call a guy who can't wait another minute to be inside you?"

I look up at him, dazed and confused.

"Me. Get on your back. Now."

Well, it's not very funny, but I haven't heard that one before.

I get on my back.

Now.

# SHANE

*I* can't stop touching this woman.

I can't stop kissing her.

I can't stop staring.

Completely naked, except for that dainty gold necklace, she pulls herself backwards from the foot of the bed up to lay her head on the pillows, my hands around her ankles as I climb onto the bed with her. Moving in sync with each other, like we're doing some choreographed dirty dancing routine, she locks eyes with me the entire time. She slowly lowers herself to the mattress, to the pillows. Her long, silky dark hair splays out around her against the white sheets, framing her beautiful face and body, and for once in my life, I am speechless. I can only touch and kiss and stare.

I stroke up from her ankles to her knees, pushing them apart, kneeling between them. She watches me intently, shifting around a bit, clawing at the covers. She's a little tense and restless from anticipation. I am too. Every part of me is straining to collide with every part of her, and I must be insane if I'm ordering her to remove her amazing mouth from my aching cock, but time is not on our side this afternoon, and I intend to spend as much of it plunging the depths of Willa's sweet, hot pussy as possible.

Her gorgeous breasts and perky nipples are beckoning to me, though. I'm not going to ignore them. I'm going to make sure they know exactly how much I like them. I'm going to massage them while my tongue circles and flicks and glides. I'm going to take in as much of this one into my mouth as I can. I'm going to suck until she cries out, and I'm going to nip at her flesh to make her gasp. She's writhing around and dragging her fingernails across my upper back. and *fuck that feels good*. She's whimpering and mumbling something I don't understand. Something about my heart line and pheromones and an allergy. She's shaking her head and repeating my name over and over in a deep, husky voice that I don't recognize as hers, but I like it just the same.

I take one last lick, hike myself up, hover over her, staring down at this pretty, flushed face that I can't get enough of. She can barely keep her blurry eyes open. I have never been this hard, but I'm completely torn between the need for release and the desire to make this last before real life comes banging down the door.

I lower myself to kiss that mouth, that swollen, moist, deep-pink mouth.

"It's been longer than a minute," she mutters between licking and biting my lower lip. "Get on your back. Now."

In the second that it takes me to lower my head and laugh, she manages to flip me onto my back. I would complain, but she's straddling me, and this view is better than any of the other views from my house. She's positioning her dripping wet pussy over my rigid cock, and I'm mesmerized. She presses into my chest with one hand for support, clutches the base of my dick with the other. I hold on to her hips. We're both holding our breaths. She's lowering herself so slowly.

Jesus, this is sweet fucking agony, and I'm feeling it all over.

She's quivering, and I'm clenching everything, trying to hold still.

When the tip of my cock gets a quick kiss of that wet heat, I know it's all over for me.

I'm a goner.

This is it.

Nothing will ever feel better than this.

Her exhale and my groan echo, chasing each other around the ceiling and she's consuming me with this soul-melting tease as she sinks down, down, down until we've merged. I've filled her up, and she's arching her back and tightening around me. "Oh, baby." I'm in deep, and she's completely still for an eternity while she gets over the shock of accommodating me. When she does, she flips her head, tossing her hair to one side, and her hips start to roll. She takes her time, smirking at me, killing me and giving me life with each swaying movement. Taking it sexy and slow.

*Fuck this shit.*

I give her ass a smack. The resulting shudder through her body is more satisfying than I'd imagined, so I do it again. She responds by picking up the pace, rocking back and forth and bearing down on me. It takes an incredible amount of effort to keep my eyes open, but watching Willa sway around and lean into the ebb and flow of this orgasm is breathtaking. Literally. I can't look away. She's drowning in it, and I squeeze her thighs to remind her that I'm here. I'm working hard to keep my climax at bay, but this is the sexiest thing I've ever seen. I want to wait for this tidal wave to crash, but I might have to wait forever. And I can't.

One swift move and I'm on top of her, thrusting like a champion right out of the gate.

"Oh, yes, Shane. Yes!"

She grabs on to my shoulders and wraps her legs around me so tight.

"Willa, Willa, Willa."

"Fuck me harder. You don't have to be Mr. Nice Guy."

*Well, fuck me.*

"Like this?" I slam into her, nailing her to the mattress. The delirious pleasure is almost unbearable. "You want that?"

"Oh God, yes!"

I grab on to the headboard for leverage and go harder, faster, deeper. Some crazy growl emerges from deep inside me. I've been on the edge of everything for so long, hanging on by my fingernails, and she's giving me permission to let go.

"Don't stop, don't stop."

The wall is shaking from the pounding of the headboard, her tits are bouncing magnificently beneath me, and I cry out, some unintelligible curse or prayer, because this is raw fucking heaven and hell and I feel so alive I might die.

I disappear into the staccato rhythm of fucking Willa and I find myself again.

The white-hot orgasm shreds me to pieces. I am somehow aware of her saying my name and holding on to me while I explode inside her. Blindly emptying into her, frozen in time.

I collapse onto her.

We cling to each other.

Both of us slick with sweat, fighting to catch our breath, exhausted and energized.

My hand finds hers, interlacing our fingers, slowly returning to the world and each other.

Finally, she reaches for the bottle of water on her bedside table, takes a sip, and then hands it to me. I sit up to drink. For the first time ever, I'm realizing I don't just have a woman in bed with me. I have a partner. It's a lot to take in—way too much to think about after ejaculating.

But this lazy thought is hovering over me like a fragrant, post-coital cloud of smoke. *This is what I want.* Pancakes and trampoline parties and a woman who can make my kids laugh *and* do sensational things to my cock.

*This* woman.

The room is filled with the delicately over-whelming scent of her.

"I want to lie here with you like this for ten minutes, and then I want to do all of that again."

"All of it?"

"Plus a few other things, in a few other places." I take one last sip of water.

"You'll have to buy me dinner first before doing certain things to one of my places."

I've done about twenty perfect spit-takes in my career, on-camera and off, but water spews everywhere and I nearly choke to death.

When I finally regain my composure, I say, "I meant other places in this house, not on you. But I can order dinner to be delivered in twenty minutes! Where's my phone?"

She laughs. "I mean, you could just make me a sandwich."

"Please, I am a gentleman. I'll make you two sand-wiches. But really, where's my phone?" My dad brain is regaining consciousness. I crawl to the foot of the bed to pick up my pants, finding my phone on the floor. "Shit." There's a voice mail, a missed call, and two text messages from Riley's mom. Two texts from Margo. All in the last forty minutes. My phone's set to vibrate, but I didn't hear a thing.

"What's wrong?"

"I don't know yet." I listen to the voice mail, trying to concentrate on what Riley's mom is saying instead of watching Willa glide out of the room, naked.

"Fuck." The twins are sick. They both barfed. Simultaneously. They *twarfed*. On the trampoline. They're resting in a back room at the gym. They want to come home. God, the poor things. This is my fault. What kind of an idiot fills his kids up with ten different kinds of food right before a trampoline party? *The horny kind.*

Willa walks back in, listening to a message on her phone too. "Ohhh, poor things. She called me too."

I hold my hand up to silence her while I call Riley's mom back. It goes to voice mail, but I tell her I'm on my way to pick the kids up in Woodland Hills. I grab my underwear, look around for my shirt. I can't go like this. It's gotta be so obvious I've been having a fuckfest.

"Should I come with you?" Willa asks as she covers herself with her dress.

"No." If we show up together, everyone will know that my nanny and I have been fucking. "I'll go. This is my fault." I rake my fingers through my hair. So much for heaven.

"They'll be fine, Shane. They just need to rest. It's not like you gave them food poisoning."

"Thanks," I say, brushing past her, out of the room.

"I'll be sure to remind people of that when I'm accepting my Father of the Year award."

I check my text messages while I head to the bathroom to clean myself up.

**MARGO: Why am I getting texts from Riley's mom about the twins being sick and needing to be picked up in Woodland Hills? What is going on?**
**MARGO: Shane. They're calling me to set. Willa won't answer me either. What is going on???**

I text Margo to tell her the twins were just sick from jumping after eating too much. And that I was stuck in traffic running errands but I'm on my way to pick up the twins. It's the first time I've ever lied to her like that. I'm a shit.

"I'll have peppermint tea waiting for them when you get home. Do you have any?"

"I have no idea," I say, looking for my wallet and keys. "See you in a bit."

I'm already backing out of the garage by the time it occurs to me that I should have kissed Willa good-bye. Something. So she knows I'm not mad at her for anything. That what just happened between us meant everything to me. But I already feel bad for making the kids wait so long to be picked up. And deep down I feel guilty that what happened between me and Willa meant everything. Because she isn't everything to me. She can't be.

I lost my head.

I may already be losing my heart to her, but I can't afford to lose my head.

*W*ell. It was not the first time a man had left my bed in a hurry before, but it *was* the first time a man had rushed off to pick up his kids after plowing me and joking about making me sandwiches before doing butt stuff.

Can't fault a guy for being such a devoted dad.

Can't blame him for forgetting to kiss me good-bye.

Can't feel bad about the fact that we didn't discuss what it means now that we've shagged and I have no idea if he regrets it or blames me somehow for distracting him.

Yeah, baby.

Yeah.

I'm clutching on to my heart pendant, something I haven't done in days, when my phone vibrates in my pocket. It's not Shane. A photo of my Grammie's beautiful, elfin face is on the screen, and I answer the call immediately, my heart suddenly racing because she usually only texts or e-mails.

"Grammie? What's wrong?"

"Nothing. What's wrong with you?"

"Are you okay?"

"Yes. I was just checking to see if your phone is working."

"Yeah. I mean, I think so."

"Oh good. I thought maybe you didn't get any cell phone reception at Shane Miller's house or something."

*Oh. It's that kind of call.* "Shit. Sorry. I haven't called you since I came here. I've been so busy. I'm an asshole."

"Well, you said it, love, not me. I did appreciate the video of Nico. Glad to see he's still a cocky little stud muffin."

"Yeah, no worries there."

"And you? Should I be worried about you at all?"

"No. I'm still a cocky little stud muffin too. Why?"

"How are Shane's children? What are they like now?"

I keep forgetting that my Grammie knew Shane better than I did for a few years, while she was out here with Nico. He probably sends her pictures or Christmas cards.

"Oh my God, they're amazing. They're so smart, and they both have really strong personalities. They're beautiful. They look so much like Shane."

"Yes. They do... And how is Shane?"

"Fine. He's really good with his kids. He's a great dad."

"Mmmhmm. And how is he with you?"

"What? Fine. Nothing—how's your foot?"

"Willa Dora Todd."

"What?"

"Are we really going to keep pretending that I have no idea how infatuated you were with that boy after you met him?"

"Infatuated? That's a strong word."

"Not from the woman who was with you when you first met him. Not from the woman who was with you when you found out he was getting married. Not from your Grammie who knows everything so why you've ever bothered trying to hide anything from her is beyond me. You can fool your brother, you can fool your parents, you can fool yourself, but you can't fool me. Tell me. Are you clutching on to your little gold heart pendant right now?"

I let go of my heart pendant immediately. "That was a long time ago."

"So it's not a big deal that you're currently living with him?"

"Pssh. It's a job."

"Willa Dora Todd."

"Dora Prunella Todd."

She snorts. "My middle name is not Prunella, you jerk."

"What are you getting at? I'm living with Shane Miller, yes. I'm his temporary nanny. It's going fine. I'm getting on with my life."

"Is that what you call it?"

"Call what?"

"Living with the boy you used to be obsessed with."

"'Obsessed?' I was hardly obsessed with him. I've dated tons of other guys—on two continents."

"Yes, we're all well aware of your astonishing, unsatisfying escapades. How's that working out for you?"

"Grammie. Are there no other pots available for you to stir today?"

"I'm just worried about you. You're brave, but you aren't tough. You're so practical, but you're prone to flights of fancy when it comes to Shane. He's a good boy—an excellent boy—but he has a big life that's filled with big responsibilities, and you're a special girl who deserves a special place in a man's life. Don't sell yourself short just because the single daddy wants a little nanny nookie."

"'Nanny nookie?' Okay, first of all, Shane is not like that, and if you think he is, then you don't know him nearly as well as you think you do—"

"Defending him already. Wonderful."

"And also, if you think I can't handle a little nookie with someone just because he's got an impressive list of credits on IMDB, then you don't know me as well as you think you do either."

"Oh, crap. You've already done the deed, haven't you?"

"Nobody calls it doing the deed anymore."

"How would you know? You're about as hip as I am."

"I love you, Grammie, but I have a lot to do today. Can I call you some other time?"

"As long as you're still doing things for yourself, yes."

"I am. Thank you for calling. I'm sure Nico would love to hear from you—maybe you could ask him why he hasn't settled down with a serious girlfriend in years!"

"I'm on it. I've got big plans for ruffling that boy's feathers today too, you'd better believe it. I love you. I love Shane too—just don't lose your head or your heart over him."

She hangs up before I can assure her that I would never.

Ugh.

Grammie. She's just lonely. She needs more hobbies.

I don't have this kind of relationship with my mother because she's always been too busy with my dad and her career to worry about the complications of my inner life.

Nice try, Grammie. You don't know everything. I am perfectly capable of enjoying a little nookie without getting hurt.

Just because I'm stomping around the house while

changing the sheets on my bed and getting a change of clothes for the twins and slamming cupboard doors looking for peppermint tea, that doesn't mean I'm mad at Shane Miller for giving me such amazing orgasms and then not letting me go with him to pick up the kids.

Just because my eyes are stinging, that doesn't mean I'm going to give him the cold shoulder for bolting before the sweat had dried.

Just because my heart starts racing and my stomach drops as soon as I hear the garage door open, that doesn't mean I'm falling in love with him and am completely, utterly fucked.

I take a deep breath, check my reflection in the hall mirror like an idiot, briefly consider changing out of my sweat pants and T-shirt like an even bigger idiot, then go to the door to the garage so I can help him bring the kids in.

He's picking Summer up out of her car seat. I go to the other door to help Lucky out of his, when Shane scoops Summer up into his arms—totally unlike the way he did that to me earlier. She is frowning and sucking her thumb—something I've never seen her do before. Lucky looks like a proud soldier who's returning from the war, battle-weary but refusing to show his emotional scars.

"Hey, buddy. How you feeling?"

"Okay."

"Yeah?" I lift him out of his car seat. He usually

insists on getting out all by himself. "Your tummy still feel funny?"

"Yeah."

I carry him inside, following behind Shane, who's carrying Summer.

"Thanks," Shane says, I assume to me. "We decided we're gonna watch movies for the rest of the day. Want to join us?"

"Sure," I answer, looking at Lucky. "For a while, anyway."

As Shane carries Summer through the hallway past the kitchen, she removes her thumb from her mouth to say, "Snacks!"

"No more food for a while, kiddo. Willa's gonna make us peppermint tea, though, right?"

"Comin' up."

Summer tries to climb over her dad's shoulder, pointing at the kitchen door. "Cheese. I want cheese!"

"Later, Summer," Shane says firmly. "We'll have a late lunch. Later."

Summer growls at him.

At least I'm not the only female in this house who's frustrated with him right now.

We set the kids down on the sofa in the family room.

"I'll go get their pajamas to change into," Shane says. "They smell barftastic."

"I got 'em." I go back out to the hall to grab the pajamas I'd left on the table.

"Thanks," Shane says as I hand him Summer's PJs, sounding so grateful it hurts.

"Welcome." I haven't made eye contact with him yet. I'm dying to look into his eyes, but I can't. "What are we going to watch first?" I ask Lucky as I help him change his clothes.

"*Mary Poppins*," the twins answer at the same time.

"Oh."

I can see Shane in my peripheral vision, watching me and shrugging. "They both wanted to watch it."

"Cool. I haven't seen that one since I was little."

"She's a nanny," Summer explains. "Like you."

*Not that much like me. Ms. Poppins never boned the dad while the kids were out.*

"She's a much better singer than I am."

"I like how you sound," she says.

"I like how you sound too," says Shane.

I finally look over at him, knitting my brows together.

"When you sing for Summer." He grins.

I frown at him. *Don't you dare grin at me while saying playfully flirtatious things with your handsome face.*

The light fades from his eyes, and he looks down at Summer. He picks up her dirty laundry, holds out his hand for me to place Lucky's clothes in it. When I do, he just nods and disappears downstairs to the laundry room, I suppose.

When Shane starts the movie, he sits on the couch, up against the corner. Summer puts a pillow on his lap and lays her head on it. I cover her with a fuzzy blanket and then cover Lucky with one and take a seat in the armchair. When I look back at Lucky, he's got *Puss in Boots* face, blinking his big eyes and pouting at me.

"You want me to sit with you?" I whisper.

"You don't have to," he whines.

"I would love to." I settle into the other corner of the couch with a pillow on my lap, so he can lay his sweet little head on it.

I can feel Shane looking over at me every few minutes, but I keep my eyes fixed on the TV screen.

About twenty minutes into the movie, I feel my phone vibrate in my pocket and try to pull it out without disturbing Lucky.

There's a text from Shane.

I glance over at him, rolling my eyes. He's holding his phone in one hand but pretending to be totally engrossed in the movie.

**SHANE: Hi. I'm really sorry I left in such a hurry. I had an amazing time with you. Wish it could have lasted longer.**

I hold on to the heart pendant of my necklace and type out a response without looking at him.

**ME: I forgot to make peppermint tea.**

ME: Did Summer used to suck her thumb? Is she regressing?

He waits one whole second before subtly checking his phone. Out of the corner of my eye, I see him typing something. I wait an entire minute before checking my phone after it vibrates.

SHANE: Yes. It still happens sometimes. She'll be fine. Probably.
SHANE: Your tits look amazing in that T-shirt.
SHANE: And mad. They look like they're mad at me. I get it. I deserve it. I just don't want you to think that I was mad at you. I was mad at myself.

I reply immediately.

ME: Yeah. You're a good guy. I get it. It won't happen again.
SHANE: I didn't mean I was mad at myself for what we did.
ME: I know what you meant, Shane. I know you have responsibilities. I'm glad you take them seriously. But if you can't be with me like that wholeheartedly,

without guilt or whatever it is you struggle with,
then I don't want to be with you like that.

ME: I have to focus on my own shit anyway. So if you
don't need me all day tomorrow, I'd like to take a few
hours off to go to a perfume supply store.

He exhales sharply. Like I just knocked the wind out of
him. Finally, he looks over at me. I meet his gaze. His
jaw is clenched. His eyes are sad. He nods and looks at
the screen.

*Happy now, Grammie?*

I leave the room when they Skype with Margo, but
I do overhear some of the conversation, and at least
she doesn't give Shane a hard time for overfeeding the
twins.

We watch TV for the rest of the day, until the kids'
bedtime, eating in front of the TV. Twice. Which is less
awkward than having to face each other at the kitchen
table.

I have to sing the chorus of "Let It Go" from *Frozen*
three times to get Summer to brush her teeth.

The twins want to sleep in bed with their dad
tonight, and he lets them. So I don't have to read to
them. I kiss them good night. I say good night to Shane
as I pass him in the hall.

"Willa," he says.

I turn back to look at him. "What?"

He looks like he's about to say something important. Something that I need to hear. Something that will change everything. And then his eyes flick to the floor.

"Good night."

He disappears into his bedroom.

I disappear into mine.

I disappear into familiar scents and the drive to create something new and beautiful. Something transformative that will last. Something that I need to smell. Something that will change everything.

## SHANE MILLER SLEEP DIARY – SUNDAY, MORNING

Went to bed at: *7:30 pm*

How long it took you to fall asleep: *Few hours.*

How many times you woke up in the middle of the night: *Five or six?*

How refreshing your overall sleep was: *Not.*

Number of caffeinated beverages you consumed throughout the day: *One.*

Number of alcoholic beverages you consumed throughout the day: *Fuck my life.*

How much time you spent exercising: *Depends on what counts as exercising.*

**Your stress level before bedtime, on a scale from 1 to 5:** *I don't know how to answer that.*

**Your major cause of stress:** *Being a dickhead.*

## WILLA TODD SCENT DIARY, MONDAY MORNING

*Just went for a walk on the bluffs to clear my head and my nose. Ocean air. Hint of eucalyptus leaves. I spent all Saturday and Sunday night, once the kids went to bed, in my room. Mixing at this desk.*

*Shane is at an appointment. He's been so grumpy since Saturday afternoon. We've barely spoken directly to each other since he brought the kids home. But when I came home this morning from dropping off the kids, I found a few sprigs of lavender at the foot of my bed. I think he cut them from the front yard. He didn't even realize he had lavender growing there before I pointed it out to him. I fucking hate that he's so sweet. And hot. He's impossible to stay mad at. Even when he's a grumpy dickhead.*

*I wish I could just roll this new perfume oil on his pulse points to alter his mood. But that would be weird. But if I*

*could, it would take him on a little journey down memory*
*lane. My memory. Of us.*

*Top notes include sweet pea. It opens up youthful and girly,*
*optimistic and not at all sexy.*

*Middle notes include the suggestion of sweet and spicy*
*freesia created with natural white verbena essential oil and*
*the clean, soothing, alluring scent of lavender of course. I*
*wonder if I should tell Shane about its aphrodisiac qualities.*
*So many benefits in the bedroom...*

*Base notes—amber and sandalwood for an unexpectedly*
*sexy drydown, with a hint of seaweed for a marine note and*
*vanilla because it's childlike and reminds me of the kids.*

*It's odd and it shouldn't work together, but it totally does. To*
*me, anyway.*
*Blended in a fractionated coconut oil, it is unassuming and*
*surprising, comforting and stimulating. I have the perfect*
*name for it, and I think I've finally found the perfect combi-*
*nation to give it long-lasting wear.*

*If it were a color, it would be peach, hot pink, red, violet,*
*deep blue. The colors of a fleeting Pacific Palisades sunset*
*over the eternal ocean.*

*I've designed and ordered the labels. Once they are deliv-*
*ered, I can open up my Etsy store and try to convince some*

*local boutiques to sell a few bottles of this new scent and the ones I've been working on for years. I'll be on my way.*

## 17

## SHANE

*I* have no idea if Dr. Gavin Shaw is actually a good physician or not, but he's oddly paternal and has a really cool Scottish accent. Since I take very little advantage of the SAG-AFTRA Health Plan myself, that was a good enough reason to select him as my primary care physician.

When I came to see him about the insomnia after I got back from Maine, he brought up the possibility of sending me to a sleep clinic if things didn't improve. Obviously, that's not going to happen, but back then I was willing to try anything. Back then, Nico's little sister was just a faint, quirky memory. Back then, all kinds of thoughts about all kinds of things kept me awake at night. Now, all other thoughts have fallen away when I'm in bed and all that's left is Willa.

"Well, yer thyroid test results came back normal, yer blood pressure is excellent today, and ya look jes' great, Shane Miller, much better than the last time, eh?"

"Better, yes. Things got worse and then a lot better, and now it's... I don't know what it is now."

"All right, well," he says, flicking at his beard while reading my sleep diary entries, "let's have a look here... Uh-huh... Mmhmm... Exercise. Hah! Indeed... Mmhmm... 'Relief.' Interestin', *innit*?... Lavender, you say? Essential oils. Great. Fantastic stuff."

"You think that stuff works?"

"Aye. I think anythin' works if it works, right?"

"Sure."

"Read a book. Have a pint. Smoke a wee bit of skunk—what have you... Guilt? Not so much. Guilt never works for anyone. Fuck guilt."

"Easier said than done."

"Fuck it and be done with it."

"Okay."

"Uh-huh... New nanny." He grins up at me. "Very nice. Good... 'Dickhead.' Ach! Come on. You're very, very hard on yourself—much too hard on yourself, boy. You worry about your kids?"

"Of course I do."

"Let me tell you—bein' a parent, jes' like bein' human, is all about makin' mistakes. Huge ones, little ones. I once forgot my children in the car at the mall for two hours. But guess what? They were fine. They didn't realize I'd gone until the battery died on their— what do ya call it—the wee game thing. The old ones."

"Game Boy."

"Aye. You know when kids worry? When they see their parents worry." He slaps the pages of my sleep diary. "So...let me get this straight... See if I can read between the lines here... New nanny at home." He gives me the thumbs up. "Relief. The right kind of exercise." He winks at me. "Everything's grand. Sleep is good."

"Basically, yes."

"Fuck things up with the new nanny?" He points his thumbs down. "Everything goes to shit. Sleep's shit. Mood's shit."

"In a nutshell, sure."

"So. Don't fuck things up with the new nanny."

"It's a little more complicated than that."

"Yeah? How so?"

"She's my best friend's little sister."

"And?"

"And she's my kids' nanny now. They love her. If I screw things up with her, I might screw things up for them too. I might screw things up with my friend."

He stares at me for a few seconds. "Forgot to check somethin'. Hang on." He reaches over and sticks his hand under my balls. I'm wearing jeans and he is a doctor, but what the fuck? "Whaddya know. Ya still got 'em." He yanks his hand away. "Had me worried there for a minute. Anythin' might screw everythin' up. Live your life. You only get this one. It doesn't have to be perfect. Set things straight with the nanny and be done with it."

"That's it? That's your professional medical opinion?"

"Whatever works, lad. For me—if I might share a wee bit of my own life with you." He leans forward, lowering his voice.

I nod, warily, as I cross my legs in a totally manly way so he doesn't try to grab my nut sac again.

"I been married to the same woman for twenty-five years, God bless her soul, and whenever I'm tossin' and turnin' in bed, keepin' her up at night...she'll jes' reach over and give me a nice slow tug on the old knob. Nothin' too excitin' you understand, jes' a nice slow tug to get me off and we're done. Simple as that. A bonnie lass and a good handy and you're all set to conquer sleep and the world... Now..." He claps his hands together. "When's the next Shane Miller picture comin' to a theater near me?"

"I've got a big Melissa McCarthy comedy coming out in a couple of months and then a little independent film coming out hopefully not long after that."

"Nothin' too artsy-fartsy, I hope."

"Not at all. I'm really excited about it." *Everyone's a critic.*

"Excellent. Off ya go."

Yeah.

I still don't know if Dr. Gavin Shaw is a good physician or not, but off I go.

When I get to my car, I find myself initiating a call that I hadn't planned to make before my doctor's appointment, but now it seems like the only call to make.

"Hey, superstar." Nico looks surprised to see that I made it to the restaurant before he did, and rightly so. It's happened maybe once before since I moved to the Palisades.

We bro-hug. His leather jacket has the vague scent of bars and some kind of incense and the perfume of dozens of women. I'm so much more aware of smells now because of Willa. In my peripheral vision, I can see the hostess and a couple of waitresses whispering to each other and giggling about us. I'm hoping that this kind of recognition and attention, if not our thirteen-year friendship, is what will prevent Nico from flipping our table at some point during brunch. But I'm also ready for anything, now that I've made a decision.

We shoot the shit and order an early lunch and a beer for each of us, catching up. I ask him about his Grammie; he asks about my mom. The usual. Until finally, he asks, "How's Willa working out for you?"

"Really well. The twins love her. She's shockingly great with them. And she's just nice to have around."

"Good." He watches me while taking a pull on his beer.

There's a long, strange silence that can only be filled with a sigh and four words: "I'm falling for Willa."

He lowers the bottle from his mouth. "What?"

"I really like your sister. A lot. I'm falling in love with her."

He slams the beer bottle on the table. "What?"

"How many times do you want me to say it?"

He continues to stare at me, incredulous. "Zero. What? Since when?"

"Since I met her, I guess. At Erewhon, I mean. Maybe since the first time, in some weird way, I don't know."

"Willa?"

"Your sister, Willa, yes. Are you clear on who we're talking about now?"

I watch his hands, which are balling up into fists while he processes this. He shakes his head and raises one hand to his temple. "I don't even... It never even... I don't know why it didn't... I didn't think she was your type."

"She wasn't. I mean. She isn't a type. She's amazing."

Nico studies my face, and I don't know what kind of expression I have, but it's obviously telling him what he doesn't want to hear. He covers his eyes. "You had sex with my sister." He groans. "I've never met one of her guys before. I can't. Ugh. Why would you do that?"

I'm arching an eyebrow at him when he finally manages to look at me again.

"Don't answer that. I feel sick."

"Do you really?"

"I don't know. I know I'm being an immature little shit, but this is weird."

"If you're pissed off, I get it. I just can't change how I feel about her. I tried. Anyway, *she's* pissed at me. I get that too. But I wanted to tell you, before I...try to make it work with her."

"Why is she pissed at you?"

"Do you really want to know?"

"Not really."

"She basically gave me an ultimatum."

"She did? That doesn't sound like her."

"Not in a shitty, manipulative way. She just told me what she wants. She's cool. She's really, really cool."

"Wow, you really like her, huh?"

"Yeah."

"Does Margo know?"

"No. Fuck, no."

"Dude."

"I know. I mean. I don't know—Margo likes her too, I think. I can't even think about that yet. I just know what I want. I want Willa. And I want you to be okay with that."

"What'll you do if I'm not okay with it?"

I shrug. "Wait for you to come to your fucking senses but do what I'm gonna do anyway."

He laughs. "Fair enough." He holds his hand out across the table for me to shake. "You got balls. Thanks for telling me. Treat her right."

"It's all I want to do."

"Just how serious are you? You better not be fooling around—if this is just a fling to you..."

"It's not. I mean, it's early days. But I don't know if I could ever get enough of her."

"Oh God. She kissed your fucking hand." He covers his face, shaking from laughter. "I just remembered that."

I can't stop smiling, now that I'm thinking about her out in the open. "She's full of surprises."

He throws his head back. "Fuck, this sucks ass. Part of me wants to high-five you for banging the nanny, and part of me wants to punch you in the balls for banging my sister."

"I feel your pain."

"Are you gonna tell the kids?"

"Not for a while. I don't even know what there is to tell at this point, other than 'Daddy's hot for Willa so if you hear noises when we're in a room together, don't come in.'"

He groans again.

"The thing is, man, I realized I've had insomnia off and on ever since I decided to marry Margo. I don't regret it, and obviously I'm glad everything happened the way it did because of the kids, but...on some level I was afraid I was making a mistake. Marrying Margo. And then worrying that because of the way my life was going that I'd never have the real thing with a woman. But when Willa's around..."

"You can sleep at night?"

"I can sleep whenever I want to."

I would never in a million years expect Nico to cry or even tear up unless he had to for a scene, but his face is contorting with some kind of emotional intensity that I've never seen from him before. He's holding his breath, and when he finally exhales, he punches his chest a couple of times. "That's some lyric-worthy shit, my friend."

"Christ, you aren't going to write a song about us, are you?"

"I gotta go where the muse takes me."

"Well, then, I'm happy if this inspires yet another ballad that will get you ridiculous amounts of pussy and royalties for years to come."

He holds up his beer bottle to clink with mine. "To family and friends and pussy and royalties and sleeping whenever you want to."

"And having balls."

"And having massive, good guy balls...that my sister has probably had her hands on—fuck."

"We don't have to talk about this anymore."

"I'd be cool with never talking about this again."

"My balls, or me and Willa?"

"Let's just never refer to your balls and Willa in the same sentence ever again."

"Done."

And that is why Nico Todd is my best friend.

And also why I will secretly be thinking about Willa's hands on my balls for the next hour.

## 18

## WILLA

*B*y the time I've finished lunch, I'm wondering where the fuck Shane Miller is. It's odd that I haven't heard from him since he left. Not that I expect him to check in and tell me that my tits look great every half an hour, but maybe let the nanny know where you are and when you'll be home so she can tell your kids or their teachers if there's an emergency? Or maybe just let her know where you are and when you'll be home because your big pretty penis was inside her a couple of days ago and that's just how you maintain a good employer-employee relationship. And now a sickening feeling settles in my stomach. I'm imagining the possible reasons why he wouldn't want me to know where he is or who he's with. He could be busy knocking up some other actress he will eventually marry. It's happened before! It could very well happen again.

Which is why I need to stand my ground and keep

my emotional distance unless he decides to nut up and own his attraction to me.

Realizing I haven't showered yet today, I go to my room to disrobe.

I tell myself to stop thinking about Shane as soon as the warm water cascades down onto my head. I wash my hair with shampoo and conditioner that I've added drops of my new fragrance to. It's a heavenly scent, not overpowering. And it reminds me of Shane. I pour the shower gel that I added my new fragrance to into the palm of my hand and rub it all over my upper body. I can no longer touch myself without thinking about Shane Miller and remembering what it was like to have his hands on me, inside me...

Fuck it, I'm going to hate-finger-fuck myself while thinking about him, and then I won't think about him for the rest of the fucking afternoon.

Before my hands venture between my legs, I hear three firm knocks on the bathroom door. I freeze for a moment, but I know in my heart and in my vulva who it is. Turning to see the door open a crack, I hear Shane's voice. "It's me. Are you decent?"

I have to clear my throat to find my voice. "Not even a little bit."

The door opens all the way, and Shane steps into the bathroom, shutting the door behind himself. "Good. If you want me to leave, tell me now," he says, unbuttoning his shirt.

I say nothing as I push open the glass shower door and then step back to let the water run down my back. My wet, soaped-up naked body is completely exposed to him again. I absentmindedly touch the little gold heart pendant at my neck, watching this man remove his clothes. He must have taken a special acting class on how to undress for the camera, and I honestly kind of wish I had a camera with me now so I could record this. His hungry eyes are fixed on me the entire time.

The expression on his face is so serious and seriously fuckable when he says, "Who's got two kids, an erection, and just told your brother he's falling for you?" He lets his boxer briefs fall to the floor and then points to himself with his thumbs. "This naked guy."

I let go of my necklace and cover my mouth. The rims of my eyes are stinging. I'm so happy I could cry. "Really? You talked to Nico?"

He steps into the shower and pulls the door shut, staring down at my breasts. "You are so fucking beautiful. I just took him to lunch and told him."

"Oh my God, Shane." I hold his face and kiss it all over, my erect nipples and this naked guy's beautiful penis the only thing standing between us now. "How'd he take it?"

"Surprisingly well. Eventually." Shane's hands slide up and down my hips and waist. He kisses my neck. Along my jaw. Across my shoulder. "He'll probably call you later. He told me to treat you right." He gives both of my ass cheeks a squeeze.

"Oh! I'm quite pleased with how you're treating me so far."

He kisses my mouth, so deeply and urgently that I nearly forget how to breathe.

When he finally pulls away to run his fingers through my hair, I gasp for air and say, "Maybe we shouldn't talk about my brother when we're both naked."

"Sounds like a plan."

"But that reminds me—I talked to my Grammie this morning. She says 'hi.'"

"Be sure to tell me how she's doing at some point in the near future, when I don't have a hard-on."

"If I were you," I say, my hand slipping down to his very hard cock, "I wouldn't plan on many points in the near future when you won't have a hard-on."

He groans. "I hope you have a simple scientific way of explaining that to five-year-olds."

"I know exactly what to say to them. 'Your daddy has a present for me in his pants. Watch Netflix in here while we go in the other room for ten minutes so he can give it to me.'"

"You are—by far—the best nanny anyone has ever had." He turns me around to face the wall, moves my hair to one side, and buries his face in my neck. "What smells so fucking incredible?"

I grin. "It's us."

His dick is pressed up between my ass cheeks, his hands roaming the curves of my hips and up to cup my breasts and tease my nipples. "Your body," he moans. "This ass. This ass is driving me crazy. Can I buy you dinner later?" His tone is playful, but that erection means business.

"You'll have to buy me dinner *first*," I say, pushing back into him and rolling my hips until he makes a thunderous rumbling sound in his throat and digs his fingernails into my flesh.

Then I turn to face him and push him back against the other tiled wall.

There is only one thing I want right now, oddly enough, and it is basically the opposite of hate-finger-fucking myself.

While kissing and nibbling on his lower lip, I say, "I want you to fist my hair and come in my mouth."

"Jesus. Willa."

And then I slowly lower myself to my knees, kissing a wet trail down his torso while watching his head tilt back, his jaw tighten, his Adam's apple bob up and down.

He finally stops talking.

I feel all ten of his fingers in my hair.

And a couple of minutes later, I get exactly what I want.

## 19

## SHANE

*T*he day isn't anywhere near over yet, and already I've had a doctor grab my nuts, straightened some important shit out with my best friend, and came in Willa's dirty, hot, eager, young mouth.

I am crushing Monday, and it's only going to get better because right now Willa's still naked and damp and straddling me on one of the armchairs in the family room.

This really says "home" to me.

I've watched a hundred family friendly movies and shows from this armchair, but not one of them was as entertaining, thrilling, or heartwarming as what's playing out on my lap right now. Willa's wet pussy is hovering an inch above my very happy cock, her tits pushed up together between her elbows while she's examining the palms of my hands. Things have really progressed since the last time she read my palm.

"Oh wow, I didn't notice this the first time," she says, tracing her fingertip up from my wrist to a spot below my index finger, and just that slightest touch is enough to make me want to come like a rocket and sing her a love song—and I hate to sing. "You have a very smooth and prominent but not overly developed Mount of Venus," she explains.

"Thank you. So do you."

She laughs and bites her lower lip. "I actually do. But your thumb..." She lightly traces her fingertip up from the bottom of my thumb to the tip of it, and *fuuuuck* it does things to me in all sorts of places in all kinds of ways. "Your thumb is very well formed. Smooth and square-tipped. The tip of your thumb is called the Will phalange."

Now it's my turn to bite my lower lip to keep myself from making a joke.

"This tells me that your willpower is strong, and you have good judgement. The second phalange of your thumb, here"—she caresses the lower part of my thumb—"is long, which shows you're clever and you take the lead in social situations. In relation to your Head Line, I can see just from looking at your palm that you're very level-headed and good at keeping strong desires in check."

I place one palm on each of her ass cheeks. "Here's a headline for you—if you don't lower yourself down onto my third phalange immediately, I will be showing you exactly how wrong you are about that."

She places her hands on my shoulders, bracing

herself. "Well, now I'm not going to tell you the really important thing I just saw on your Mount of Venus."

"Stop saying 'mount' and mount me." I take one pretty, perky nipple into my mouth and suck until she moans, arches her back, gives more of herself to me. I position the crown of my cock right where it needs to be, and her breath hitches, her back straightens. She can be as kooky as a sitcom character, but she is very serious about fucking me. I like that.

She eases herself down, inch by devastating, life-affirming inch, holding her breath.

She stares into my eyes. Her lips are millimeters from mine and they're barely moving, but I know what she's saying. "We fit. We fit together so perfectly." She gasps, and I dig my fingers into her thighs.

As soon as she has taken me in as much as she can, she exhales like she's sunk into a hot bath, wriggles around a little, squeezing and releasing and instantly making me forget everything that isn't this burning, necessary connection. And then she holds my face in her hands. She tilts her chin up that tiny bit, pressing her lips to mine, and everything that I am is hers now.

I can be quippy as fuck with this woman, but as soon as my mouth is on Willa's, it forgets how to do anything other than kiss her.

Hot and frantic and deliberate and desperate for more.

My lips were made for this.
My tongue was made for this.
My teeth were made for this.

My breaths are meant to be shared with hers.

Her little sighs and moans are just for me.

Fuck this poetic shit—my dick and her pussy were made for each other.

I recognize the scent of lavender and those flowers that I bought her on her skin, along with something earthy and sexy that I can't picture or name, but I do recognize it. She's right. It's us. She's wearing me on her skin, and it both awakens and satisfies some primal need to mark her as mine. I want to be all over her, inside her, on top of her, beneath her, beside her, around her. I want to inhale her so my lungs can bring her to every part of my body.

None of this can be expressed with words, only gripping hands and vigorous thrusts and caveman grunts.

Willa is a sleek, bouncing beauty. Panting, eyes closed, head thrown back, lost in whatever it is I'm making her feel as I drive up into her. I am definitely firing my trainer—this is the only abs workout I'll ever need. I am relentless, and she is taking everything I give her, and it only turns me on more. Instead of staring at her tits, in order to keep from erupting, I stay fixated on the slender gold necklace. She is so damp from the shower and sweat that the little gold heart sticks to her skin, even though she's experiencing extreme turbulence.

"Oh my God, Shane, don't stop!"

"I'd fuck you like this forever if I could, baby."

"Yes! Fuck me forever. Oh God!" Her entire body

contracts, and then she comes apart in a screaming, wailing, cursing jumble of tremors and waves and convulsions. I try to watch for as long as I can because it's so fucking beautiful, but feeling it happen all around my cock sends me right over the edge.

I see stars and the abyss and a flash memory of Willa's smiling face when I first met her.

The guilt only lasts a second, because I mean—I'm coming—but it is not okay to picture a twelve-year-old girl during sex, even if you're doing it with the grown-up version of her.

I might have to schedule another appointment with Dr. Shaw.

Willa is plastered to me, arms wrapped tight around my neck, still straddling me while we catch our breaths.

I already know that every time with her, it will be perfect, but I could do a million takes and never feel like I got it just right.

Because I didn't get to be her first.

Because she wasn't my first.

But if I can be her best and last, I might come close to showing her that it's the first time that anything I've ever done with a woman has ever felt this good and real.

*Fuck guilt.*

I stroke the back of her head. "Tell me what you saw on my Mount of Venus."

She pulls back and smiles. "You have a trident."

"A trident?"

"Yeah. See?" She takes hold of my hand and points out a little fork indentation at the base of my thumb. "It's a very lucky sign. It means you'll find your true love," she whispers.

I take her hand in mine. If someone had told me this even a month ago, I wouldn't have believed it. Now I do. "What about you?" I flip her hand over so I can see her palm. "Do you have one too?" I have never wanted so badly to see a trident on someone's Mount of Venus. The little lines at the base of her thumb are so faint. She sees me struggling to find what I'm looking for and curls her fingers inward a bit, making the lines more obvious.

And there it is.

A trident.

Right around the same place mine is at.

I place my hand over hers.

She rests her forehead against mine.

We're so fucking cute, we might have to do something extra filthy really soon, but for now, I'm going to lift her hand to my lips and press a kiss to the back of her hand.

It's worth the cheese to hear her sigh and see her blush and smile.

I touch the heart pendant on her neck. "I like this. I like that you're always wearing it."

"Oh... That's...ironic."

"Why?"

She takes a deep breath and shrugs, reaching for her towel as she lifts herself up off me. "I bought it for myself after I found out you were going to marry Margo. To remind myself to protect my heart."

"To protect your heart from me?"

"To remind myself not to give my heart away so easily. I mean, it was just a crush. I had an overactive imagination." She's sighing and blushing and smiling again, but this time she's embarrassed.

*Fuck.*

*Guilt again.*

"I hate that. I hate that you felt that way."

"It's not your fault. Honestly, I mean, it's no different from having a crush on Zac Efron, except that I happened to meet you once because of my brother... Oops. I'm not supposed to mention Nico when we're naked."

"Don't tell me it's not a big deal if it was a big deal. You're still wearing the necklace. Also—fuck Zac Efron."

"It was a big deal and then it wasn't. I like the necklace. And I didn't say I had a crush on him."

"Good, because the guy's a dick."

"Is he really?"

"No, not at all. But stay away from him." *Fuck, I'm losing my mind. But fuck Zac Efron.*

"I mean, I'll try to stay away from him, but I can't promise anything."

I grab her hand. I want to promise her everything, but I can't. "I'm going to make it up to you."

"There's nothing to make up for. You didn't do anything wrong. You didn't even know how I felt.

Nobody did." She gives my hand a squeeze. "You have good judgment. You did the right thing. I don't want to change the past." She lets go of my hand to wrap the towel around herself and then leans down to kiss my cheek. "And I don't want to protect my heart anymore."

Goddammit.

This woman.

Her heart isn't the one that needs protecting.

## 20

## WILLA

*I*t was so sweet, how upset Shane seemed to be about the meaning of my heart necklace. He told me that next month, Margo would be in town for five days during spring break, so she'll have the kids at her house. He told me that he wants me to stay with him for those five days, even when the kids aren't around. He told me that he wants to take me out for a real grown-up date and do all the things that twentysomething Angelenos do, all night long. I said sure, as long as "all night long" means until ten p.m. After showering together again, we went to pick up the kids from school—together—for the first time since my first day on the job. We got frozen yogurt on the way home. I had the kids help me cut blooms from the front yard, and we made bouquets for them to give to Mrs. Babcock for her birthday. I took a bunch of pictures of them with the flowers and posted my favorite one of them—where you can only see them from the back—

on my Instagram. Shane and I both gave them a bath together, and then once the twins were asleep, we made out in the laundry room downstairs for fifteen minutes and then he went off to read while I worked on the fragrance for Margo. It was perfect.

This morning, after one of the greatest Mondays ever, I woke up to an e-mail from Margo Quincey, informing me that by posting an image of her children on Shane's property on Instagram, I have violated one of the terms of the nondisclosure agreement. She told me that she would let it slide since I didn't name them, as long as I take down the post immediately. Then she asked me how her fragrance is coming along. *My fragrance*, she called it.

I deleted the post and wrote her back, apologizing once and telling her that I think she'll be pleased with *my* design when she samples it next month.

I didn't hear back from her.

And I've been annoyed about it ever since. I was annoyed about it while I fed the kids breakfast and while I took them to school. I was annoyed about it while I bought groceries with the credit card that Shane gave me for buying things for the kids. I was annoyed while I went to the stationary store and the toy store to get gifts for the birthday party the twins are going to next weekend. I'm annoyed now that I'm putting away the groceries that I bought for us and getting out the things I'll need to bake cookies for the kids to snack on after their karate class.

I get that she's the mother and I'm just the nanny. I

get that she's the ex-wife and I'm just the girl who had a massive crush on her ex-husband many years ago and is currently having awesome sex with him for who knows how long. I get that I did not pay close enough attention to the NDA when I started working here because I was so overwhelmed by Shane's pheromones.

But fuck.

This feels like my family.

This feels like my home.

It feels like Grammie was right about me—I'm still prone to flights of fancy when it comes to Shane Miller.

No matter how I've grown. No matter how confident I may be. No matter how direct I can be with him. I can't stop feeling like he's mine. That I belong with him. And his kids.

Oh my God, am I like the psycho nanny from that movie?

Have I imagined everything?

I haven't seen Shane yet this morning because he had a breakfast meeting with a producer and then he had his personal training session at the gym afterwards.

I don't want to feel like this when he comes home. I need to get these feelings out of my body. So, I go to an open space in the kitchen, take a deep breath, and jump around, punching and kicking the air. I huff and puff like a furious maniac. It feels good.

Until I hear someone quietly laughing behind me.

I freeze and cover my face.

"No, please, don't stop."

"Oh God. You're never going to want to put your pretty penis in me again, are you?"

"On the contrary." I feel his warm hands on my shoulders. "I'm actually hoping you still have a little of that angry energy left for when my penis is inside you."

My own hands drop from my face so I can inhale the air around him. Without seeing him, I can tell that he is still glistening with sweat from his workout, and *oh God the pheromones*. I spin around to face him. His skin is flushed, and his fitted sleeveless Nike shirt is damp, his muscles are taut, and I want to lick every single inch of him. "I have all kinds of energy left for when your penis is inside me." I kiss him on the mouth, but he pulls back, letting his hands slide to my waist.

"There are a few things we need to discuss first, but I'd be happy to undress you while we talk."

"Proceed." I stand straight so he can remove my clothes.

He starts to unbutton my blouse. "First of all, I got an e-mail from Margo this morning. She told me she asked you to take down a picture from Instagram. I'm sorry about that." I start to apologize, but he continues. "I Skyped her and told her not to communicate with you directly regarding nanny issues, since I'm the one who hired you. She can run things through me, and I'll decide if it's something I need to bring up with you or not."

"Really?"

"With everything you do for me and the kids, it just pissed me off that she reprimanded you like that for something so insignificant." He pulls my shirt off and lets it fall to the floor.

"Thank you," I say as he stares at my bra. "You're such a thoughtful boss."

He shakes his head, grinning. "Don't even joke about that." He unbuttons and unzips my pants. "Second item of business..." He pulls his phone out from the pocket of his workout shorts and taps on his e-mail app. "My publicist forwarded something to me. Apparently someone got a few shots of us picking up the kids at school yesterday and getting Froyo after. Must have been a slow celebrity news day."

He shows me the online images on his phone. There's a shot of us walking toward the school from his car with his hand barely touching the small of my back. Just thinking about the way it had felt to have his hand on the small of my back in public makes me swoon. The shots of us through the window of the frozen yogurt place make the tip of my nose tingle. We look like such a fun, happy little family. "Does that bother you? That these pictures are out there?"

"I mean, I'm not crazy about the expression on my face in this one, but...of course it doesn't bother me. I'm a little surprised someone bothered to follow us all the way to the Palisades from the school, but... Does it bother you?"

I shake my head. He pushes my pants down past my hips, and I step out of them.

"Good." He reaches into another pocket and pulls out a small box. "Final item of business." He looks down at my lacey bra and panties, clearing his throat. "You are so fucking hot." His fingertip traces the edges of my bra. He squeezes one breast and grunts.

"Final item of business?"

"Right." He pulls his hand away from my boob and uses it to open the box, holding it up for me to see. There is a gold heart necklace inside. He removes the necklace, drops the box to the floor. The chain is slightly longer than the one I'm wearing now, and the heart is a little bit bigger. He unhooks the clasp. "Turn around. Hold your hair up."

I do as he says.

"This is my heart," he whispers into my ear as he places the necklace around my neck. "I want you to wear it to remind yourself that it belongs to you now."

The new heart pendant hangs just below the old one.

"Shane. I love it." I have to bite my lower lip to keep from saying "I love you." I let my hair down and turn to face him again. "That is so sweet."

"I know. I'm going to do filthy things to you right here on the counter now so we can both forget how fucking adorable I am." He picks me up and places me down on the center island. The smooth cement is cool on my skin, but his hot breath over my panties warms me up immediately. "I've been thinking about you all morning." He rubs his hands up and down my thighs, pushes my panties to the side, and licks me. "I've been thinking about this since last night."

I lean back on my elbows, sighing. "I know I'm not supposed to joke about this, but I really like this job... Before I forget—Summer wanted to know if you're coming to their first karate class today."

"Wouldn't miss it."

"They're really excited about it. Oh shit, that feels so good."

"Maybe don't talk about my kids while I'm going down on you."

His tongue flicks rapidly at my clit, and I forget what we were saying. "Oh my God, Shane!"

"*Ay, Dios mio!*"

It takes me a second to realize that what I just heard was not, in fact, my vagina crying out in Spanish.

Plastic items fall to the floor somewhere behind me, near the entrance to the kitchen.

Shane pops up from between my legs, wiping his mouth with the back of his hand. "Consuelo!"

"Ay! So sorry, Mr. Miller! So sorry! I clean upstairs first!"

I am too mortified to turn around, but I hear her hurry down the hall.

"Consuelo!" Shane picks up my clothes and hands them to me. "Shit. I forgot she was coming today." He goes to the door to call out to her. "I'll pick this stuff up for you!"

I can hear her apologizing again from the stairwell.

"That poor woman," I mutter, covering myself with my shirt. "I should probably bake her some cookies."

"Or possibly something that won't remind her of me eating your cookie. And *this* is why we have NDAs."

I slide down off of the counter and find Shane putting bottles of cleaning liquids back into the plastic carrier the housekeeper dropped.

"Are you saying you've had domestic employees walk in on you like that before?"

"I've never had sex with a woman besides you in this house before, Willa. I usually only hook up when I'm out of town."

This is a shocking but welcome revelation. "Really?"

He stands up, shaking his head. He is so flustered. I don't want to tell him he's sweet and adorable again, but he's so fucking sweet and adorable.

"Does that surprise you?"

I pull my pants on and shuffle over to kiss him on the cheek. "So I'm the first?" I whisper into his neck.

"Yeah. You're the first. You're driving me insane. And I'm going to have to give Consuelo a fucking raise." He adjusts the front of his shorts and turns to take the cleaning supply carrier up to her. "We'll continue that after she leaves, hopefully."

I hold up my crossed fingers.

We do not continue that after Consuelo leaves,

because she was still at the house when we had to leave to pick the kids up at school to take them to the dojo. Shane drives the Land Rover and his hand is on my thigh for most of the ride. "If their art teacher asked for something blue from home for them to paint today, I'd give them my balls," he mumbles as we park at the curb.

I pat his hand. "I'll be sure to mention that at your Father of the Year ceremony."

He mutters something about "dad dick" as he gets out of the car.

Summer and Lucky are already exiting the building as we walk down the sidewalk. When they see us, they are both so happy and start running toward us, each of them holding a big sheet of art paper in one hand. Summer hops in front of me, her face all lit up.

"I made this for you!" She presents me with a painting. "We had to paint someone we like to be with, and I did you!"

Through watery eyes, I'm staring down at a colorful portrait of a woman with a huge head, enormous brown eyes, giant smile, big long dark hair, massive boobs—*thank you Summer!*—and a yellow heart on her neck.

"Summer. This is so beautiful." I bend down to hug her. I don't know why I'm so surprised that she'd pick me, but I am. "I love you," I whisper in her ear. I've never said it to her before, and it immediately feels like I just crossed a boundary, but I don't regret it.

She says, "Okay," gives me an extra squeeze before

letting go, and looks at me like we have a shared secret now. "Heyyyy," she says. "You got another heart on your neck."

"Yes. I got it today. Isn't it pretty?"

She nods and takes my hand.

Shane is admiring Lucky's painting of him. He mostly painted a bunch of hair that's standing up and big blue eyes inside an upside-down triangle face, but it's unmistakably Shane.

"You guys are so talented," he says. "I love it. You ready to go kick some ass at the dojo?"

"Yaaaahhhh!!! What's a dojo?" Lucky asks, as Summer asks, "Are you going to stay and watch us?"

"We both are," I tell her.

"A dojo is where you're going to go once a week to kick some ass."

"But why's it called that?"

"It's a Japanese word," Shane says, winking at me, like "I got this." "For a room or hall where karate or other kind of martial arts is practiced."

"What's martial arts?"

"It's what you'll be learning. It's a kind of self-defense fighting that just uses hands and feet. No weapons."

"We get to fight each other?" Summer claps her hands. "And we won't get in trouble?"

"Well, not by me or Willa, but you'll have to do what the karate teacher tells you to do."

"Why is it called karate?"

. . .

Fifteen minutes, four cookies, a baggie of baby carrots, and twenty-seven questions later, we make it to the dojo in the Palisades, help the kids change into their karate uniforms, chat with the instructor and some of the other parents, and then take a seat in the folding chairs at the edge of the room to watch the half-hour-long class.

It is so stinking cute, watching Summer and Lucky and eight other three-and-a-half to five-year-old kids line up, shout out "yes, *sensei*!" and imitate the instructor when he tells them to. Honestly, I could watch this all day. But Shane appears to be a bit restless. In my peripheral vision, I see him surreptitiously typing something out on his phone. When I feel my phone vibrate in my pocket, I casually look around to see if anyone will notice me pull it out. I look down and almost laugh out loud when I see the message.

SHANE: I cannot fucking wait to get back up in your dojo later.
ME: Does this mean you'll be using your hands AND feet to defend yourself against me?
SHANE: It means get ready for some full-contact sparring with my Sammo Hung.
ME: <eye roll emoji> Is that a martial artist joke?
SHANE: I would never joke about hiding my dragon in your crouching tiger.
ME: <three eye roll emojis> Are you drunk?

**SHANE: I wish. Are you still wearing those lacey panties?**
**ME: Watch your children.**
**SHANE: <two blue circle emojis>**

I stifle a giggle as I look over at him. We both slide our phones back into our pockets, but it's too late. Summer is watching us from the blue mats, attacking us from across the dojo with the most devastating frown I have ever seen.

If it's bad parenting to let five-year-olds watch *The Karate Kid* during dinner on a school night, then Shane Miller is perfectly content to be a bad parent. He feels so guilty for letting his blue balls get the best of him during the class, I wouldn't be surprised if he never makes Summer brush her teeth again. Lucky was so focused on the instructor that I don't think he noticed when we weren't paying attention.

I'm so focused on how cool Elisabeth Shue is in this movie that I don't even realize how long Summer has been gone after saying she had to go to the bathroom. When she returns, she is silent and doesn't make eye contact with anyone, but I notice her sneaking peeks at me out of the corner of her eyes. When I try to meet her gaze, she snaps her head back to the TV, frowning.

I get a sinking feeling in my gut.

After taking the dishes to the kitchen sink, I go to my room to have a look.

The top of my desk is completely empty, except for my perfumer's organ, which is upright and closed.

That wouldn't be a problem if it hadn't been half-covered with twenty bottles of the roll-on perfume oil that I'd spent the past few days mixing and bottling and labeling.

I check the wastebasket beneath the desk—empty.

I check the wastebasket in my bathroom—no perfume bottles.

I check my closet, because *maybe just maybe* Summer decided to line them up in an orderly fashion on one of the shelves. Nope.

I check all of the drawers in the desk and dresser.

"What's going on?" Shane asks from the doorway.

"Nothing. I need to talk to Summer."

"Shit. What did she do?"

"It's fine." I go into the family room and find Summer sitting at the edge of the sofa, arms crossed, lower lip quivering, staring at the floor. I kneel on the floor in front of her. "Summer. Where did you put my perfume bottles?"

She shakes her head.

"Summer. I made those. Do you understand? I'm going to sell those in a store. That's my job."

"Your job is our nanny!"

"Yes, it is. But my other job is making perfume."

"Oh, shit!" I hear Shane say from the kitchen.

I watch a solitary tear fall from Summer's eye and then go to the kitchen. Shane is looking in the wastebin from under the sink. "They're empty," he says, holding one of the cylindrical bottles up. The label has a tomato sauce stain on it. "I think all the labels are messed up. I'm so sorry."

I shake my head and calmly march over to the bathroom in the hallway. As soon as I open the door, I can smell my perfume oil in the sink.

I can hear Shane telling Summer that she's grounded. I can hear him tell her that she doesn't get any dessert tonight, that she doesn't get to go to her friend's party this weekend. I can hear Summer saying there were too many bottles on my desk and clutter is bad. And my first instinct is to go in there and defend Summer.

I put my hand on Shane's arm. "Shane, it's not her fault. I should have locked my stuff away or put a lock on the door like you said."

"Summer, go to your room." His voice can be so commanding when he's talking to his daughter.

"But clutter in the room makes clutter in your head!"

"Go brush your teeth and get ready for bed. Now."

"Shane."

"I will pay to replace everything, obviously," he tells me as Summer skulks out of the room.

"It's really not that big of a deal. I can mix the oils again, I can order more labels and bottles. It'll just delay my store opening for a week or so."

We both look over to see that Lucky is on the verge of tears, watching us. "Can I finish watching the movie?"

"Yes, buddy. You're not in trouble. You can finish watching the movie with Willa. I'll go talk to Summer."

"Let me go. Let me talk to her. Okay?"

He studies my face, his forehead and jaw relaxing. "Okay." He kisses the top of my head.

I go up to Summer's room, knocking on the closed door before entering. She is lying flat, facedown on her bed. I go to the side of her bed and sit down.

"I'm sorry," she says, the words completely muffled because they're spoken into a blanket.

"I know. The thing is, Summer, I think one of the things you're supposed to ask yourself when you're decluttering is 'does this thing bring me joy?' Right?"

She nods.

"Sit up."

She slowly pushes herself up and sits next to me at the head of her bed.

"Making perfume brings me joy. And I make it to sell to other people because I hope it will bring them joy too. So it's not clutter. And besides, it's mine. You can't throw out or put away things that aren't yours without the other person's permission. Do you understand that?"

"I'm sorry."

"I know."

We both sigh.

"Are you mad at me?"

"Kind of. But I'll get over it. Are you mad at me? Because we weren't paying attention to you during karate class?"

She nods.

"Think you'll get over it?"

She nods. "He doesn't pay as much attention to us now when you're here."

*Oh shit. Dagger to the heart.* "That's not true. That can't be true. Your daddy pays so much attention to you. He loves you so much, just as much as he always has."

Her lower lip sticks out.

"Do you wish I wasn't here?"

"No."

"You want me to stay?"

"Yes."

"You just want your dad to pay more attention to you?"

She nods.

"Okay. I'll send him up. Do you promise to stop throwing things out and hiding them?"

She nods. When I stand up, she says, without looking at me, "You know that thing you said today?"

"When you gave me the painting?"

She nods. "Do you still?"

"Yes, Summer. I still do. People don't stop loving someone just because they're mad."

"Okay."

.   .   .

When the twins are asleep, Shane pours us both a glass of wine in the kitchen. Instead of letting Shane enter my dojo again, I tell him that we should probably try not to get each other all sexed-up for a while. Maybe wait until spring break, when the kids are with Margo, before doing filthy things to each other again. "It's not that I don't want to go all Cobra Kai on your Sammo Hung, but...I like it here. I don't want to mess things up."

*I am so not the psycho nanny from that movie.*

"I like you here too," he says, clinking glasses with me. When we've both taken a sip of wine, he leans over to kiss me on the cheek. "I cannot fucking wait for spring break."

## 21

# SHANE

*I*t's spring break.

I didn't go to college. I was home-schooled by on-set tutors from the age of fifteen. I've played horny teenage guys who go nuts trying to get laid in March or April, but I never really understood what the big deal was. I could have gotten laid whenever I wanted to when I was eighteen—I was the star of two different cable TV shows that year. You know who finally gets why spring break is such a big deal? My dad dick.

The sun is shining. The twins are in the back seat, and their little suitcases are in the trunk. Willa is in the passenger seat next to me, and our bags are packed too —for a two-night stay at a beautiful luxury ranch resort in Santa Barbara. And my dick is going to party like it's 2009 because it hasn't been inside Willa for almost three weeks.

She was right, though. It was a good idea to hit the

brakes and fool around a lot less so we could focus on the kids. I got by on a well-timed handy or two, as per doctor's advice, and returned the favor with a practical, level-headed cunnilingus session in the laundry room or three. She had more time to work on her fragrances. and I got a lot of reading done. Now we can head into the next five days without any guilt whatsoever and about a gallon of baby batter.

"Why can't you and Willa stay at Mommy's house too?" Lucky asks.

"Because we aren't masochists," I mutter to Willa.

"Your mom has been missing you so much, she wants you all to herself," Willa says.

"But who's going to be our nanny while we're there?"

"Nobody," I say. "Your mom's going to be with you the whole time. She came back just so she can see you."

"But is she going to have to go to bed in the afternoon?"

"That's actually a really good question." Willa turns to look at him. "Your mom will probably have something that's called 'jet lag,' which means that even though it's the same time for her here as it is for you, her body clock will think she's still in Poland."

"What's a body clock?"

"Why can't she just bloomin' fix it so it works right, eh? Wouldn't it be loverly?" Summer asks in a Cockney accent.

"You know what—I bet your mom would be better

at answering that than we would," Willa says, grinning at me.

Well, well. Sounds like Little Miss Post-Graduate Degree has learned a thing or two from the undereducated actor for a change.

"Oy say, cap'n—is Landon 'ere too? Oym a good gurl, I am!" Summer asks, again in her weird English accent. She looks out the window, at the mansions in the exclusive Riviera neighborhood that Margo and Landon live in. It's only a ten-minute drive from my house, but the properties are twice as expensive and the streets have names like Amalfi and San Remo, and the residents have last names like Spielberg, Hanks, and Schwarzenegger.

Whatever. I'll watch their movies, but I wouldn't trade neighborhoods with these people if they paid me.

"Landon had to stay on set in Poland. They're still shooting the movie. Your mom will have to go back to work on the weekend. Willa and I will pick you up Saturday morning."

I turn onto the long slate-paved driveway and watch Willa's face as I park. She looks as unimpressed by this estate as I am, bless her heart. She helps Summer out of her car seat while I get Lucky, but as soon as the front door opens and they see Margo, they go running to her. Willa looks a little surprised by how happy they are to see their mom, and maybe a tiny bit jealous too. I feel that way every time I drop them off.

But I'll get over it faster than I usually do, because—spring break.

Willa gets her purse from the front seat and waits for me to get Summer and Lucky's bags and walk with her up the path to the house. I touch the small of her back because I know what it does to her. Her breath catches and I feel her shiver every time. We don't hold hands in front of the kids because we haven't had a talk with them yet, but I told Margo that I'm taking Willa up the coast. She doesn't like surprises, and I trust that she isn't going to create some sort of emergency to fuck up our plans, because she hasn't seen the twins in so long.

"Go to the kitchen, my darlings—there are snacks waiting for you," Margo says to the kids. "Wash your hands first! With soap!" Her hair is blonder than it was before she left, and she's wearing one of her $250 tank tops with a pair of wide-leg pants that have a ridiculously large bow at the waist. Perhaps she was expecting us to come with a camera crew. Or maybe she's trying to look more glamorous than my gorgeous nanny. Either way, her toothy smile seems genuine as she holds her arms out to welcome Willa with a hug. "So good to finally meet you in person! You're even prettier than you were on Skype."

"Oh, thank you," Willa says. "So are you."

"Oh my God, no. I'm exhausted and dehydrated from the flight. Hey, you," she says as she gives me a friendly hug and pat on the back. "Do you have time to come in?"

"We should get on the road," I insist.

"I brought the perfume sample," Willa says, pulling a small box out of her purse and handing it to Margo. "You can try it out for a few days, let me know what you think."

"Oh, look at this pretty box. How cute!"

Willa gives her a folded-up piece of fancy letter paper. "Here's a list of the ingredients."

"Thank you." Margo holds the paper up to her nose. "Oh my God—did you put my fragrance on the paper? Is this it?"

I notice Willa wincing when Margo says the words "my fragrance." "Yes, I did. It is."

"Willa, I love it!"

"I want to smell that." Margo holds the paper out for me to get a whiff, and gosh darnit, it somehow smells like some idealized version of Margo. I don't know how Willa did that without actually spending time with her. "That's amazing."

"Willa—I'm so excited. We'll talk more later—you'll come by to pick up the kids, and I'll have my lawyers draw up the paperwork by then."

"Sure."

"Would you mind if I talk to Shane about the kids for just one second? Have so much fun at the Ranch."

"Thanks. Bye, kids!" she yells out through the open doors.

"The Ranch, huh?" Margo says to me in a low voice, eyes sparkling. "Pretty special."

"Yes, she is."

Once Willa is inside the Land Rover, she gets a stern look on her face and says, "I hope you know what you're doing, Shane. Word has gotten out. I keep in touch with Jill, you know."

"Who?"

She rolls her eyes. "Abby's mom. She told me about the zoo."

"So?"

"So—she's the nanny. You know how those moms gossip. I'm not mad. It just better not affect the kids."

"You mean the way you snuck around with Landon while you were married to me didn't affect the kids? Thanks for the tip, Marg. I'll try real hard to meet your high standards. Make sure they practice their karate stance and punches. Oh, and Willa's been teaching Summer songs from *My Fair Lady*, so she talks like Eliza Doolittle now. Have a great visit." I call out through the open doors too. "See you on Saturday, kids!"

I lean in to give Willa a kiss when I turn on the engine while Margo is still standing there and pull away from her a second before the kids run out to wave good-bye.

I will miss those little people, but there's a private hot tub, an outdoor rain shower, and a king-size bed with Italian linens waiting for us, ninety minutes away.

♥

I don't know why it's so important to me to stake my

claim as the first guy to do certain things for Willa, but being the first person to drive her up the 101 between Ventura and Santa Barbara felt good and it was fun—almost as good and fun as being the first guy to get a blow job from her in the shower. Driving her down the olive tree and lavender bush-lined lane that leads up to the front desk cottage of the resort as she leans out the window to inhale the scented air is a singular delight. Because I knew she'd love it, and I know I'm the only person who'd ever think to bring her here.

"Shane! It's so pretty here!"

"This is just the beginning."

I chose the accommodations, but my business manager's office made the reservation. I've been checking into hotels under the name Milton Shine for the past couple of years—an alias I came up with when I was sleep-deprived, but it amuses me that it sounds like I'm a producer from the golden age of Hollywood or a vaudeville comedian in the Catskills. I can't help but crack up when the front desk clerk calls me "Mr. Shine." Willa is outside, taking pictures of the gardens and the view of the Santa Ynez mountains. The property's designed like a French country garden, but every cottage has its own cobblestone parking spaces and total privacy. The Gardenia Cottage that I booked is right next to a little orange grove, and it has a view of the wildflower garden. I called yesterday to make sure the orange trees are in bloom—don't ask me what kind of strings I would have pulled to get them to bloom if they weren't, but I definitely would have made more calls.

Fortunately, orange blossoms are abundant this time of year, and as soon as I open the French doors, Willa dashes through the 1800 square foot cottage, through the bedroom, to the enclosed back patio with her nose raised. "Orange blossoms! Jasmine! Geranium! Lavender! Rosemary! Oh, Shane! *Holy shit! Do you smell that?*" She spins around, runs back to me, and leaps. I catch her, hiking her up so her legs can wrap around my waist. "They're all aphrodisiac scents!" she says, peppering my neck and face with kisses.

"I don't think I need any help in that department, but it does smell nice."

"We're going to have to be quiet," she whispers into my ear as I carry her to the bed.

"Why?"

"Because I want to keep the doors open while we fuck." She winks at me. "Oym a good gurl, I am!"

*Fair enough!*

"Eliza, where the devil are my slippers?" I say as I quietly rip apart her blouse and bury my face in her tits.

"Hey! I like this blouse."

"I'll buy you ten new ones."

She pushes me away to pull my T-shirt over my head, leaning in to lick and bite my chest. "This is the nicest place I've ever had sex in, Mr. Shine."

"*You're* the nicest place I've ever had sex in." I stop

just short of calling her "Mrs. Shine," but dammit it just feels right.

The performer and the perfumer.

Us.

I grab her face, devouring her lips, invading her mouth with my tongue. The drive to be inside her in every way possible consumes me. It could be the weeks of missing her body, it could be the aphrodisiac scents, it could be that I know for certain that nothing and no one is going to interrupt this for us, or it may just be that I am completely stone cold crazy about this girl.

All of the desire that I've been keeping under control is being unleashed on her now, and she meets me head-on with the same furiously happy kisses.

She wriggles around beneath me as she unzips my pants and reaches inside them with one hand, pushing my underwear down with the other.

Heavy breathing, blinding passion.

I'm lost in the waves of her dark hair and the divine scent of the pulse point behind her ear and then down to the base of her throat where her gold heart meets mine.

I've never craved anything as much as this, on any level.

She is wearing a loose skirt, clever girl, and I am pressing myself inside her as soon as I get her panties down.

No fanfare this time, just sweet fucking heavenly relief.

The moan that escapes me isn't loud, but it is deep, and it vibrates through me.

*I'm home.*

Tight. Warm. Wet. Pulsating. Highly sensitive. Always responsive. Endlessly engaging. Definitely the nicest place.

"Willa. Baby."

Her hands are in my hair, and I have no idea what's going on with the rest of our bodies or the rest of the world, because all that matters is that I'm inside her and we're moving together and this is the only thing we have to do today.

Her sighs and gasps are as quiet as a gentle breeze, but when she whispers my name, it sets my soul on fire, and I start pumping harder and faster, and *fuck it* this is the first of many times we'll be doing this.

She cries out, clenching around my cock. Somebody heard and nobody in this room cares.

"Shane. More. More!"

Spring.

Break.

The magnificent darkness is closing in as I thrust, ruthlessly, with wild abandon.

"Everything, everything." I don't even realize I'm saying it out loud until I've probably said it five times, but I can't stop. "I'm gonna give you everything."

Even in my delirious state I know that it can only be completely true until Saturday morning and then maybe in thirteen years when the twins are off in college, but it is true.

"I'll take it," she says, digging her nails into my back. "Give me all of it."

Jesus.

Christ.

And I do.

Dinner is at the resort's formal restaurant so we could stroll through the grounds to get here, drink wine, and stumble back to the cottage for more grown-up spring break sex.

I've never seen Willa dressed up before, and although she is wearing a simple knee-length black dress with red lipstick and sandals, I am awestruck and fully aware that she is turning more heads than I am tonight.

We dine on a patio, surrounded by small trees that are covered with warm white lights. There are heat lamps, a wood-burning fireplace, and potted plants everywhere. Willa is thrilled, and my only complaint is that the tabletop hides her slamming bare legs.

I've only ever shared one glass of wine with her before, and she is already on her second glass of Merlot before we've finished the appetizers. Tipsy Willa is nearly indistinguishable from sober Willa, except that her cheeks are more flushed and she never stops smiling or swaying, almost imperceptibly. in her seat.

"Do you miss the kids already?"

"What kids?"

She giggles.

"I always miss them when I haven't seen them for a day or more. Do you miss them?"

She nods and then squints at something or someone behind me.

"Is that Al Pacino?"

I look over my shoulder and see a tanned, dark-haired elderly man in a white shirt and black pants. "Who—the waiter?"

"I think it is."

"I think you've had enough wine."

"*Hoo-ah!*"

"That is literally one of his worst performances. It's a joke that he won an Oscar for that."

"I like that movie."

"Why? Because it has the word 'scent' in the title and he talks about perfume?"

"Yeeesss."

"You honestly like that piece of crap but you hate my movies?"

Her eyelashes flutter and her lower lip sticks out. It's a total Summer Miller move, but I think this is Willa's natural response. "I never said I hate your movies."

"You just hate the scripts for the movies I've done?"

She shakes her head. "I mean, I didn't love them, but the truth is..." She sits up straight, her eyes searching mine until she comes to some decision and nods. "The truth is, it was just hard for me to watch them because I hated thinking about how you were with Margo when you made them. Some of them, I mean. I guess you were already divorced when you shot most of them, but still..."

I reach across the table to touch her hand.

"I mean, it wasn't my idea to watch them. Chantal, the mother of the family in Versailles, she happened to be a fan of yours. I didn't even tell her that I'd met you or that my brother knew you. She had the DVDs and always went to see your movies on opening weekend. I went with her and the kids and sometimes her mother."

"So you saw my comedies in French? *Mon Dieu.*"

She shakes her head. "In English. With subtitles."

"Did people laugh?"

She nods vehemently. "Your charm and attractiveness transcend cultural boundaries."

I have to laugh at the earnest way she delivered that line. "Shut up."

"I mean it! I mean, would I have chosen to spend my time watching those movies if you weren't in them? Probably not. But they make people happy. And you're always really good and likable."

"I guess."

"Don't tell me *you* don't like those movies either."

"No, I do. I want to do more serious stuff. The indie I did—the one we're going to see a rough cut of this week—it's a comedy drama. It's the first time I was able to show some range since I was a sexy vampire... Did you watch that show?"

"Not once I found out you were dating Margo."

"You didn't miss much. Anyway... It's really hard to transition from teen star to serious actor. First-world problems, though."

"Yeah." She sighs and polishes off her second glass of wine. "Careers, huh?"

"Well, yours is starting out pretty well."

She stares at me, blinking, and I can tell she's trying to decide if she should say something again. Finally, she nods and says, "I got an e-mail from my mentor in Versailles. Yesterday."

"Oh yeah?"

"He told me he spoke to someone at a big company about me. They're based in Germany, but they're global suppliers of fine fragrance and flavors. And they have a perfumery studio in New York. I guess they're expanding there." She watches me for a reaction.

My reaction is immediate and gut-level and I fucking hate how I feel, but thank fuck I'm an actor so I can keep my expression neutral. "And?"

"And they're looking for perfumery technicians. It's lab work. I'd—the technician—would be supporting the perfumer by doing compounding. Something like 280 pours a day, so it's a lot of lab work. No designing. But it's a good company. I'd—the technician—would be part of a team. I'm more than qualified and the salary is good, but you know...I've had sales and good reviews on Etsy already, and I'm going to try to get some local boutiques to carry a couple of my scents."

"That's great. You should do that. How can I help?"

"Oh, you don't have to help me."

"I want to."

She smiles and gives me a *what do you know about perfume* look.

I get it. I mean, I probably know more about perfume than Al Pacino does now, but I get it. "Let me know if you change your mind."

"Okay. Thank you."

"Do you want to live in New York?"

"I used to. I always assumed I would one day. Anyway—I'd still have to interview. I haven't set anything up yet."

"Well, I hope you get to do whatever it is that you want to do, wherever you want to do it."

She tilts her head. "Thank you." She leans in and says, perhaps a little too loudly, "I want to do what we did in the hot tub again after dinner."

"We're on the same page, then."

The waitress brings us our entrees, but I can't take my eyes off Willa. I don't want to take my eyes off her. Ever. In the glow of the candle and string lights, she has gone from unique everyday beauty to beguiling and stunning. When the waitress leaves, I finally have to ask the thing that I'm wondering every time I look at her: "Do you have any idea how beautiful you are?"

She smiles and looks down, rearranging the napkin in her lap. "I have an idea. I just don't think about it very much."

"Really? Because I think about it all the time. Ever since I saw you at Erewhon."

"So, just over a month."

"Feels longer."

"Well. I've been thinking about you ever since I met you twelve years ago."

God, it breaks my heart a little every time she brings that up.

She shivers and rubs her bare arms before picking up her fork.

"Are you cold?" I stand up to remove my blazer. I'm only wearing a T-shirt underneath, but I'm a thick-skinned stud. "Here."

"Oh, I don't need that."

I stand behind her and help her put it on. She sniffs the collar and smiles up at me. "It smells like you. Thank you."

"You're welcome."

When I sit back down, she's grinning mischievously. "This blazer reminds me of your Greyson outfits from *That's So Wizard*. You were so cute."

I roll my eyes. "Thanks. I didn't wear blazers or high-tops for like five years after the show was cancelled."

"Oh, but you were so cute! I loved your little ties and your button-down shirts. There was a guy at my school who tried to dress like you, but he just couldn't pull it off." She purses her lips, and I can tell there's something else she wants to tell me, but she doesn't. She takes a bite of her pasta.

"What?"

She raises her eyebrows and shrugs. "Nothing."

"What?"

"Okay, but it's so dumb. But I never told anyone—oh my God, I can't believe I'm telling you this, but here goes. Before I met you..." She smacks her lips together, places her fork on the side of the dish before continuing. "I did an online quiz. *Which Disney Channel Character Should be Your Boyfriend?* Guess who my boyfriend was?" She covers her face.

"Me?"

"Greyson Manning."

"Fuckin' A. That's so wizard."

"It was! I mean, I don't even remember the questions."

"Liar. You remember every word of the quiz."

"Yeah. I do. One of them was 'which song would you pick to dance to with your boyfriend at Homecoming?' The choices were, 'Bye Bye Bye' by NSync, 'Livin' La Vida Loca' by Ricky Martin, 'Get This Party Started' by Pink, and 'Just My Imagination' by The Temptations."

"What'd you pick?"

"'Just My Imagination' of course."

"Because Greyson liked Motown."

"So did I. Which was why we were so perfect for each other." She giggles and wiggles around in her chair, and it's so adorable I can't even eat.

*Shit.*

I already know what I'm going to have to do before she's even finished telling me all of the questions she answered. If Nico finds out, he'll never speak to me again. Not because of what I'm going to do to her but because it's so fucking cheesy. But I know I'm going to do it, just as surely as I know why.

I am hopelessly in love with this woman, and I don't want her to go anywhere without me.

## 22

## WILLA

*O*range blossom. Jasmine. Geranium. Lavender. Rosemary.

I'm going to blend all of these heavenly scents together as essential oils when we get home, but for now I'm going to lie here on this chaise lounge on the enclosed patio while Shane is out "running an errand." We had breakfast in the room. We had in-room massages. We made out in the hot tub. We even Skyped with Summer and Lucky. Summer wanted me to sing "Wouldn't It Be Loverly" with her, but I was so blissed out I forgot half the lyrics.

It's like I lose an IQ point every time Shane gives me an orgasm.

I'll be down to zero by the time we're back in LA.

This is such a beautiful place, and I don't want to leave it.

I want to wake up with Shane Miller between gazillion thread count Italian sheets every morning.

I don't want spring break to end, but it will.

I don't want to think about the New York job, but I have to.

I don't want to think about what I'll do or what it will be like for me and Shane once I stop working for him and Margo hires a permanent nanny, but I have to.

But not yet.

For now, I will lie here with my eyes closed and the sun on my face, enjoying the orange blossom, jasmine, geranium, lavender, and rosemary.

I'm not sure how much time passes, but I'm suddenly hearing music from inside the cottage.

Motown. The Temptations. "Just My Imagination."

"Aren't you Nico's little sister?" asks a familiar voice.

Without opening my eyes, I reach up, take hold of the waist of Shane's jeans, and pull him down to me. Just like he did to me that time he fell asleep watching Austin Powers. I squint up at him, but it's not Shane Miller that I see. It's Greyson Manning.

His hair is gelled straight up, and he's wearing a blazer, white button-down shirt, and a loose skinny tie. I open my eyes, sit up, and look down at his feet— Converse high tops!

"You wanna dance?" he asks, grinning as he holds his hands out and stands up.

I cover my mouth, nod, and take his hand so he can pull me up.

He leads me over to an open area on the patio, pulls me in, placing both hands on the small of my back. I hold my hands behind his neck and gaze up at him, head shaking in disbelief, heart bursting. "Wow. This is even cheesier than the necklace. I can't imagine how filthy you're going to have to be to get me to forget how fucking adorable you are this time."

"Let's just say I went to the mall to buy the skinny tie, high tops, hair gel, and some lube."

I chuckle at that—well aware that he's kidding but also completely aware that I would probably do anything he wanted me to. "That's really thoughtful of you, thanks. You are so wizard."

"You are so welcome." He kisses the top of my head, and I rest my forehead against his chest. "Never, ever speak of this to Nico."

"Which part?"

"All of it."

"Don't worry. I'm used to not talking about you with my brother. Or anyone else, for that matter."

"You can, you know?"

"Can what?"

"Talk about me with people. I was thinking we should tell the twins, since Margo knows."

Oh God, my cheeks are burning. First the slow dancing with Greyson Manning and now this? It's too much. "Knows what?"

"About us. That we're...going to Homecoming together."

I look up at his handsome face and see that patented Disney Channel star expression—so earnest and yet playful.

"Well, I would love to. But I think we should wait

until I'm not working for you anymore. So it's less confusing."

"For them or for you?"

"Both."

"Are you confused?"

"About you? Never. Not when I'm with you, anyway. That's the problem. I always feel so sure of things, even though I can't really know for sure."

"What'll it take for you to know for sure? Because I don't dress up as Greyson Manning and buy lube for everyone. You're the first, since the show was cancelled, and hopefully the last."

I tug on that skinny tie around his neck and bring his lips to mine.

"I just want to finish being your nanny before I'm officially something else. Okay?"

He nods once, eyes closed. "You really are something else, though," he whispers. "I wish I could have taken you to Homecoming. And prom. And the Kids' Choice Awards. And the Golden Globes. And my movie premieres. I wish I could have taken you to France."

"Is that a euphemism for something?"

"Yes. And no."

"You know where you can take me now?" I ask as I unbutton his shirt.

"Where? Name it and I'll take you there."

"Bed."

"You really are a swell girl."

♥

We had to leave that amazing bed in Santa Barbara eventually, and now that we're back in the Pacific Palisades and I don't have to look after the kids, I am using my free time to visit a few of the fancy boutiques in the village to see if the owners will stock a few bottles of my perfume oil. The first attempt was a bust, even though the lady seemed to really love the fragrance and was super interested in hearing about my Scent Design and Creation degree and the education of a perfumer in general. I left her with samples, a business card, and a pamphlet that I had printed up— with my logo and pretty pictures and little stories about my fragrances and the ingredients. It's a great package. I'm a great package! I just don't get LA store owners. How many more degrees does a girl need to get a break around here?

Now I'm in a pretty shop that sells fashionable organic clothing and handmade jewelry as well as a small selection of scented candles, organic cosmetics and perfume. If any shop in this neighborhood should be selling Aura perfume oils, it's this one. I do a lap around the store, looking at the displays. A tanned blonde woman who is probably in her fifties comes by to welcome me and asks if she can help me with anything, and miracle of miracles—she tells me that I smell amazing.

I tell her that it's my own perfume blend called Sleeper and that I just happen to have a sample of it right here. I ask if she's the owner of the store, and she is. I don't launch into a hard sell or anything. It's very conversational, and Christina seems really interested. She asks to see the bottles and loves everything she smells. But when I ask if she'd be interested in carrying a few bottles of each fragrance in her store, she says she's not really looking to stock more perfume right now.

And then I hear the bell above the door jingle, and when the lady looks over my shoulder, her face lights up. "Well hello, stranger!" she says, hand on her hip. "Long time no see, you!"

I glance over to get a look at who she's ignoring me for, and wouldn't you know it? Shane Miller is strolling towards us, lifting his aviator glasses to the top of his head and grinning. "Been waiting for a special occasion to buy a new dress. You know how it is."

"Ohhh! I mean I haven't seen you at breakfast in ages. The kids on spring break?"

"They are, yeah. I was just checking on Willa." He comes over to put his arm around me. I don't have a fucking clue how he found me here, but I did tell him I was going to scout out the boutiques in the Palisades. "Oh, you got your perfumes out."

"Yeah. Do we have to get ready for your screening?"

"No, we have a little time. Are you going to be stocking Willa's perfume here, Christina? They're selling like hotcakes on Etsy. She just sold a fragrance design to Margo—they're going to sell it on her website later this year."

"Well, we were just discussing that, actually. They smell fantastic, and I'm very interested. Let's discuss prices."

And just like that, Christina and I are discussing prices and filling out paperwork.

When I leave the store with Shane, I'm carrying nine fewer bottles of roll-on perfume oil than I had walked in with.

I wait until we've turned the corner and started walking back toward home to slap his arm. "How did you know I'd be there?"

"Process of deduction. I'd already been to the other two stores that looked like the kind of place you'd want to sell your stuff in."

"You know, she was not at all interested in selling my stuff until you walked in."

He rests his arm around my shoulder again. "This is LA, babe. Celebrity endorsement is the name of the game. No matter what game you're playing."

"Well, thank you. Part of me was really looking forward to walking in there with you tomorrow if she had turned me down outright and I'd ask if she worked on commission, and then I'd say, 'Big mistake. Huge!'"

"Your perfume will sell itself one day. I just wanted to help in any way I could. Hope you don't mind."

"I don't. I hope I can return the favor. *Ha-ha*."

"Well, you can. Just go easy on me and the movie tonight."

"I'm not that big of an asshole! Are you really worried that I won't like it?"

"I don't know, I've been talking it up. I just don't want you to be disappointed."

"I don't think you could ever disappoint me, Shane."

*Unless you marry someone else again.*

We're in a small screening room at some fancy private Hollywood club called SoHo House, on Sunset Boulevard. We have a drink at the bar first. Everyone looks like they just had a facial and a hair appointment, and I recognize every third person I see here. Shane introduces me simply by name, to his agent and the producers and writer-director, a couple of his costars. But he has his hand around my waist almost the whole time we're standing together.

The film is called *Hard Shell*, and Shane is the lead. He "carries" the film, as his agent said, but there are some amazing middle-aged and older character actors, and the teenager who plays his nephew is fantastic. It's about this sarcastic, troubled, but privileged teenage boy who runs away from home to stay with his very young uncle who lives in Maine. The kid's workaholic dad comes out from New York to get him, and you see the strained and awkward relationship between him and his much younger brother. This old lobsterman has a monologue about the exoskeleton as armor but how difficult it is for a lobster to molt and how vulnerable they are when they have their new soft shell. It's subtle but obvious that the story is about manhood and masculinity and the vulnerabilities of these men who are trying to be tough but also trying to change.

Shane is the young uncle who is a functional alcoholic. He works on a lobster boat. He's funny and charming but sometimes he's a mess and just so angry one minute and heartbreaking the next. And he looks tired. In a good way, that's right for the character, but it's so poignant for me to watch, knowing that he really couldn't sleep back then. I would totally fall in love with him because of this movie if I hadn't already been head over heels.

Watching him is thrilling. Hearing the twenty or so other people in the audience laugh at his lines makes me so happy. Every time I look over at Shane, he's either wincing at the screen or he's watching me. I cry three times, and each time, he squeezes my leg.

When the credits roll, everyone applauds, and I still have a huge lump in my throat. People descend upon Shane as soon as he stands up, so all I can do is smile at him and try to convey to him with my eyes just how much I loved the movie. I can tell that Shane's agent is as excited about the performance as I am, but Shane seems to be taking it all in stride.

When the agent asks if we'll join him for drinks, Shane says we have to be getting home, takes my hand, and doesn't let go until we're alone in the elevator to the parking level. I can tell he's a little overwhelmed, so I don't say anything until he looks over at me.

"Shane, you were so wonderful. Truly. The movie is great. I loved every minute of it."

"Really?"

"Of course, really—didn't you?"

"Yeah, I think it's really good. I just wish I'd done certain things differently. It's hard to watch myself. But the cinematography is great."

"It's beautiful! Maine looks so beautiful, and the score is beautiful, and the script is fantastic, and all of the actors—it's so funny and sad and heartwarming. It's going to be a hit."

"I hope so."

"I have no doubt. You'll see. Once people start seeing this, you'll get to play any kind of role in any kind of movie you want."

He laughs. "Except a period piece."

"Aw, who cares. I hate period pieces. Unless they're about perfume."

He kisses my cheek. "It really means a lot to me that you liked it."

"Well I loved it. I'm really proud of you. Is that weird to say? I don't even care. I am. I'm so proud of you. I can't wait to see what happens next for you."

And I mean it.

I am so proud of him that I don't even wonder what happens next for *us*. I just want him to get what he wants in life. And I hope that one of the things he wants in life is me.

## 23

**WILLA**

\* One Month Later\*

"*O*y vey! We made it! Mazel tov!" I got a little tired of Summer's Eliza Doolittle impression, so we watched *Fiddler on the Roof* a couple of weeks ago, and now she wants to be Jewish.

"Mazel tov!" I tickle her waist as I help her out of the car seat. "Let's go see some flowers!" It took almost an hour in Saturday traffic, but since the kids don't have any parties or play dates today, I decided to bring them to a botanical garden that's over thirty miles away from home, in the hills of Northeast Los Angeles. I want to get some photos of the roses and camellias that are in bloom here, for Instagram, and the twins needed to get out of the house.

Summer was in a mood this morning, probably

because her daddy hasn't been around as much as usual lately. The premiere for his big summer comedy is on Thursday, and he's been so busy with publicity stuff for the past couple of weeks. We've all been a bit stressed and moody lately. Shane isn't thrilled that I don't want to be his date to the premiere, but he understands why. He wanted me to keep sleeping in his bed once the kids came back home, but I think I should sleep in the nanny room any time they're around. If he and Margo always think of the children first, then he and I should too. Boundaries. I know how hard it was for Shane to cross the line when he talked to Nico about me, but I still need the nanny-employer boundaries to define my life right now. Because there aren't any boundaries in my heart.

Fortunately for everyone, the *Fiddler on the Roof* soundtrack is on Spotify, so we listened to it all the way here. It cheered us up a bit. Summer wanted to sing "Matchmaker" over and over again, and Lucky wanted to hear "If I Were a Rich Man" because he's fascinated by the singer's deep voice and all the funny noises he makes.

"Come with me," I tell Summer while I go around to the other side door to get Lucky out of his car seat.

"Bahdahbahdahbahdbahduhbahduh biddy biddy bum!" Lucky's arms are up in the air, and he's wiggling his shoulders, the way the father in the movie dances.

"Let's get your biddy biddy bum out of here." I pull him out and realize that Summer is not by my side. "Summer!"

"Yabba dibba dibba dubba dabba dibba dibba dum!" Her voice comes from about twenty feet away. The parking lot isn't too busy, but still.

"Summer! Stop where you are and wait for us!" I shut the door.

"Daidel deedle daidel daidel hurry up!"

I grab Lucky's hand, and we jog over to where Summer is standing.

"We all need to stay together," I say to Summer. "Take my hand."

"You forgot to make the car beep," Lucky says.

"What? Oh right." I lock the car with the key fob, and then I take Summer's hand as we cross the lot to the entrance to the gardens and wait in the short line.

"Are there animals here?" Lucky asks.

"Good question. It's not a zoo, but I'm sure we'll see some birds and squirrels, maybe lizards."

"I wanna see lizards!"

"Me too!"

"Is Papa going to meet us here?" Summer has started calling Shane "Papa" and Margo "Mama" while pointing out that there aren't any nannies in the "fiddler family." She now refers to me as "Tzeitel," the eldest daughter.

"No. I told you, we'll see him at the house for dinner."

"Tzeitel?"

"Yes, Summer?"

"When is matchmaker going to make you a match?" There's a teasing tone to her voice, but I still don't like it. She has been such an adorable little turd, ever since they Skyped with Margo last night.

"What makes you think I need a matchmaker?"

"Because you don't have a husband."

"Well, *Fiddler on the Roof* takes place in Russia in 1905. Things are a little different here and now."

"But Abby's mom uses match dot com to find husbands."

"Good point. But I'm not looking."

"Why not?" She eyes me suspiciously. "Do you already have one?"

"No." Fortunately, I'm up next to pay for admission, so I can ignore her when she asks me if Papa should have a matchmaker.

"But where will you go when the new nanny moves in?"

"I don't know for sure yet. Probably back to Nico's place for a while."

"I don't want you to go," Lucky whines. "I don't like the new nanny."

"What new nanny?"

Summer lets go of me so she can jump in front of Lucky and cover his mouth with her hands. "You're not supposed to say anything, 'member? Oy vey!"

"You already met your new nanny?"

Summer lets her head drop back and smacks her forehead. "Yes!" She takes my outstretched hand again. "At spring break. Mommy made us meet her. I mean, Mama. I liked her. She brought cookies."

This is news to me, although I guess I shouldn't be

surprised that Margo would want to interview nannies while she was in town. It's just odd that Shane hasn't mentioned it. And that somebody didn't want the twins to mention it to me. And it's ridiculous that I'm feeling a pang of jealousy about being replaced, because it's not like I want to be their nanny forever. I'm just hoping—perhaps it's irrational of me to be *expecting*—to be in their life forever and ever.

But I can't think about that now.

This garden is the perfect size—not small, but it doesn't feel expansive. It's blissfully peaceful and quiet. There are so many trees that provide shade and dappled light. I can tell I'm going to love it here. I let go of the twins' hands for a few seconds to study the map handout. There are a lot of different sections and paths. Some paths are paved around the perimeter, and some go through the woods in the center of the property.

After making the twins close their eyes and inhale the incredible scent of the wisteria near the entrance, after agreeing to buy Summer a soft pretzel for her to share with Lucky, and after taking them both to the bathroom, we've finally made it to the Japanese Garden. The kids are happy to stand here on the little bridge and watch the koi in the pond. I check my phone to see if there are any messages from Shane. After seeing how he was constantly surrounded by people before and after the screening a month ago, I have some idea of why he doesn't have much time to keep in touch when he's working.

There aren't any messages from Shane. But there is an e-mail from my mentor in Versailles, letting me know that the German perfume studio in New York still has one lab tech position available. I had politely declined to interview after he first told me about the job because I still had two months of nanny work left and I didn't want Shane to worry about finding someone to replace me. But Margo will be back from Poland in just under a month. I need to figure out my next move.

I have a good chunk of change saved thanks to Shane, but it would only be enough for a deposit and a few months' rent, given the money I have to put into my new business. Christina at the boutique keeps ordering more of my perfume oil every week—she sells out within days every time. I have steady sales on Etsy now, but it's not enough to cover rent yet since I don't have time to produce and ship more than thirty bottles a week now. So I'd pretty much have to stay with my brother again. I've been designing my own website storefront, which I plan to launch once I'm done working for Shane, but I'll need space for all of my supplies. I haven't talked to Nico about setting up a work area yet.

I'm starting to panic just a little bit. Shane's busy schedule has meant that we don't get much time to talk, much less kiss each other, and I keep getting glimpses of what his life would be like when I'm not living with him anymore. I need to have a plan. I can't ignore this job opportunity.

By the time I look up from my phone, Summer and Lucky are no longer on the bridge. I see Summer dragging Lucky over to the Japanese Tea House. "Summer! Wait for me!" I am already questioning my decision to bring them here by myself. I usually just shuttle them around, picking them up and dropping them off, or I take them to the beach where it's easy to keep an eye on them. The other times we've gone on outings like this, it has been the four of us.

"You have to stop running off like that."

"We weren't running!"

"You need to stay with me. Both of you. Always."

"But you were looking at your phone! Oy!"

"I was just checking to see if your papa sent a text or not."

"Did he?"

"No. Let's keep walking."

"Can I get a hot dog?"

"You just ate a pretzel."

"But I finished it."

"We'll have lunch in an hour, Summer. You'll just have to wait." I don't mean to snap at her, but oy vey.

She doesn't growl at me or stick out her lower lip like she usually does. She just frowns and goes silent. Which is even more troubling.

Lucky looks up at me apologetically, taking my hand.

"Let's go see the rose garden. Does that sound good?"

"Okay. Is it far away?"

"I don't think so. We'll just cross back over the bridge and then follow the main path to the right."

"Okay."

Summer continues her silent rage, staring at the ground while walking hand-in-hand with Lucky. She doesn't even look at the koi when we cross the bridge.

"Hey. Where do fish keep their money?"

Lucky wrinkles his brow. "Their pockets?"

"A river bank!"

No reaction from the twins. I don't blame them. That one's a thinker.

"Knock knock."

"Who's there?"

"Honeydew."

"Honeydew who?"

"Honeydew you want to hear some more jokes?"

Lucky laughs. He may or may not actually get the joke, but he definitely wants to lighten the mood. Summer is still sulking. I glance over at the snack bar as we pass by and briefly consider buying her a hot dog just to cheer her up so she'll like me again. But no. Nope. I'm in charge. Not her.

The rose garden is in full bloom, and I get dozens of gorgeous close-up shots. I take a picture of Summer and Lucky dancing around on the lawn like Russian Jewish villagers and immediately e-mail it to Margo and text it to Shane because it looks like they're having fun. Maybe Lucky managed to cheer his sister up, bless his heart.

My phone immediately vibrates with a text notification from Shane.

**SHANE: Mazel tov!**

I laugh and look up at the kids before replying. "Hey guys, I'm going to sit here on this bench, okay? Your dad sent a text." They completely ignore me, but the bench isn't far away, so I guess they'll figure it out.

**ME: Diddle daidle biddy bum.**
**SHANE: Fuck, I love it when you text dirty to me.**
**You having a good day?**
**ME: Yes.**
**SHANE: So that's a no, then? Wish I could be there.**
**I'm so sick of answering the same questions over and over again, and there's still a couple of weeks of this dog and pony show to go.**
**ME: I think I speak for everyone when I say we really fucking miss you.**
**SHANE: I really miss you guys too.**
**SHANE: If it wasn't clear...by 'you guys,' I meant your tits.**

ME: If it wasn't clear...by 'everyone,' I meant all of my lady parts.
SHANE: Tell your lady parts they have a standing invitation to join me in my bed every night. And by 'standing invitation' I mean...
ME: Pretty sure I know what you mean, Papa.
SHANE: Oy vey.
SHANE: Gotta go. They're calling me back inside. See you at dinner.

I can't stop smiling. I could be in the center of an actual shitstorm while being attacked by aliens, and a text from Shane Miller would still put a smile on my face and make me feel like I can face the rest of my day. I slide the phone into my pocket and look up to tell the kids that it's time to move on to the next garden.

But the kids aren't on the lawn where I last saw them.

They aren't anywhere that I can see.

I even made sure they were wearing brightly colored clothes today—both of them are wearing sunflower-yellow tops.

I instinctively reach for the heart pendant that Shane gave me, stand up, and do a slow spin around to survey the entire rose garden. It's not all that crowded. They could certainly be on the ground, ducking beneath the rose bushes. I call out their names. No answer. I jog over to the covered patio and call out for them again. I go into the ladies' room, check under the stalls, calling out their names. I open the door to the men's room and call out for them, but no one answers. I go inside to check under the stalls—empty.

Their legs are shorter than my arms. They could not have gotten very far in the couple of minutes that I was looking at my phone. There's no need to panic. I just need to walk around. I just need to scour every inch of this 150-acre property as quickly as possible. The first logical place to look is the snack bar, but I see that there's a miniature train stopped outside the rose garden, so maybe they went to check it out.

I run over to the enchanted fucking railroad station, but I don't see Summer or Lucky anywhere.

It occurs to me that maybe I should return to the bench where I was sitting, in case they go back there to find me.

I run back to the bench in the middle of the rose garden and sit there, calmly, for thirty seconds. Thirty-one seconds later, I'm in full-on panic mode. Thirty-two seconds later, I'm sprinting to the snack bar near the entrance to the gardens. I check the restrooms near the snack bar. I check all of the tables on the patio. I check the gift shop nearby. I run back to the Japanese Garden and the tea house, because maybe they wanted to go back there.

Or maybe I should go back to the bench again so they know where to find me?

I should have told them to meet me in a specific place if we got separated.

Shit.

How do single parents handle more than one kid?

"Are you all right, dear?"

I spin around to find two sweet elderly ladies looking at me with concern and realize that I'm practically hyperventilating.

"I...I can't find my kids." Oh shit, I'm tearing up. This is so unprofessional.

"Oh no. How old are they?"

"Five. They're five. They're wearing yellow shirts, a boy and a girl."

"Well, we haven't seen them, but you should talk to the people in the front office. I'm sure they have a way of dealing with this kind of thing."

"Yes. Yes—good idea." I run back to the front entrance, but I mean—it's not a supermarket. They can't make an announcement on a loudspeaker telling them where to meet me. Can they?

On my way to the front entrance, out of the corner of my eye, I see a flash of yellow.

"Lucky!"

Lucky is wandering around the tables on the patio by the snack bar, his lower lip quivering, but he's trying so hard not to look upset.

I grab him and pick him up. As soon as he's in my arms, he starts crying. Summer is not with him.

"Oh, honey, I got you. It's okay. It's okay."

"Summer said to follow her, and then I saw a lizard and I followed the lizard."

"Ohhh, okay. You followed the lizard and then what?"

"He went into the woods and then under a rock."

"Uh-huh, and then what?"

"I went out of the woods, and Summer was gone."

"Okay. So you haven't seen Summer since then?"

He shakes his head. "I'm sorry! I lost her."

"No no no no, this is not your fault, sweetie. You didn't lose Summer. We didn't lose Summer. She's probably just hiding from us. We'll find her together, okay?"

I carry him to the ticket booth at the entrance and tell the man there that we can't find his sister. Turns out they *do* have loudspeakers around the gardens, because they sometimes have concerts and nighttime events with music. He tells me to go around to talk to someone who meets us in the gift shop. They tell all of the employees who are on walkie talkie to look out for a five-year-old girl with light brown hair and a yellow top and jeans, to bring her to her family at the gift shop if they find her. Before they make an announcement on the loudspeakers, they ensure that there is an employee stationed at all of the exits to make sure no one else leaves with her. Then they make an announcement asking Summer to find the nearest wide path and wait there for someone in a golf cart to pick her up. Four employees in golf carts are told to drop what they're doing to drive around looking for her.

Fifteen agonizing minutes later, Summer is

dropped off in front of the gift shop. She's crying and sucking her thumb, but she thanks the man who's driving the golf cart for the ride when I pick her up out of the back seat. And then she waves to him and says, "Mazel tov."

The drive home was a long one. It took the same amount of time as the drive to the garden, but this time no one sang along to *Fiddler on the Roof*. I finally turned it off, but Summer said she wanted to listen to it.

For lunch, I make turkey dogs for them, give them each a double helping of dessert, and we all eat, mostly in silence. I ask them if they want to talk about what happened, but all Summer says is, "No. You were on your phone. You're always looking at your phone."

"I'm not always looking at my phone, Summer, but I'm very sorry that I wasn't watching you for two minutes."

She clams up after that.

I haven't texted Shane since there's no need to worry him and nothing for him to worry about now. I consider hiding all of the phones, iPads, and computers in this house so they can't Skype with their mother today. Maybe they'll forget by tomorrow.

But sure enough, Summer tells me she wants to Skype Mama. I can't tell them not to tell her about what happened, because then they'd either just tell her that I told them not to tell her or they'd feel guilty because they're keeping a secret from their mother. At least Summer isn't sucking her thumb anymore and Lucky seems fine.

I set up a Skype call for them and then go to my room and shut the door. I don't want to hear what they're saying. If they tell Margo about it, I'll find out sooner or later anyway.

When Shane gets home, the kids abandon the movie they were watching to run to him. I can tell he's feeling overwhelmed from his day and just wants to chill out. But I have to tell him what happened. I get him a glass of water and a snack and ask him to join me in the kitchen when the twins are done climbing all over him.

"What happened?" he asks, sliding the kitchen door mostly shut behind him.

"What do you mean? Did they tell you?"

"Tell me what? You look totally freaked out."

It isn't until he puts his arms around me and brings my head to his chest that I cry. I cry like a big baby. I cry while telling him that I lost his children at the garden while I was texting with him and they had to make an announcement on the loudspeaker. He doesn't understand a word I'm saying the first couple of times I try to explain it to him.

"Shane, I'm so sorry. It was so stupid of me. I was so scared."

"Hey hey hey, it's okay. They're here."

"But Lucky was crying and Summer was sucking her thumb again. They were traumatized."

"They don't seem traumatized to me."

"They were traumatized. It was all my fault."

"Wow. I thought I was hard on myself, but you really are."

"I lost your children, Shane."

"But you found them. They're here."

"You really aren't mad?"

"I mean, if you had come home without them, I would have been really fucking pissed off, and I wish they hadn't gotten lost, but it happened and they're safe and it's okay. My doctor told me he once forgot his kids in the car at the mall for two hours."

"I don't think that's the same thing. Have any of your other nannies lost them? Have *you* ever lost them?"

"No. But I always worry about it."

"What about Margo?"

"I don't think so. But it happens all the time. To other parents. You can't keep kids on a leash. Well, I guess you can. But we don't. I'll talk to them at bedtime. I'm sure it's fine."

I can tell he's concerned, but he's trying so hard not to show it.

"Okay. Well, dinner's almost ready."

He rubs his forehead. "Okay. Great."

*I'm not going to ask about the new nanny.*

*I am not going to ask about the new nanny.*

"Hey, did you know that Margo and the kids

already met with a nanny to replace me? Over spring break?"

I am half-expecting him to be surprised and perhaps a tiny bit outraged by this news. But he sighs. "Yeah. I actually had a Skype meeting with her."

"You did? When?"

"Few weeks ago."

"Oh. Why didn't you tell me?"

"I guess I didn't think it would be of interest to you, and also I sort of forgot because as soon as I got off of Skype with her, I had back-to-back interviews about the movie." He sighs again, raking his fingers through his hair. He's tired and he doesn't want to talk about this anymore. But he continues. "Her name is Margarita."

*Shit. She sounds hot.*

"She's about sixty, I think. Her kids are all grown up. She's pretty serious. She's basically the opposite of you." He kisses me on top of my head. "I'm gonna go sit with the kids."

"Okay. They already Skyped with Margo today."

He nods again, looking a little concerned.

"You haven't heard from her?"

He shakes his head and leaves the room.

And that's it.

Now all I can do is wait to see if the other shoe is going to drop.

## 24

## SHANE

*I*t has been two days since the garden incident, and I hadn't heard from Margo, so I'd almost forgotten about it. Willa has been so much quieter than usual. I know it's still weighing on her mind, and I'd give anything to make her feel better, but I can't promise that it was inconsequential. Because I know that Summer told Margo about it when they Skyped. And because I know Margo.

I know why Margo is Skyping me right now.

And I know that no matter what my feelings are for Willa, no matter how much my kids adore her, this nanny job was always going to end for her eventually. She is taking the kids to school, and I have about an hour before I have to leave for another day of photo shoots and interviews. I have to take this call.

"Hello, Margo," I say once the video is connected on my phone. She isn't in costume, and I can see that she's in her hotel room. She is frowning me. "What's up?"

"Well, let me tell you what's up, Shane, in case you don't already know. Willa lost our children when they were at a garden the other day, while she was busy texting with you."

"Yes. She feels terrible about it. But, as you know, she found them. They're fine."

"So you do know about it?"

"Willa told me about it as soon as I came home. She was really upset about it."

"And you didn't think it was necessary to talk to *me* about it?"

"That's what we're doing now, isn't it?"

"Shane. If this were anyone else, you wouldn't have hesitated to discuss it with me—the mother of your children."

"Kids first. I talked to the twins about it. I know that Summer told you about it. You and I are talking about it now. Why don't you cut to the chase?"

"I've spent the last day getting in touch with the nanny agency. Margarita is available to start now, so I've hired her. Her employment as *our* nanny begins tomorrow. I'm paying for the first month, but she'll stay with you. And don't tell me you don't need her to stay with you—I know how busy you are for the next couple of weeks. I'll forward her contact information, as well as the contract for you to sign. You should call Margarita to arrange a time for her to go to your house. As per your wishes, I have not communicated with

Willa to let her know that she has been replaced as the twins' nanny. I'll leave that to you."

"You are aware that the twins are going to be devastated if she leaves this abruptly?"

"Yes, I am. And if you play your cards right, maybe she won't leave."

I'm about to spew something biting and sarcastic and then I realize what she just said.

My ex isn't giving me the holier than thou look I was expecting.

It's the *I know you better than you think* look that I usually give her.

"Wait. What? What are you saying?"

"I saw the way you looked at her. You never looked at me that way. Not when we first got together. Not even during our love scenes on the show." She wipes a tear from her eye.

Holy shit. She's crying.

"I don't even know why I'm crying. That's not true. It's not about you—get that look off your face. It's because I know how much the kids love her too."

Well, shit. Now she's really crying.

"And I don't want them to love her more than they love me." She covers her face, and her whole damn body is shaking

Well, fuck. That never occurred to me. For the second time ever, Margo Quincey has surprised me.

"Marg...you'll always be their mother. You can't be replaced by anyone, any more than I was replaced by Landon."

She wipes her eyes and blows her nose. "Yeah, but Willa's so much more lovable than Landon is."

We both laugh at that. "True."

"Maybe if you guys aren't so worried about hiding your relationship from the kids, you'll both be a little more clearheaded."

"Yeah. Maybe."

"But if anything ever happens to my children because of her—"

"It could have happened with either of us, you know that."

"Look, I don't want to create trouble. I'm trying to make things easier for everyone. I do like Willa, Shane. And not just because she designed an amazing perfume for me. I like her for you. I could see us all going on family vacations together one day. I hope you don't fuck it up."

"That's very Gwyneth of you, Margo. Thanks. I hope I don't fuck it up too."

"I think we should tell the kids together, you and I, on a Skype call after they get home from school."

"I won't be home until dinner my time."

"We'll work it out. Bye." She ends the call.

And *that* is why I'm friends with my ex-wife.

I put my phone away and go downstairs to take a look at the lower level of the house, where the laundry room and my workout area is. There's room for a workspace for Willa. She could stay in my room and mix her perfumes down here. Or she could turn the guest room into an office. I think it should be pretty easy for her to see that this is a good thing—the early termination of her position as a nanny. She'll be able to get on with the very important business of creating and selling perfume and being my girlfriend. And sleeping in my bed. Without hiding it from the kids or anyone else.

I can't fucking wait for her to get home.

Fortunately, I don't have to wait long.

As soon as she's through the door from the garage, I take her in my arms.

She drops her purse and wraps her arms around me. "Hi."

"Hi." I'm not going to let go of her until she understands that she doesn't have to leave. "Drop-off went okay?"

"Yeah, I dropped them off at a 7-Eleven. Is that cool? They should be able to find their way to school eventually." She buries her face in my chest, shaking her head. At least she's able to make jokes again, even if she doesn't find them funny.

"They're really smart. They'll figure it out. I need to talk to you about something." When I feel her loosening her grip, I hold on tighter. "Margo called just now. Summer told her about what happened at the garden, and she decided to hire Margarita to start tomorrow. She isn't mad. She just thinks it would be better if—"

"I'm going to go to New York for the job interview," she blurts out. She hugs me so tight, the side of her face flat against my chest. I can't tell if she's happy or consoling me or hugging me good-bye.

"What?"

"The lab technician job I told you about last month?" Her voice is shaky now. "There's still one position left, and they're holding it for me. There aren't many people in the US who are as qualified as I am."

"What about your own business?"

"I'll close my Etsy store for a few days and then figure things out after the interview."

"Willa. I want you to know that you can stay here. Even when the new nanny is here. I want you to stay here, if you want to. You can use the guest room as an office, or I'll set up a workspace for you downstairs."

She grabs my face and kisses me on the mouth, and as always, I can't say or do anything other than kiss her. It's all I want to do. I can feel how hard it is for her to pull away from me when she does, and that's how I know how important it is to her to be able to pull away from me.

"Thank you. I need to go. I have to." Her eyes are shiny and about to spill over. Uncertainty flickers across her pretty face.

I want to tell her not to go, plead my case. I know exactly what to say and do, how to look at her, the tone of voice to use, to get her to say she'll stay. God knows, if I were twenty-one and it was just her and me, I probably would. But I don't want her to resent me for manipulating her. I know why she needs to go. I can't blow off my work responsibilities today or next week, so I can't ask *her* to.

She's a perfumer. It's what she's wanted to be since she was twelve. I'm a performer. I've been giving things up for my career since I was a child. Even when I have to give up seeing my kids all the time for a few months, it doesn't mean that I don't want to see them.

Still.

I don't want her to choose anything else over me or my kids.

But I have to let her choose.

"It sounds like a great opportunity for you."

"I think I should say good-bye to the kids tonight instead of in the morning before school."

*Jesus. This girl is giving me whiplash again.*

"Yeah. I agree. The kids will miss you. I will miss you."

"I'll stay with my brother."

"But you can always come back here if it doesn't work out. Or come back just because you want to. Just come back."

She nods and gulps back some sad little sound, picking her purse up from the floor and running to her room. The door clicking shut echoes all through the house. Just a hint of how empty this place will feel when she's gone.

I did not see this coming.

I can't even think about how much I'll hate not having her around, even for a few days, because the twins are going to take this so hard.

I vaguely remember when my only problem was that I had insomnia, no nanny, two kids who took up all my time and energy, and no love life to look forward to.

Now all of a sudden, I've got an upcoming press junket and movie premiere, two nannies, two kids, three broken hearts to look forward to, and the terrible knowledge that the only woman I can see myself spending the rest of my life with needs to be able to see herself living her life without me.

I get it.

I fucking hate it.

But I get her. Even when she surprises me and knocks the wind out of me, I understand Willa Todd. Even if I give her everything that I can give her, she needs to know that she can concoct something that will make her feel like she's in control of her world and her heart.

So all I can do is try to figure out how to explain all of that to two five-year-olds.

## 25

# WILLA

*I*t felt like everything was happening in slow-motion—like I was wading through water ever since I brought the kids home from the garden. Now things are happening so fast. Everything is spinning, and I'm circling the drain.

I e-mailed my mentor and the people in New York right after Shane told me about the new nanny starting.

I have an interview set for Wednesday.

I've booked a flight to JFK.

I've texted my brother to let him know I'll be bringing my things back to his place tonight. I told him that I'll explain why when I see him.

I've called my grammie to let her know I'm going to visit her in Michigan right after my interview and gave her two minutes to explain to me why I had made the right decision.

I've started packing everything up.

I've posted a note on my Etsy shop that I won't be shipping anything for the next week.

I've eaten dinner with Shane and the kids, and he and the kids have Skyped with Margo in the family room.

I've dotted my pulse points with lavender and neroli oil.

I keep reminding myself to breathe.

I keep reminding myself that I can't blame anyone for anything, especially not Shane.

I keep reminding myself that I spent seven years in post-secondary school to be a perfumer and I can't ignore a job opportunity just so I can play house with Shane and his kids. Shane wouldn't do that. It might not be my dream job, but it's a great job and it's my reality.

Now I just have to be a grown-up and say good night and good-bye to the kids without falling to pieces or breaking their sweet little hearts.

When it was time for me to leave Versailles, I was sad to say good-bye to Noelle and Leo and their mother too, but nobody got emotional. They weren't a particularly expressive family, but I never really felt like a part of their family either. When I said good-bye to the grandmother and told her that I was going to Los Angeles, she studied my palm and said, "Yes. You will be reunited with much family there." At that point, I figured she meant my brother. A month ago, it occurred to me that she may have meant Shane's family. Now I'm wondering if maybe palmistry is just a load of crap.

Shane is letting the twins sleep in his bed tonight. They're all washed-up, and for the first time since I met her, Summer brushed her teeth without any fuss. They've both been acting like they've been told that Santa won't be coming this year and it's all their fault. Neither of them has cried yet, but they've also barely made a sound. Maybe they can't wait for me to go. Shane went downstairs to give me a chance to talk to them, and I've just been sitting on the bed watching the twins lie there quietly while staring at their stuffed animals for a couple of minutes.

"Is there anything that either of you would like to ask me?"

Lucky takes a deep breath and sighs. "How are you going to go to New York?"

"I'm going to fly there. On an airplane. Have you been to New York?"

He nods. "Our grandma and grandpa live there. Are you going to see them?"

"No. I'm only going to be there for a short while, this trip. I'm going to meet some people and talk to them about a job."

"To be someone else's nanny?"

"No, it's not a nanny job. It's another kind of job. Working in a big building instead of a house."

"But why do you have to go to New York?"

"Because that's where the job is."

"But are you going to come back to here?"

"Yes. And if I have to move to New York, I promise I will come back to see you before I go. If you want me to. Do you want me to?"

He nods and wipes his nose.

I kiss him on the cheek. "You're a very good, smart boy, and I love you very much."

"You're supposed to kiss me on both cheeks," he whispers. "Like French people."

"You're right." I kiss him on both cheeks. "*Bonne nuit, mon chéri.*"

Summer still hasn't said a word or made eye contact with me, so I go over to sit closer to her. I brush hair out of her face and lean in to kiss her on both cheeks, and as soon as I do, she bursts into tears. "I made you in trouble, didn't I?"

"No. *I* made me in trouble."

"I'm sorry I told on you."

"You don't have to say you're sorry to me. I am not mad at you, Summer. I love you."

"But you're going away anyway?"

"I have to go to New York for the job interview. It's not because I want to leave you and Lucky or your dad. People don't stop loving each other just because they aren't around all the time. You know that, right? Just like your mom still loves you, even though she's working in Poland now. And your dad always loves you, even when he's doing a movie somewhere else. I might have to go to New York to work for a while, but I'll still love you and think about you guys all the time."

This seems to make sense to both of them, and Summer calms down.

She wipes the tears from her eyes. "You're not taking us to school tomorrow?" she asks.

"No, I have to go to the airport tomorrow. I'm going to my brother's place tonight."

"Will you wait here until we're asleep?"

I give her a hug, and she hugs me back. I have to hold my breath because the scent of her baby shampoo is the thing that might finally break me. "I have to go downstairs to finish packing and putting things in the truck. But I'll send your dad up to stay with you. Okay?"

She nods.

"Knock knock."

They both ask, so cautiously, "Who's there?"

"Toodle"

"Toodle who?"

"See you later, alligators."

Shane is sitting at the bottom of the stairs. He stands up as soon as he hears me coming down.

"Can you stay with them until they fall asleep?" I whisper.

"Don't you need help loading up the truck?"

My mind flashes back to the first day I got here, when he helped me unload the truck in a haze of pheromones, and the first time he said good-bye to me in the garage when I was leaving to go to Nico's show. "I think it would be best if we just say good night right now."

I hug him, looking down, because if he kisses me, I will forget to leave.

He strokes my hair instead. "Text me when you get to Nico's."

"Okay."

"Text me when you're in New York."

"I will."

"Text me anytime you want to. It doesn't even have to be dirty. I'll be busy, but I'll get back to you when I can."

I nod and pull away from him.

He stares at me for a few seconds before saying, "We love you, you know?"

"Yeah. I love you guys too." I glance up at him to confirm that he regrets what he just said as much as I do, but neither of us says anything else. "Go be with the kids. Good night."

"Good night."

My brother patiently listens to everything I have to tell him about what's happened in the past few days and why I'm going to New York for the job interview before staring at me blankly and saying, "Go back to Shane. Now."

"What?"

"You're punishing yourself because the kids got lost on your watch."

*Am I?*

"Well, that may be part of the reason why I'm not hesitating to go to New York right now, but I still have to go. It's not just for me, even. My professor highly recommended me. It wouldn't reflect well on him or the school if I just blew off this interview—I already turned down that job in Paris when I decided to move here."

He waves his hand dismissively. "You're being an idiot. I mean, do what you gotta do." He gets up from the coffee table he was sitting on, returning with his guitar. "You have the best brain of anyone I know, but you need to trust your heart on this one. You should trust *his* heart. God knows I love Grammie and she's right about most things, but she's wrong about you and Shane."

"You talked to Grammie about us?"

"I talk to Grammie about almost everything."

"Really?" Am I jealous that Grammie talks to my brother more than me? A little.

"Who do you think I talked to about the real shit when you were in France? Mom and Dad? It's been Grammie and Shane for half my life almost."

He sits back down in front of me, tuning his guitar.

"Oh God. Are you going to serenade me?"

"I'm gonna show you what's what in a minute. Hang on." He continues tuning.

I check my phone when it buzzes. It's not Shane. Harley has been texting me nonstop ever since I told her that I was fired and I'm going to New York for the job interview. Texts like "Yeah, girl! Boss up and change your life!" and "Walk that fine ass out that door."

HARLEY: I've got a bottle of tequila I've been saving for you!
ME: I'm fine and I can't go out. I have a flight to catch tomorrow. Stop quoting Lizzo songs at me. XOXO
HARLEY: Holy shit. I'm so impressed that you actually know who Lizzo is, I'm backing down.
ME: Peace out, sister.
HARLEY: Okay, that's just lame. Dork.
ME: <shrugging woman emoji>

I look up to find my brother staring at me. "You ready to have your mind blown?" He starts strumming his guitar. "This is a song I started working on after Shane told me about you guys. It's called 'Sleeper Hit.'"

"What? You stole my name."

"What are you talking about?"

"I called my perfume that's inspired by Shane and me 'Sleeper.'"

"You didn't tell me that. I'm not changing the title."

"Fine. People will just think I copied you anyway."

He shrugs and starts singing. He sings about an actor who can't sleep because he's afraid he'll be alone in bed for the rest of his life, tired of acting like everything's okay. And then he meets the girl of his dreams and all of that chemistry he's been pretending to have with other girls is finally real. I'm curled up on the futon, in tears, before he's finished the song.

It doesn't change the fact that I'm leaving tomorrow. But for the first time ever, my brother lies down beside me and comforts me, and I am realizing that he might not be as big of an asshat as I thought he was. Even if it is completely ridiculous to think of me as the girl of Shane Miller's dreams.

## SHANE MILLER SLEEP DIARY – WEDNESDAY, 5 AM

**Went to bed at:** *This shit again. I don't have a fucking clue. I got a call from the director of Hard Shell at around ten last night, letting me know that our movie is going to be screened at the Toronto International Film Festival in September. It's a big deal. A huge deal. And the only person I wanted to tell was Willa. But she has her job interview today. I didn't want to bother her with my career crap.*

**How long it took you to fall asleep:** *How the fuck should I know? Keeping track of this shit when you're trying to sleep is stressful. Who came up with these fucking diary questions anyway? How do they sleep at night?*

**How many times you woke up in the middle of the night:** *Seriously, what difference does it make?*

**How refreshing your overall sleep was:** *Like lying in a fucking bed of daisies that won't stop asking where Willa is* *or what she's up to or why you thought it would be better for her if you let her go.*

**Number of caffeinated beverages you consumed throughout the day:** *Five. You try getting through a day of pretending to give a shit while entertainment journalists ask you the same questions over and over again. It's sort of like answering these stupid sleep diary questions, except with lights and a high-definition camera in your face.*

**Number of alcoholic beverages you consumed throughout the day:** *One beer last night, and don't try to tell me that's why I couldn't sleep.*

**How much time you spent exercising:** *None. Fired my trainer as soon as he asked me what happened to the hot nanny.*

**Your stress level before bedtime, on a scale from 1 to 5:** *Fuck this scale.*

**Your major cause of stress:** *I can't let her go. And I can't cancel out of the press junket today or the premiere tomorrow.*

## 26

## SHANE

*M*argarita Vasquez has been a professional child caregiver for well over four decades. She has been our nanny for almost two days now. She enjoys cooking healthy meals, being organized, staying on schedule, reading quietly in her room when the kids are asleep, and she knows CPR. She speaks fluent English, but when either of the twins says or does something that she considers to be misbehavior—like request pocket snacks or insist that she sing a showtune or ask why flies like dog poop or why she isn't married—she expresses something very rapidly in Spanish. I have no idea what, because the word *si* is never involved. This causes the twins to shut up and do whatever she wants them to do immediately, and then everyone gets on with their day. I respect and appreciate her and hope to never see her naked.

It's not her fault that she is the living, breathing embodiment of Willa's absence.

I'm sure that Summer and Lucky will like her eventually.

I'm pretty sure that they will stop staring at me like they're waiting for me to have a nervous breakdown any minute now.

I know what a broken heart looks like.

I have always known how to act heartbroken.

I've played five different guys who've been crushed by the girl he's in love with.

I've been the guy whose wife fell in love with someone else.

And part of me knew that if I gave my heart to Willa in the way that she deserves, I'd have to be willing to let her go if she still felt she needed to protect her own heart.

But for fuck's sake... Missing Willa, wondering how she feels right now, and seeing how much my kids miss her—there's an emptiness that no thirty-second montage that's underscored by a contemporary sad love song could ever convey.

And I don't want my kids to see me sad or worried or empty, even though I may not be as good of an actor as I thought I was.

Every day for more than five years, I've been living with the knowledge that I would do anything for my kids, even though I almost never feel like I've said the exact right thing or done enough. That's just being a parent. But ever since I left Willa at the bottom of the stairs on Monday night, I have been thinking about the one thing I could have said that might have changed everything.

I tried calling Nico while I was driving home for dinner earlier, but I got his voice mail. A little while ago he sent a text, asking if I'd be home tonight. When I told him I would be, I didn't hear back from him. I just want to get an idea of how things went for Willa today, but now it's bedtime.

This is the third night in a row I've let the kids sleep with me—even though Margarita thinks I'm spoiling them. To be honest, after the press junket today, it feels good to be flanked by two people who *aren't* going to ask me what it was like performing in front of a green screen or if I think Melissa McCarthy and I would make good detectives in real life too. When I come to the end of *Miss Nelson is Missing*, the three of us are silent for an awkward five seconds, as we're all probably wishing that Margarita is just Willa in disguise, trying to teach us a lesson.

"Papa?"

"Yes, my child?"

"Can I be a matchmaker like Yente when I grow up?"

"Sure. If that's what you want to be."

"Can I be one now?"

"Not according to child labor laws. But you can pretend to be one, sure. You gotta go to sleep now, though."

She sits up, claps and then rubs her hands together. "But Papa. Oh, Papa! Have I got a match for you! She's pretty! She's young! Actually, I don't know how old she is. But she's a nice girl! A good catch! Right? Right."

I don't know if it's possible for me to love my daughter more than I do right now, but part of me is a little terrified that she wants to set me up with Abby's mom.

Lucky sighs dramatically. "Do you think we waited long enough?"

"For what, buddy?"

"You said. Sometimes girls get weird and we have to wait. For them to be not weird again. Do you think we waited long enough for Willa?"

I turn to Summer. "Please tell me that's who you're talking about."

"Duhhh! Knock knock."

"Who's there?"

"Nobody! Because Willa is in New York!"

"Wow, that's kind of dark, honey. Are you saying you want Willa and me to be together?"

"Duhhh! Oy vey, dummy!" She smacks her forehead with one hand. "You're so sad and grumpy when she's not around. You're *sarumpy*. Such a man is this!"

"Diddle daidle deedle deedle daidle deedle deedle dum!"

And now both of my offspring are flat on their backs in a fit of giggles that's shaking the mattress and forming words that make absolutely no sense to me. There's a good chance none of us are going to get any sleep tonight, but at least we aren't sarumpy anymore.

I guess now's as good a time as any to have The

Talk. "You know what that would mean, though? If Willa and I are a match? Like a couple? If she lives here, she'd be sleeping here with me at night. In this room. In this bed."

"What if we want to sleep with you too? Can you get a bigger bed?"

"We'll figure something out. But there will be times when Willa and I will be in here and the door will be closed. That means we need to be alone together for a while."

Summer rolls her eyes. "Like when mommy and Landon close their door?"

"Exactly. Exactly like that."

My kids simultaneously shrug their shoulders. *Whatever.* Mommy and Landon must have their door closed a lot.

"But it would mean Willa and I will be phoning and texting each other when we aren't with each other."

"What about when you are with each other?"

"We're probably going to text each other when we're in the same room sometimes too. We can't seem to stop doing that."

Summer scrunches up her entire face for a few seconds and then exhales and throws her hands up in the air. "Fine. Just pay attention to us at the dojo."

"Deal."

Lucky asks, "Can we Skyped her? Or is she still being weird?"

"I guess we can try Skyping her tomorrow. I'm not

sure which one of us is being weird. I just don't want you guys to get your hopes up about her moving back in with us. I mean, she loves you a lot, but she might have to move to New York for work."

Summer rolls her eyes at me for the nine hundredth time in her life. "Yeah. We know she loves us. Do something to make her love *you*!"

"Oy vey. That's harsh."

All three of us are startled by the sound of the buzzer to the front gate. People don't usually come by the house at night.

Summer bolts upright. "Maybe it's Willa!"

"Unlikely. Maybe Margarita has a visitor." While I slide down to the foot of the bed, the phone in my pocket vibrates. There's a message from Nico: **It's me. Open up.**

"It's Uncle Nico."

Summer jumps up on the bed. "I wanna see him!"

Lucky starts to climb out from under the covers. "I'm coming too then."

"Both of you get back in bed right now and go to sleep, or I'll send Margarita up."

Their heads hit the pillows immediately, eyes shut tight. I don't know... I kinda like this new nanny situation.

"Love you. Good talk. Nighty night."

Margarita is by the front door, wearing pajamas and a robe, clutching an iPad to her chest and staring at the intercom. "Mr. Miller, I didn't know which button to push."

"I got it, Margarita. Sorry to disturb you. It's a friend of mine."

She nods and steps away, giving me the side eye. "Are the little ones asleep?"

"Almost." When I turn on the front gate video, I see Nico holding up a six pack over his head, like John Cusack with a boom box in *Say Anything*. "You here to tell me you love me?" I say into the intercom. "Because you should have brought more beer."

"Let me in, superstar. I haven't got all night."

I buzz him in and open the front door. I cannot believe he drove all the way out here and I didn't even beg him. "Is everything okay?"

"I'm in the fucking Palisades at eight on a Wednesday night. What do you think?" He narrows his eyes at me. "Wow. You look like shit, bro. Good."

"Did you expect to see sunshine shooting out of my ass? I'm a broken man. Also, keep your voice down— it's bedtime." I lead him to the kitchen, and he's twisting open a bottle when I'm shutting the doors. "What's up?"

He takes a pull of his beer and hands me one. "Remember that very special Valentine's Day episode of *That's So Wizard*?"

"'The Love Potion Notion?'"

"Season Two."

"'Hocus Refocus?'"

"Yes. Jesus. It's kind of a miracle either of us ever got laid."

"Did you bring me a pair of magical glasses that

will change the way I see the nerdy girl who has a crush on me? Because I don't need them."

"Okay wait, it was Season Three."

"Ahh. 'Prince Charmingest.' You're here to encourage me to fight for love. Thanks for not coming to punch me in the balls."

"I would have if you didn't already look like you've been doing it to yourself."

"How is she?"

He shakes his head and stares at his beer bottle. "I've realized recently that she's a better actor than I am. She's been hiding how she felt about you ever since she was a kid. But I've never seen her so sad."

*Now* I feel like I've been punched in the balls.

"I mean, she came around once it was time for her to leave for the airport."

"Oh." And now it feels like his combat boot is up my ass.

"She had a really good interview with the perfume people today, I guess. She said it went really well. She has until Friday afternoon to give them an answer."

And a sucker punch to my heart. "They offered her the job?"

"Course they did. She's a genius."

"Yeah. Course she is. So she hasn't given her an answer yet?"

"I can't believe I'm about to say this out loud in real life, but did you tell her that you love her?"

"I told her we love her."

"We, like you and the kids?"

"Yeah."

"Dude."

"Honestly, even if I'd told her I love her, I don't think that would have been enough."

"It would have been a good fucking start. I don't want her to live in New York. I mean, I love it there, but I don't want my sister to live there by herself. I don't think she really wants to, but they made her a good offer. You need to make her a better one."

My mind is racing. "Is she still in New York?"

"Yeah, she's going to Grammie's in the morning."

As always, I have so much to do and very little time in which to do it.

Tonight, I've got one beer to drink, one friend to hug, one text to send, and one very important call to make.

And then four lives to change if I can just make it through tomorrow with no sleep.

# REASONS WHY SHANE IS TOTALLY WRONG FOR ME AND IT WOULD NEVER WORK OUT FOR US

*1. Margo.*

*2. His hair is better than mine, which is obviously unacceptable.*

*3. He can't harmonize with me (or anyone else for that matter).*

*4. He's way too generous in bed. Like we get it—you're good at giving a girl an orgasm or twelve. Let her do a little work, yeesh.*

*5. Way too much time wasted staring into those blue eyes. Get a life, Willa. Read a book or something.*

*6. Too much time wasted staring at his hands. See above.*

*7. Obviously I'm allergic to his pheromones. Fuck you, science—it's a thing.*

*8. His kids are too cute. Way too cute. Give your ovaries a break, Willa.*

*9. Margo. I mean, maybe she's not all that terrible, and I can't really blame her for anything. But still. Margo.*

*10. He forgot my name.*

*11. Every time he says my name, my uterus screams like it's at an Elvis concert. This is no way to live.*

*12. Loving someone this much is terrifying.*

*Maybe I'm just a big baby.*

*Maybe everyone is this scared when they're in love and nobody tells you.*

*I don't know.*

*Fuck this list.*

# WILLA

*Friday Morning*

*I* had decided to make that list while I was at the airport in LA on Tuesday. I've only ever tried to get over my feelings for Shane Miller, so I have no idea if it's this hard to get over anyone else. But trying to get over Shane Miller is a joke. Especially now.

There aren't any billboards in the part of town that he lives in and I don't watch TV, so I had no idea what a big deal this upcoming Melissa McCarthy movie is. Driving to Nico's place, I had passed two billboards and a bus that was advertising the movie. I don't know why they felt the need to put his handsome smiling face on the poster—I mean, isn't Melissa McCarthy a big enough star to sell a movie on her own? More billboards on the way to the airport, and then as soon as I finished writing up my list, I looked up and saw his beautiful face on the TV in the airport bar. Some daytime talk show.

If he were laughing and smiling like most talk show guests, I would have added that to the list. But he was barely keeping up appearances. He was still handsome, of course, but he looked tired. I ran to the bar and asked the guy to turn the volume up, but it was too late. It cut to commercial, and Shane's segment was over.

I thought things would get easier once I left LA, but the in-flight movie was that damn action comedy that he starred in with John Cena. There was a huge digital screen advertising the new movie around the corner from my hotel in Times Square. And even if he weren't in movies, it wouldn't have mattered. Because I still see his face every time I close my eyes.

The good news is, I haven't been able to sleep more than a few hours since I left his house. So my eyes have been open a lot. Always looking on the bright side. But I miss the twins just as much. I miss hearing their voices. I miss their little hands. There's an emptiness inside, and I'm so afraid I won't be able to fill it, but I also don't feel right being so attached to them because they aren't mine.

My talent and skills and work. My own family. These are the only things that are mine. I just need to focus on that.

The job interview was good. It actually felt good to

be in a lab again, surrounded by other chemistry nerds who like to make things smell good. I mean, the job itself gives me no opportunities for creativity, but I can do my own thing on the weekends. And at night, if I'm not too tired. Manhattan gave me a headache, but I'm sure I'd get used to it eventually.

I'm at Grammie's house now, and I haven't heard from Shane since he sent me a text on Wednesday night, asking me not to accept the job until I've talked to him. But I haven't talked to him. I told him that I only have until this afternoon to make my decision. I know how busy he is, but come on. Don't leave a girl hanging. I'm not calling him. If I haven't heard from him by four o'clock, I'm accepting the job.

"Why are you shaking your head at me, young lady?" Grammie asks.

I realize my arms are crossed in front of my chest and I'm frowning.

"Nothing. I just can't believe you won't let me take you to the arboretum. It's a beautiful day. Don't you want me to take you anywhere? Somewhere in Detroit?"

"Well..." She smirks. "If we stay here, there's less chance of you losing me."

"Too soon, Grams." Now I'm really frowning at her. "Too soon."

We're sitting in her living room, and the scent of my grandfather's cherry vanilla tobacco smoke still permeates everything. It has mellowed a bit over the years, but it's still here, stubborn and lovely. Kind of like my grandmother, although she's not being very lovely at the moment. She's just being a stubborn ass.

"Well, I'm only going to be here for a couple more days. What do you want to do? Should we visit Mom and Dad?"

"No, just calm down. I want to talk to you."

"I am calm. You calm down."

"You are not calm. You're miserable."

"Well, you're not exactly helping to change that situation at the moment."

"I just want to tell you that I was wrong."

Ten words I never thought I'd hear this woman say. "Sorry, what?"

"You heard me."

"Regarding?"

"This job. I don't think you should take it."

"Well, I don't think I can afford not to. I mean, I can get a job waiting tables in LA until I'm making enough from my own sales, but that'll just drive Nico nuts and he'll be impossible to live with."

"Then live with Shane."

"*You're* telling me to live with Shane? Dora Cruella Todd. You?"

"That's not my middle name. Let go of that heart pendant."

I let go of it. I've been unconsciously rubbing it so much for the past few days, I'm surprised it hasn't melted. The other one, the one that Shane gave me, just makes me sad, so I try to ignore it. But I'm not ready to stop wearing it yet.

"That's what I was wrong about," she continues. "You and Shane. I shouldn't have worried about you." She closes her eyes and inhales deeply. "I loved your grandpa so much. Losing him was the worst thing that ever happened to me, and I never wanted anyone I love to go through that. I saw how meeting Shane sparked something in you. Something big and beautiful, and it all happened without him even being around. I was afraid that when you moved in with him, you'd hang on to that fantasy of him, even though it wasn't real for Shane."

"Well. I wouldn't say you were wrong to think that."

"No, I was. It just took Shane about twelve years longer to realize what you knew when you met him."

I bark out a laugh while wiping a tear from my eye. "I think perhaps you're the one who's prone to flights of fancy, Grams."

She smiles at me. She's so pretty when she isn't being a bossy know-it-all. "I wouldn't trade the pain of losing the love of my life for anything if it meant not having all that time with him. It took me so long to grasp that. Fortunately, you and Shane are more clever than I am. So forget what I said before. Don't listen to me. About this one topic, I mean. You're a wonderful girl. Of course you can live without him. But you don't have to."

I'm about to get up to hug her when the doorbell rings.

"Finally," she says on an exhale. "I've been expecting a delivery. Go get that for me, will you? I have to check on something." She disappears out of the room without any hug or explanation.

*Thanks, Grammie.* She never was much of a hugger.

I wipe my nose with the back of my hand and go to the front door. I suddenly get this ridiculous idea that maybe Shane had a big flower arrangement delivered here and Grammie knows about it. I run my fingers through my hair as I peer through the peephole. But I don't see anyone there.

I open the door, and the reason I didn't see anyone through the peephole is that the two people who are standing on the porch are under four feet tall. Shane is getting out of the passenger side of a parked car at the curb. His tired blue eyes are still magnetic, even from this far away. Even when they aren't illuminated on screen.

"Knock knock!" Summer says, laughing.

I am so happy to see them I can barely speak. "Who's there?"

"It's us! Trick or treat!" Summer and Lucky say in unison.

I drop to my knees to hug them. The scent of their baby shampoo and the feel of their little hands and arms on my back is confirmation of something I haven't been able to admit to myself, even though I've known it for two months—that I want my home to be wherever these three people are. I want it, and I'm going to let myself have it.

"I can't believe you're here," I say to the twins, in between kissing their cheeks.

"We took the red eyes plane!" Lucky exclaims. "It's called that because everyone on the plane is tired, not just Daddy."

"And we got to miss school today because Daddy's sick!"

"Oh no." I look up at Shane, who is walking up the steps. "You're sick?"

"Yeah," he says. "Sick of missing you."

The kids go inside the house while I melt into Shane's arms. "You could have just sent me a text begging me to come home, you know? It didn't even have to be dirty."

"Ahh, but then I wouldn't have had the pleasure of leaving the red carpet to get home and get two five-year-olds out the door in time for the red eyes flight to Detroit."

"You rushed to the airport for me? That's so romantic."

"Didn't feel very romantic, with two tired kids and a grouchy nanny in tow, to be honest."

I pull him inside the house and glance out at the car parked outside. "Where's the grouchy nanny?"

"At the hotel in Detroit, sleeping. I hired a driver to bring us here. Didn't want to risk driving in my state."

"Which state is that?" I shut the front door and wrap my arms around his waist.

"Michigan, I think."

Summer and Lucky are in the living room, talking

to Grammie, who has that elfish glint in her eye. "Welcome to Michigan, Shane Miller. You're a little late." While Shane hugs her, she looks over her shoulder and winks at me.

Summer and Lucky run over to me, pulling little boxes out of their jacket pockets and holding them up to me.

"This is a present for you!" Summer says, opening the box herself. "It's a pretty necklace!" She takes the gold necklace out of the box and holds it out for me. "It has a heart on it like the ones you have, 'cept this one's mine. For you."

Lucky holds his little box out to me. "And mine too. You can open it yourself."

"Thank you. It's so pretty." I take the necklace and box from them. "Thank you. I'm going to wear them all the time."

"Why don't we give these two kids some privacy, Mr. Lucky and Miss Summer. Come to the kitchen with me."

"I'm hungry," Summer says. "What kind of snacks do you have?"

"Prunes."

"What are prunes?" Lucky asks.

"They're dried plums that relieve constipation. You'll love them."

Summer looks back at us, pouting.

"I also baked some chocolate chip cookies last night. Would you like those instead?"

The twins cheer as they follow Grammie out of the room.

Shane helps me put my new necklaces on. I lift my hair up, and the touch of his fingertips on the skin of my neck almost makes my knees give out.

"If you're going to do something disgusting to me to make up for how sweet this is, we should at least go into the guest room."

"Oh, I've got big plans for you, believe me. But they'll have to wait."

"Not too long, I hope." When I have four pretty gold necklaces and four pretty gold hearts around my neck, I let my hair down.

"You could also just put all of these pendants on one necklace, I guess. Right?"

"Yes." I kiss him on the right cheek. "I can." I kiss him on the left cheek. "So, you told Grammie you were coming?"

He nods. "She good at keeping a secret?"

"A little too good. It's disturbing."

Shane takes a deep breath. "It still smells like cherry vanilla in here," he says.

"Have you been here before?"

"No. You told me about it. When we met."

"I can't believe you remember that."

He looks at me so seriously all of a sudden. "I know I got your name wrong at first, but I was really tired. I remember everything about that first time I met you. I remember everything about every second I've spent with you. I want to spend all the seconds with you.

Don't take that job. I want you to live with us, and I want you to make your own perfume, and I want you to feel good about being with us. I want you to live with us as my future wife." He pulls another small box out of his blazer pocket.

Oh my God. I was so excited to see everyone, I didn't even notice that he's wearing a blazer, button-down shirt, and a skinny tie! I look down at his feet. And the high-tops!

I'm so excited that he's dressed up like Greyson again for me that when he opens the box and I stare at a beautiful diamond ring, it takes me a few seconds to understand that it's an engagement ring. For me.

"I am so in love with you, Willa Todd. I want you to know that you're the first. I asked Margo to marry me because I got her pregnant and I cared about her and it was the right thing to do. I'm asking you to marry me because you're the only woman I've ever been in love with, and my kids love you, and one day when you're ready, I want to get you pregnant. And you're the only woman I want to go to sleep with and wake up next to for the rest of my life."

Shane Miller is looking at me like I'm the most beautiful woman in the world, but I feel like a twelve-year-old dork. My mouth is dry. My hands are trembling. My right eye might be twitching.

"Yes," I blurt out, at the same time that he asks, "Will you marry me?"

He laughs, and as he takes my hand to slide the ring onto my finger, his index finger touches the pulse point on the inside of my wrist, and once again I don't see our future life together, but I *feel* it. Comforting and exciting and romantic and light and important and there's a home and kids, and...I feel it all in this moment, and this time I know that he feels it too.

## SHANE

*M*ost days, I think it's ridiculous that I get paid so much to be a good-looking funny guy. Today, I am incredibly grateful for everyone responsible for overpaying me, because I'm able to afford a chauffeured SUV, two suites in the nicest hotel in Detroit, and a nanny to look after my kids in one of them. In the other one—that is not next door but across the hall—I get to undress the love of my life.

Willa called to turn down the New York job before we left Grammie's house. For the past forty minutes, I've been doing a half-decent job of pretending to be an attentive father who enjoys listening to his kids sing along to *Singin' in the Rain* and who definitely isn't thinking about sticking his head under his fiancée's dress. But as soon as I pull Willa inside our suite, I lift that dress up over her head.

This dress. I will always think of this as the dress she wore the first time I saw her naked and the one that she wore on the day I asked her to marry me. And underneath the dress—four necklaces, a beige full-coverage bra, and granny panties.

"I wasn't expecting to see you today," she explains, covering her face. "And I definitely didn't expect you to propose to me. or I would have worn something a little less geriatric."

"You are making this ensemble work, I promise you."

She groans. "I'm humiliated."

"I can fix this." I swiftly remove her bra and panties, taking in her beautiful naked body. "Better?"

"You tell me," she mutters.

"It's better than anything." Honestly, I'll never get tired of looking at and touching and kissing this woman. "We need to plan on another little vacation when Margo is back and the kids are with her."

"Maybe don't talk about the kids when I'm completely naked and you're squeezing my ass."

"Mmm, you're gonna have to get used to talking about all kinds of things when you're completely naked and I'm squeezing your ass. I told the twins that you'll be sleeping with me from now on and that they aren't supposed to bother us if the door is closed. I plan to spend a lot of time in the bedroom with my naked fiancée."

"That's a lot of talk about your naked fiancée for a guy who's fully dressed as Greyson Manning of TV's *That's So Wizard*."

"I'll stop talking now."

"I'll start undressing you now."

We're a fucking awesome team.

My mom called me yesterday, from Florida, to tell me that she and Hank are going to see my movie this weekend. When I told her that I had fallen in love with Nico's little sister and was in the middle of shopping for an engagement ring for her, she was not at all surprised. She reminded me that the day I met Willa on the *Wizard* set, I said to her, "Something weird happened. I met Nico's sister, and when I held her hand to pull her up, I think I had a vision. Not something I could see, exactly, but a feeling. Like a flash of what it would be like to be married with kids one day. And I liked it."

I had completely forgotten about that. Blocked it out, probably, as soon as I asked Margo to marry me, because I knew on some level that it would never feel like that with her. But as soon as my mom said it, I remembered the feeling. It was the feeling I had as soon as I introduced Willa to my kids. I'll tell Willa about that, one of these days, because if anyone would understand that kind of thing, it's her. But I'm way over my cheese quota for today.

Now is the time for me to make my bride-to-be forget how fucking adorable I am. I'm gonna make her forget so hard. But it seems I'm still fully dressed as Greyson Manning, aside from being unzipped.

My bride-to-be is gripping my cock and looking up at me pensively. "Actually, I think I'd like to engage in sexual activity with Greyson Manning today."

"What?" I slam my hands flat against the wall behind her, on either side of her head. "You would rather engage in sexual activity with a fictional teenage wizard who doesn't have full control over his wand yet than with me—the world-famous star of motion pictures who asked you to marry him?"

She purses her lips and shrugs. "Just this once?"

"Well, you're in trouble, because Greyson Manning is secretly a dirty horndog who will bewitch your tits and enchant your pussy."

"Sounds charming." She slowly removes her hand from my jeans. "Get that wand out. Let's see what you can do with it."

I lick my lips, lowering myself to my knees. "I may still be a student, but I know how important it is to work some magic with my mouth first." This woman. Her eyes and voice are unflinching, but her thighs are quivering. She gasps and tenses up when my thumb gently brushes against her clit, still sensitive to my touch as if it were the first time. I will be worshipping at this temple for the rest of my life. "You're so wizard."

She tilts her head back against the wall, threading her fingers through my hair. "*You* are."

I get a quick taste of forever and the shuddering pleasure I'll be giving her. "You."

# EPILOGUE I – Willa

# WILLA TODD-MILLER SCENT DIARY, TUESDAY AFTERNOON

*Provence in early July smells of lavender, rosemary, basil, sage, fennel, fresh air, true love, and dirty sex. Lots and lots of sleep and sex. It's so beautiful here—fragrant and scenic. The sunflowers are blooming too, so it's just like sunflowers —pow! Lavender—bam! Tah dahhhh—evergreen trees everywhere! I basically came in my pants for the entire drive from Nice. Or something more ladylike, since I am a blushing bride.*

*But if I'm being honest, I really have been in a constant state of orgasm. We've been here for two nights already, on our honeymoon. Shane chose a spa hotel in the hills above the Luberon, in the south of France. An elegant chateau, surrounded by a vineyard and lavender fields. The view from our suite is spectacular. We have our own terrace, pool, jacuzzi, and garden. It's all very private and low-key, but it feels so extravagant. One more week here, a few days on the coast, and then it's back to the Palisades to get ready for Summer's and Lucky's seventh birthdays.*

*It feels like we're celebrating all the time now.*

*We had a small wedding in Santa Monica—mostly a family affair. The twins were the cutest flower girl and ring bearer ever, Nico was Shane's best man for the second time, and Grammie made for a surprisingly helpful and dazzling matron of honor. Margo even gave a moving and not at all nauseating speech. I do not hate her.*

*One thing I will say about Margo Quincey—the woman knows how to market herself. Her "Margo" perfume oil launched half a year ago to great success. At first it was sold exclusively on her online store, but now it's being carried at posh department stores in New York, LA, and Chicago. I get a cut of the profits. I own a piece of Margo. We are connected in many ways, as mothers and entrepreneurs. Ever since she posted an interview with me on her website, sales of my own line have skyrocketed. I pay Margarita to help me with shipping orders when she isn't busy with the kids. Turns out people really want to smell like me and Shane. The Sleeper fragrance is now available as a roll-on perfume oil, eau de toilette spray, soap, body lotion, and candle. A girl could make her whole house smell like the beginning of our relationship if they wanted to.*

*But only I have the pleasure of basking in the glory of Shane Miller's pheromones. He's all mine for two weeks, mine and the kids' for a couple of weeks, and then he starts work on his next movie. After the Toronto film festival, Hard Shell got a limited release in December and Shane was nominated for an Independent Spirit Award. He wasn't even annoyed that Zac Efron ended up winning because Hard Shell went on to become a surprise sleeper hit, and as I had predicted, he's getting offered all kinds of parts.*

*Fortunately, the only parts he's interested in right now are mine. My skin is pink and raw all over and thoroughly loved. Shane is slowly waking up from a long nap, naked and blissed out under soft white sheets, caressed by the gentle lavender-scented breeze that blows in through the open windows. His hair is perfect. Eyes closed, he's reaching for my leg.*

*I don't know that it would even be possible for me to capture the way I feel right now in a perfume. It's a remarkable thing, to know that a person is yours but to still long for him. To be married to your first celebrity crush. To choose to love someone with an unguarded heart because he has proven to you, time and again, that he will be the one to protect it.*

*We blend well together. I suppose I didn't need a post-graduate degree to figure that out, but who knows. Maybe that's why our chemistry is so spectacular. The performer and the perfumer.*

*I'm reaching behind myself with my free hand to hold his.*

*Shane Miller.*
*My brother's best friend.*
*My brother's former costar.*
*My first non-Disney prince crush.*
*My best friend.*
*The best dad of the best kids I know.*
*My husband.*

## EPILOGUE 2 – SHANE

Oliver Sage Miller Sleep Journal – One month old - no idea what day of the week it is

**Morning Wakeup:** *5:30 a.m.*
**Nap #1** *7:10 a.m. – 8:30 a.m.*
**Nap #2:** *10 a.m. to 11:45 a.m.*
**Nap #3:** *1:30 p.m. to 3:10 p.m.*

*Etc., etc. We're doing an approximate 90-minute sleep/wake cycle thing, and it seems to be working.*

*The first few weeks were a fucking adorable sleepless shit show, but we seem to be figuring things out now thanks to the science of observing and recording baby's sleepy signals. As you know, Dr. Sun, our little devil was a fussy "problem sleeper," despite being constantly swaddled in soothing essential oil-scented blankets and living in a home that has a lavender oil diffusing cool mist humidifier in every room. Literally. Every room.*

*Willa and I are very grateful that we've been blessed with such a beautiful, healthy boy who loves to eat and shits like a dream, but he almost never slept for more than forty-five minutes at a time and preferred to sleep while being driven in a car, pushed in a stroller, or held in my rocking arms. This made it nearly impossible for me to do anything else.*

*Our nanny Margarita is tasked with caring for the twins all day, and we've found that it's best for all of us if she gets a good eight hours of sleep each night. She helps out with the baby when the kids are in school. Willa is getting ready to launch a new line of fine fragrances and she has a team to oversee, so I've put my career on hold for two months in order to devote myself to Oliver's body clock and getting him the fuck to sleep, while also somehow managing to remind the twins and my wife that I love them just as much as I did before I started obsessing about this beautiful, diabolical infant.*

*I've read the books. I've read the Internet. I've logged every vacant stare, slow blink, yawn, head tilt, ear tug, eye rub, and Mr. Cranky Pants Dance. We've created a comforting, monotonous sleep environment for him in his bedroom.*

*We have all become experts at keeping this baby enter-tained for ninety-minute periods before winding things down and soothing him to sleep again. Turns out Ollie*

*really likes it when Summer sings showtunes to him, he's
very alert when Lucky tries to explain everything he knows
about the world to him, and he practically stands at attention when Margarita goes on one of her Spanish rants. Like
me, he could just stare at his mother and nuzzle her breasts
all day. He is infuriatingly happy and calm when she's
around. He coos and farts roses and burps rainbows for
Mommy.*

*But it turns out, to my horror, that it's my singing voice that
lulls him to sleep when all else fails. Apparently, my limited
vocal range provides him with exactly the right amount of
unstimulating monotony. That's the good news. The bad
news is, the more I sing to him, the better I seem to be
getting. It is totally conceivable that one day in the near
future I will no longer sing "Baby Mine" off key. But one
step at a time, as my lovely wife continually reminds me.
On the bright side—I will finally be able to do a musical
with Zac. Or maybe I'll do one without him—because fuck
you, Zac Efron. You try maintaining a six-pack with three
little kids.*

*I honestly don't even know how I got through life without
Willa. I'm getting on average three to five hours of sleep
lately. On a good day. I have no complaints. I get to live
with my four favorite people on earth. And Margarita.
When I do get to crawl into bed at night, my gorgeous wife
is lying there naked, and if I'm having trouble drifting off,
she always remembers a little trick that Dr. Shaw told me
about. On occasion, I have been known to slumber with my*

*head between her legs, because sometimes I sleep better knowing that I can still make the mother of my child scream my name into a pillow.*

*I know this is supposed to be about Oliver, but until he can write this thing himself, I'll be including my own musings about handjobs and cunnilingus.*

*Sorry if you don't like swearing, nudity, or sex, Dr. Sun, but this baby sleep journal is rated R because I can't get through this period of infant neurological development without swearing, nudity, or my wife.*

*It has been four years since I first realized that I can't sleep unless Willa is living under my roof. It's still true. I don't always get to sleep as much as I want to, but I get through every waking moment as long as I know that she'll be in my bed at night. There was a time when I was afraid I wouldn't be able to give her everything that she deserves because of the kids, but I never stop trying and she's never stopped blossoming. I think the truth is that she is every- thing—all on her own. She doesn't need me to give her anything. She just wants me. And that is really fucking comforting.*

*Hopefully it won't take Oliver twenty-eight years to find what he's looking for, but he has us to help him figure it out. Me and Willa, and the twins, and this fucking amazing sleep diary.*

**THE END**

Printed in Poland
by Amazon Fulfillment
Poland Sp. z o.o., Wrocław